THE CRITICS MAKE WAY FOR LUCIA
by E. F. Benson

"If you have not met Lucia, you must do so now. In this big new volume you will find everything held in reverence by those of us who kept the cult-fires burning when the novels were out of print." —*Cleveland Plain Dealer*

"It is seldom one can read through 913 pages with unflagging delight. Without this reissue I might have gone to my grave without ever knowing about Lucia or Miss Mapp. It is not a risk anyone should take lightly."
—Auberon Waugh
New York Times Book Review

"Memorable!"   —*Saturday Review*

"Delightful!"   —*Springfield Republican*

"Benson created a small scale world that is a pleasure to enter. More than 50 years after the first of them appeared, these books are fresh and funny. Benson was at least mildly infected by genius."   —Walter Clemons
Newsweek

"An extravaganza of altogether satisfying entertainment!"
—*The London Times*

MAKE WAY FOR LUCIA is—or soon will be—available from Popular Library in six volumes.

QUEEN LUCIA • I

LUCIA IN LONDON • II

MISS MAPP* • III

MAPP AND LUCIA • IV

THE WORSHIPFUL LUCIA • V

TROUBLE FOR LUCIA • VI

* Though the character "Lucia" does not appear in the novel MISS MAPP, nevertheless MISS MAPP has always been known as a "Lucia" novel and is, in fact, volume III in the series. Mapp is furious.

LUCIA IN LONDON

MAKE WAY FOR LUCIA · II
LUCIA IN LONDON
by E. F. Benson

Foreword by Nancy Mitford

POPULAR LIBRARY • NEW YORK

Published by Popular Library, a unit of CBS
Publications, the Consumer Publishing Division
of CBS Inc., by arrangement with Thomas Y. Crowell
Company, Inc.

March, 1978

Library of Congress Catalog Card Number: 76-783

ISBN: 0-445-04193-5

Foreword

by Nancy Mitford

AT LONG last, here she is again, the splendid creature, the great, the wonderful, Lucia. What rejoicing there will be among the Luciaphils! Those of us who lost her chronicles during the war and have never, by Clique, by barrow or by theft, been able to replace them, now find ourselves armed against misfortune once again; when life becomes too much for us we shall be able to take refuge in the *giardino segretto*. The publishers, in reprinting *Lucia in London* (and by degrees, the whole saga) have deserved well of all who like to laugh.

Lucia (Mrs. Emmeline Lucas) is a forceful lady who lives in the South of England in two small country towns—that is, when we meet her first, in the late Twenties, she is the Queen of Riseholme, but half way through her story (which ends just before the war) she transfers, presumably so that her creator can pit her

against the formidable Miss Mapp, to Tilling. Tilling, I
believe, is Rye, where E. F. Benson himself lived in the
house formerly occupied by Henry James; this is the
very house which Lucia finally worms out of Miss
Mapp.

Lucia's neighbours in both towns are almost all, like
herself, middle-aged people of comfortable means.
Their occupations are housekeeping, at which most of
them are skilled (there is a good deal about food in the
books, and lobster à la Riseholme plays an important
part), gardening, golf, bridge and bickering. None of
them could be described as estimable, and they are certainly not very interesting, yet they are fascinated by
each other and we are fascinated by them.

All this fascination is generated by Lucia; it is what
happens with regard to her that counts; she is the
centre and the driving force of her little world. As she
is a profoundly irritating person, bossy, horribly energetic and pushing, the others groan beneath her yoke
and occasionally try to shake it off: but in their heart of
hearts they know that it is she who keeps them going
and that life without her would be drab indeed.

The art of these books lies in their simplicity. The
jokes seem quite obvious and are often repeated: we
can never have enough of them. In *Lucia in London*,
Daisy gets a ouidja board and makes mystical contact
with an Egyptian called Abfou. Now Abfou hardly
ever says anything but "Lucia is a snob," yet we hang
on his lips and are thrilled every time Georgie says, "I
am going to Daisy's, to weedj." Georgie is the local
bachelor who passes for Lucia's lover. Then there is
the Italian with which Lucia and Georgie pepper their
conversation: "Tacete un momento, Georgie. Le do-

mestiche." It never, never palls. On at least two occasions an Italian turns up and then we learn that Lucia and Georgino mio don't really know the language at all; the second time is as funny as the first.

I must say I reopened these magic books after some thirty years with misgivings; I feared that they would have worn badly and seem dated. Not at all; they are as fresh as paint. The characters are real and therefore timeless; the surprising few differences between that pre-war world and its equivalent today only add to the interest. Money of course is one of them—the characters speak of £2,000 as we would of £20,000. At least two people have Rolls-Royces; everybody has *domestiche*. When listening-in begins, Lucia refuses to have a wireless until Olga, a prima donna whom she reveres, owns to having one and listens-in to Cortot on it. None of them ever thinks of going abroad. When Lucia and Georgie want to get away from Riseholme for a little change they take houses at Tilling for the summer; that is what leads to them settling there.

But the chief difference is that, in Lucia's words, "that horrid thing which Freud calls sex" is utterly ignored. No writer nowadays could allow Georgie to do his embroidery and dye his hair and wear his little cape and sit for hours chatting with Lucia or playing celestial Mozartino, without hinting at Boys in the background. Quaint Irene, in her fisherman's jersey and knickerbockers, would certainly share her house with another lesbian and this word would be used. There are no children in the books—"Children are so sticky," says Georgie, "specially after tea."

I was a fellow guest, at Highcliffe, with Mr. E. F. Benson soon after Lucia had become Mayor of Tilling.

We talked of her for hours and he said, "What must she do now?" Alas, he died in the first year of the war; can we doubt that if he had lived Lucia would have become a General?

1

CONSIDERING THAT Philip Lucas's aunt who died early
in April was no less than eighty-three years old, and
had spent the last seven of them bedridden in a private
lunatic asylum, it had been generally and perhaps reasonably hoped among his friends and those of his wife
that the bereavement would not be regarded by either
of them as an intolerable tragedy. Mrs. Quantock, in
fact, who like everybody else at Riseholme had sent a
neat little note of condolence to Mrs. Lucas, had, without using the actual words "happy release," certainly
implied it or its close equivalent.

She was hoping that there would be a reply to it, for
though she had said in her note that her dear Lucia
mustn't dream of answering it, that was a mere figure
of speech, and she had instructed her parlormaid who
took it across to The Hurst immediately after lunch to
say that she didn't know if there was an answer, and

11

would wait to see, for Mrs. Lucas might perhaps give a little hint ever so vaguely about what the expectations were concerning which everybody was dying to get information. . . .

While she waited for this, Daisy Quantock was busy, like everybody else in the village on this beautiful afternoon of spring, with her garden, hacking about with a small but destructive fork in her flower beds. She was a gardener of the ruthless type, and went for any small green thing that incautiously showed a timid spike above the earth, suspecting it of being a weed. She had had a slight difference with the professional gardener who had hitherto worked for her on three afternoons during the week, and had told him that his services were no longer required. She meant to do her gardening herself this year, and was confident that a profusion of beautiful flowers and a plethora of delicious vegetables would be the result. At the end of her garden path was a barrow of rich manure, which she proposed, when she had finished the slaughter of the innocents, to dig into the depopulated beds. On the other side of her paling, her neighbor Georgie Pillson was rolling his strip of lawn, on which during the summer he often played croquet on a small scale. Occasionally they shouted remarks to each other, but as they got more and more out of breath with their exertions, the remarks got fewer. Mrs. Quantock's last question had been "What do you do with slugs, Georgie?" and Georgie had panted out, "Pretend you don't see them."

Mrs. Quantock had lately grown rather stout owing to a diet of sour milk, which with plenty of sugar was not palatable; but sour milk and pyramids of raw vegetables had quite stopped all the symptoms of consumption which the study of a small but lurid medical

manual had induced. Today she had eaten a large but
normal lunch in order to test the merits of her new
cook, who certainly was a success, for her husband had
gobbled up his food with great avidity instead of turning it over and over with his fork as if it were hay. In
consequence, stoutness, surfeit, and so much stooping
had made her feel rather giddy, and she was standing
up to recover, wondering if this giddiness was a symp-
tom of something dire, when de Vere, for such was the
incredible name of her parlormaid, came down the
steps from the dining room with a note in her hand. So
Mrs. Quantock hastily took off her gardening gloves of
stout leather, and opened it.

There was a sentence of formal thanks for her sympathy which Mrs. Lucas immensely prized, and then
followed these ridiculous words:

> It has been a terrible blow to my poor Peppino
> and myself. We trusted that Auntie Amy might have
> been spared us for a few years yet.
>
> Ever, dear Daisy, your sad
> LUCIA

And not a word about expectations! . . . Lucia's
dear Daisy crumpled up the absurd note and said,
"Rubbish," so loud that Georgie Pillson in the next
garden thought he was being addressed.

"What's that?" he said.

"Georgie, come to the fence a minute," said Mrs.
Quantock. "I want to speak to you."

Georgie, longing for a little gossip, let go of the
handle of his roller, which, suddenly released, gave a
loud squeak and rapped him smartly on the elbow.

"Tarsome thing!" said Georgie.

He went to the fence and, being tall, could look over
it. There was Mrs. Quantock angrily poking Lucia's
note into the flower bed she had been weeding.

"What is it?" said Georgie. "Shall I like it?"

His face red and moist with exertion, appearing just
over the top of the fence, looked like the sun about to
set below the flat grey horizon of the sea.

"I don't know if you'll like it," said Daisy, "but it's
your Lucia. I sent her a little note of condolence about
the aunt, and she says it has been a terrible blow to
Peppino and herself. They hoped that the old lady
might have been spared them a few years yet."

"No!" said Georgie, wiping the moisture off his forehead with the back of one of his beautiful pearl-grey
gloves.

"But she did," said the infuriated Daisy; "they were
her very words. I could show you if I hadn't dug it in.
Such a pack of nonsense! I hope that long before I've
been bedridden for seven years, somebody will strangle
me with a bootlace, or anything handy. Why does
Lucia pretend to be sorry? What does it all mean?"

Georgie had long been devoted henchman to Lucia
(Mrs. Lucas, wife of Philip Lucas, and so Lucia), and
though he could criticize her in his mind, when he was
alone in his bed or his bath, he always championed her
in the face of the criticism of others. Whereas Daisy
criticized everybody everywhere. . . .

"Perhaps it means what it says," he observed with
the delicate sarcasm that never had any effect on his
neighbor.

"It can't possibly do that," said Mrs. Quantock.
"Neither Lucia nor Peppino has set eyes on his aunt
for years, nor spoken of her. Last time Peppino went
to see her she bit him. Sling for a week afterwards,

don't you remember, and he was terrified of blood p
soning. How can her death be a blow, and as for her
being spared—"

Mrs. Quantock suddenly broke off, remembering
that de Vere was still standing there and drinking it all
in.

"That's all, de Vere," she said.

"Thank you, ma'am," said de Vere, striding back
toward the house. She had high-heeled shoes on, and
each time she lifted her foot, the heel which had been
embedded by her weight in the soft lawn came out with
the sound of a cork being drawn. Then Daisy came
closer to the fence, with the light of inductive reasoning, which was much cultivated at Riseholme, veiling
the fury of her eye.

"Georgie, I've got it," she said. "I've guessed what it
means."

Now though Georgie was devoted to his Lucia, he
was just as devoted to inductive reasoning, and Daisy
Quantock was, with the exception of himself, far the
most powerful logician in the place.

"What is it, then?" he asked.

"Stupid of me not to have thought of it at once,"
said Daisy. "Why, don't you see? Peppino is Auntie's
heir, for she was unmarried, and he's the only nephew,
and probably he has been left piles and piles. So
naturally they say it's a terrible blow. Wouldn't do to
be exultant. They must say it's a terrible blow, to show
they don't care about the money. The more they're left,
the sadder it is. So natural. I blame myself for not having thought of it at once. Have you seen her since?"

"Not for a quiet talk," said Georgie. "Peppino was
there, and a man who, I think, was Peppino's lawyer.
He was frightfully deferential."

"That proves it," said Daisy. "And nothing said of any kind?"

Georgie's face screwed itself up in the effort to remember.

"Yes, there was something," he said, "but I was talking to Lucia, and the others were talking rather low. But I did hear the lawyer say something to Peppino about pearls. I do remember the word 'pearls.' Perhaps it was the old lady's pearls."

Mrs. Quantock gave a short laugh.

"It couldn't have been Peppino's," she said. "He has one in a tiepin. It's called pear-shaped, but there's little shape about it. When do wills come out?"

"Oh, ages," said Georgie. "Months. And there's a house in London, I know."

"Whereabouts?" asked Daisy greedily.

Georgie's face assumed a look of intense concentration.

"I couldn't tell you for certain," he said, "but I know Peppino went up to town not long ago to see about some repairs to his aunt's house, and I think it was the roof."

"It doesn't matter where the repairs were," said Daisy impatiently. "I want to know where the house was."

"You interrupt me," said Georgie. "I was telling you. I know he went to Harrod's afterward and walked there, because he and Lucia were dining with me and he said so. So the house must have been close to Harrod's, quite close I mean, because it was raining, and if it had been any reasonable distance, he would have had a taxi. So it might be Knightsbridge."

Mrs. Quantock put on her gardening gloves again.

"How frightfully secretive people are," she said.

"Fancy his never having told you where his aunt's house was."

"But they never spoke of her," said Georgie. "She's been in that nursing home so many years."

"You may call it a nursing home," observed Mrs. Quantock, "or if you choose, you may call it a post-office. But it was an asylum. And they're just as secretive about the property."

"But you never talk about the property till after the funeral," said Georgie. "I believe it's tomorrow."

Mrs. Quantock gave a prodigious sniff.

"They would have, if there hadn't been any," she said.

"How horrid you are," said Georgie. "How—"

His speech was cut off by several loud sneezes. However beautiful the sleeve links, it wasn't wise to stand without a coat after being in such a heat.

"How what?" asked Mrs. Quantock, when the sneezing was over.

"I've forgotten now. I shall get back to my rolling. A little chilly. I've done half the lawn."

A telephone bell had been ringing for the last few seconds, and Mrs. Quantock localized it as being in his house, not hers. Georgie was rather deaf, however much he pretended not to be.

"Your telephone bell's ringing, Georgie," she said.

"I thought it was," said Georgie, who had not heard it at all.

"And come in presently for a cup of tea," shouted Mrs. Quantock.

"Should love to. But I must have a bath first."

Georgie hurried indoors, for a telephone call usually meant a little gossip with a friend. A very familiar voice, though a little husky and broken, asked if it was he.

"Yes, it's me, Lucia," he said in soft firm tones of sympathy. "How are you?"

Lucia sighed. It was a long, very audible, intentional sigh. Georgie could visualize her putting her mouth quite close to the telephone, so as to make sure it carried.

"Quite well," she said. "And so is my Peppino, thank heaven. Bearing up wonderfully. He's just gone."

Georgie was on the point of asking where, but guessed in time.

"I see," he said. "And you didn't go. I'm very glad. So wise."

"I felt I couldn't," she said, "and he urged me not. It's tomorrow. He sleeps in London to-night—"

(Again Georgie longed to say "where?" for it was impossible not to wonder if he would sleep in the house of unknown locality near Harrod's.)

"And he'll be back tomorrow evening," said Lucia without pause. "I wonder if you would take pity on me and come and dine. Just something to eat, you know; the house is so upset. Don't dress."

"Delighted," said Georgie, though he had ordered oysters. But they could be scalloped for tomorrow. . . . "Love to come."

"Eight o'clock then? Nobody else, of course. If you care to bring our Mozart duet."

"Rather," said Georgie. "Good for you to be occupied, Lucia. We'll have a good go at it."

"Dear Georgie," said Lucia faintly. He heard her sigh, again, not quite so successfully, and replace the earpiece with a click.

Georgie moved away from the telephone, feeling im-

mensely busy: there was so much to think about and to
do. The first thing was to speak about the oysters, and
his parlormaid being out, he called down the kitchen
stairs. The absence of Foljambe made it necessary for
him to get his bath ready himself, and he turned the
hot water tap half on, so that he could run downstairs
again and out into the garden (for there was not time
to finish the lawn if he was to have a bath and change
before tea) in order to put the roller back in the shed.
Then he had to get his clothes out, and select something which would do for tea and also for dinner, as
Lucia had told him not to dress. There was a new suit
which he had not worn yet, rather daring, for the
trousers, dark fawn, were distinctly of Oxford cut, and
he felt quite boyish as he looked at them. He had ordered them in a moment of reckless sartorial courage,
and a quiet tea with Daisy Quantock, followed by a
quiet dinner with Lucia, was just the way to make a
beginning with them, far better than wearing them for
the first time at church on Sunday, when the whole of
Riseholme simultaneously would see them. The coat
and waistcoat were very dark blue; they would look
blue at tea and black at dinner, and there were some
grey silk socks, rather silvery, and a tie to match them.
These took some time to find, and his search was interrupted by volumes of steam pouring into his bedroom
from his bathroom; he ran in to find the bath full
nearly to the brim of boiling water. It had been little
more than lukewarm yesterday, and his cook had evidently taken to heart his too sharp words after breakfast this morning. So he had to pull up the plug of his
bath to let the boiling contents subside, and fill up with
cold.

He went back to his bedroom and began undressing.

All this news about Lucia and Peppino, with Daisy Quantock's penetrating comments, was intensely interesting. Old Miss Lucas had been in this nursing home or private asylum for years, and Georgie didn't suppose that the inclusive charges could be less than fifteen pounds a week, and fifteen times fifty-two was a large sum. There was income, too, and say it was at 5 per cent, the capital it represented was considerable. Then there was that house in London. If it was freehold, that meant a great deal more capital; if it was on lease, it meant a great deal more income. Then there were rates and taxes, and the wages of a caretaker, and no doubt a margin. And there were the pearls.

Georgie took a half sheet of paper from the drawer in a writing table where he kept half sheets and pieces of string untied from parcels, and began to calculate. There was necessarily a good deal of guesswork about it, and the pearls had to be omitted altogether, since nobody could say what "pearls" were worth without knowing their quantity or quality. But even omitting these, and putting quite a low figure on the possible rent of the house near Harrod's, he was astounded at the capital which these annual outgoings appeared to represent.

"I don't put it at a penny less than fifty thousand pounds," he said to himself, "and the income at two thousand six hundred."

He had got a little chilly as he sat at his figures, and with a luxurious foretaste of a beautiful hot bath, he hurried into his bathroom. The whole of the boiling water had run out.

"How tarsome! Damn!" said Georgie, putting in the plug and turning on both taps simultaneously.

His calculations, of course, had only been the

materials on which his imagination built, and as he dressed, it was hard at work, between glances at his trousers as reflected in the full-length mirror which stood in his window. What would Lucia and Peppino do with this vast increase of fortune? Lucia already had the biggest house in Riseholme and the most Elizabethan decor, and a motor, and as many new clothes as she chose. She did not spend much on them because her lofty mind despised clothes, but Georgie permitted himself to indulge cynical reflections that the pearls might make her dressier. Then she already entertained as much as she felt disposed; and more money would not make her wish to give more dinners. And she went up to London whenever there was anything in the way of pictures or plays or music which she felt held the seed of culture. Society (so called) she despised as thoroughly as she despised clothes, and always said she came back to Riseholme feeling intellectually starved. Perhaps she would endow a permanent fund for holding May Day revels on the village green, for Lucia had said she meant to have May Day revels every year. They had been a great success last year, though fatiguing, for everybody dressed up in sixteenth-century costume, and danced Morris dances till they all hobbled home dead lame at the merciful sunset. It had all been wonderfully Elizabethan, and Georgie's jerkin had hurt him very much.

Lucia was a wonderful character, thought Georgie, and she would find a way to spend two or three thousand a year more in an edifying and cultured manner. (Were Oxford trousers meant to turn up at the bottom? He thought not; and how small these voluminous folds made your feet look.) Georgie knew what he himself would do with two or three thousand a year more; indeed he had often considered whether he would not try to do it without. He wanted, ever so much, to have a little flat in London (or a couple of rooms would serve), just for a dip every now and then in the life which Lucia found so vapid. But he knew he wasn't a strong, serious character like Lucia, whose only frivolities were artistic or Elizabethan.

His eye fell on a large photograph on the table by his bedside in a silver frame, representing Brunnhilde. It was signed "Olga to beloved Georgie," and his waistcoat felt quite tight as, drawing in a long breath, he recalled that wonderful six months when Olga Bracely, the prima donna, had bought Old Place, and lived here, and had altered all the values of everything. Georgie believed himself to have been desperately in love with her, but it had been a very exciting time for more reasons than that. Old values had gone; she had thought Riseholme the most splendid joke that had ever been made; she loved them all and laughed at them all, and nobody minded a bit, but followed her whims as if she had been a Pied Piper. All but Lucia, that is to say, whose throne had, quite unintentionally on Olga's part, been pulled smartly from under her, and her scepter flew in one direction, and her crown in another. Then Olga had gone off for an operatic tour in America, and after six triumphant months there, had gone on to Australia. But she would be back in England by now, for she was singing in London this season, and her house at Riseholme, so long closed, would be open again. . . . And the coat buttoned beautifully, just the last button, leaving the rest negligently wide and a little loose. Georgie put an amethyst tiepin in his grey tie, which gave a pretty touch of color, brushed his hair back from his forehead, so that the toupee was quite indistinguishable from his own hair, and hurried downstairs to go out to tea with Daisy Quantock.

Daisy was seated at her writing table when he entered, very busy with a pencil and piece of paper and counting something up on her fingers. Her gardening fork lay in the grate with the fire irons; on the carpet there were one or two little sausages of garden mold, which no doubt had peeled off from her boots, and her gardening gloves were on the floor by her side. Georgie instantly registered the conclusion that something important must have occurred, and that she had come indoors in a great hurry, because the carpet was nearly new, and she always made a great fuss if the smallest atom of cigarette ash dropped on it.

"Thirty-seven, forty-seven, fifty-two, and carry five," she muttered, as Georgie stood in front of the fire, so that the entire new suit should be seen at once. "Wait a moment, Georgie—and seventeen and five's twenty-three—no, twenty-two, and that's put me out; I must begin again. That can't be right. Help yourself, if de Vere has brought in tea, and if not ring— Oh, I left out the four, and altogether it's two thousand five hundred pounds."

Georgie had thought at first that Daisy was merely doing some belated household accounts, but the moment she said "two thousand five hundred pounds," he guessed, and did not even go through the formality of asking what was two thousand five hundred pounds.

"I made it two thousand six hundred," he said. "But we're pretty well agreed."

Naturally Daisy understood that he understood.

"Perhaps you reckoned the pearls as capital," she said, "and added the interest."

"No, I didn't," he said. "How could I tell how much they were worth? I didn't reckon them in at all."

"Well, it's a lot of money," said Daisy. "Let's have tea. What will she do with it?"

She seemed quite blind to the Oxford trousers, and Georgie wondered whether that was from mere feebleness of vision. Daisy was short-sighted, though she steadily refused to recognize that, and would never wear spectacles. In fact, Lucia had made an unkind little epigram about it at a time when there was a slight coolness between the two, and had said "Dear Daisy is too short-sighted to see how short-sighted she is." Of course it was unkind, but very brilliant, and Georgie had read through *The Importance of Being Earnest*, which Lucia had gone up to town to see, in the hopes of discovering it. . . . Or was Daisy's unconsciousness of his trousers merely due to her preoccupation with Lucia's probable income? . . . Or were the trousers, after all, not so daring as he had thought them?

He sat down with one leg thrown carelessly over the arm of his chair, so that Daisy could hardly fail to see it. Then he took a piece of tea cake.

"Yes, do tell me what you think she will do with it?" he asked. "I've been puzzling over it, too."

"I can't imagine," said Daisy. "She's got everything she wants now. Perhaps they'll just hoard it, in order that when Peppino dies we may all see how much richer he was than we ever imagined. That's too posthumous for me. Give me what I want now, and a pauper's funeral afterward."

"Me, too," said Georgie, waving his leg. "But I don't think Lucia will do that. It did occur to me—"

"The house in London, you mean," said Daisy, swiftly interrupting. "Of course, if they kept both houses open, with a staff in each, so that they could run up and down as they chose, that would make a big hole in it. Lucia has always said that she couldn't live in London, but she may manage it if she's got a house there."

"I'm dining with her tonight," said Georgie. "Perhaps she'll say something."

Mrs. Quantock was very thirsty with her gardening, and the tea was very hot. She poured it into her saucer and blew on it.

"Lucia would be wise not to waste any time," she said, "if she intends to have any fun out of it, for you know, Georgie, we're beginning to get old. I'm fifty-two. How old are you?"

Georgie disliked that barbarous sort of question. He had been the young man of Riseholme so long that the habit was ingrained, and he hardly believed that he was forty-eight.

"Forty-three," he said, "but what does it matter how old we are as long as we're busy and amused? And I'm sure Lucia has got all the energy and life she ever had. I shouldn't be a bit surprised if she made a start in London, and went in for all that. Then of course, there's Peppino, but he only cares for writing his poetry and looking through his telescope."

"I hate that telescope," said Daisy. "He took me up on to the roof the other night and showed me what he said was Mars, and I'll take my oath he said that the same one was Venus only a week before. But as I couldn't see anything either time, it didn't make much difference."

The door opened, and Mr. Quantock came in. Robert was like a little, round, brown sarcastic beetle. Georgie got up to greet him, and stood in the full blaze

of the light. Robert certainly saw his trousers, for his
eyes seemed unable to quit the spreading folds that lay
round Georgie's ankles; he looked at them as if he was
Cortez and they some new planet. Then, without a
word, he folded his arms and danced a few steps of
what was clearly meant to be a sailor's hornpipe.

"Heave-ho, Georgie," he said. "Belay there and
avast."

"What is he talking about?" said Daisy.

Georgie, quite apart from his general good nature,
always strove to propitiate Mr. Quantock. He was far
the most sarcastic person in Riseholme and could say
sharp things straight off, whereas Georgie had to think
a long time before he got a nasty edge to any remark,
and then his good nature generally forbade him to
slash with it.

"He's talking about my new clothes," he said, "and
he's being very naughty. Any news?"

"Any news?" was the general gambit of conversation
in Riseholme. It could not have been bettered, for
there always was news. And there was now.

"Yes, Peppino's gone to the station," said Mr.
Quantock. "Just like a large black crow. Waved a
black hand. Bah! Why not call a release, a release and
have done with it? And if you don't know—why, I'll
tell you. It's because they're rolling in riches. Why, I've
calculated—"

"Yes?" said Daisy and Georgie simultaneously.

"So you've been calculating, too?" said Mr. Quantock. "Might have a sweepstake for the one who gets
nearest. I say three thousand a year."

"Not so much," said Georgie and Daisy again simultaneously.

"All right. But that's no reason why I shouldn't have a lump of sugar in my tea."

"Dear me, no," said Daisy genially. "But how do you make it up to three thousand?"

"By addition," said this annoying man. "There'll be every penny of that. I was at the lending library after lunch, and those who could add made it all that."

Daisy turned to Georgie.

"You'll be alone with Lucia then tonight," she said.

"Oh, I knew that," said Georgie. "She told me Peppino had gone. I expect he's sleeping in that house tonight."

Mr. Quantock produced his calculations, and the argument waxed hot. It was still raging when Georgie left in order to get a little rest before going on to dinner, and to practise the Mozart duet. He and Lucia hadn't tried it before, so it was as well to practise both parts, and let her choose which she liked. Foljambe had come back from her afternoon out, and told him that there had been a trunk call for him while he was at tea, but she could make nothing of it.

"Somebody in a great hurry, sir," she said, "and kept asking if I was—excuse me, sir, if I was Georgie—I kept saying I wasn't, but I'd fetch you. That wouldn't do, and she said she'd telegraph."

"But who was it?" asked Georgie.

"Couldn't say, sir. She never gave a name, but only kept asking."

"She?" asked Georgie.

"Sounded like one!" said Foljambe.

"Most mysterious," said Georgie. It couldn't be either of his sisters, for they sounded not like a she but a

• • •

he. So he lay down on his sofa to rest a little before he took a turn at the Mozart.

The evening had turned chilly, and he put on his blue cape with the velvet collar to trot across to Lucia's house. The parlormaid received him with a faint haggard smile of recognition, and then grew funereal again, and preceding him, not at her usual brisk pace, but sadly and slowly, opened the door of the music room and pronounced his name in a mournful whisper. It was a gay cheerful room, in the ordinary way; now only one light was burning, and from the deepest of the shadows, there came a rustling, and Lucia rose to meet him.

"Georgie, dear," she said. "Good of you."

Georgie held her hand a moment longer than was usual, and gave it a little extra pressure for the conveyance of sympathy. Lucia, to acknowledge that, pressed a little more, and Georgie tightened his grip again to show that he understood, until their respective fingernails grew white with the conveyance and reception of sympathy. It was rather agonizing, because a bit of skin on his little finger had got caught between two of the rings on his third finger, and he was glad when they quite understood each other.

Of course it was not to be expected that in these first moments Lucia should notice his trousers. She herself was dressed in deep mourning, and Georgie thought he recognized the little cap she wore as being that which had faintly expressed her grief over the death of Queen Victoria. But black suited her, and she certainly looked very well. Dinner was announced immediately, and she took Georgie's arm, and with faltering steps they went into the dining room.

Georgie had determined that his rôle was to be sympathetic, but bracing. Lucia must rally from this blow, and her suggestion that he should bring the Mozart duet was hopeful. And though her voice was low and unsteady, she did say, as they sat down:

"Any news?"

"I've hardly been outside my house and garden all day," said Georgie. "Rolling the lawn. And Daisy Quantock—did you know?—has had a row with her gardener, and is going to do it all herself. So there she was next door with a fork and a wheelbarrow full of manure."

Lucia gave a wan smile.

"Dear Daisy!" she said. "What a garden it will be! Anything else?"

"Yes, I had tea with them, and while I was out, there was a trunk call for me. So tarsome. Whoever it was couldn't make any way, and she's going to telegraph. I can't imagine who it was."

"I wonder!" said Lucia in an interested voice. Then she recollected herself again. "I had a sort of presentiment, Georgie, when I saw that telegram for Peppino on the table, two days ago, that it was bad news."

"Curious," said Georgie. "And what delicious fish! How do you always manage to get better things than any of us? It tastes of the sea. And I am so hungry after all my work."

Lucia went firmly on.

"I took it to poor Peppino," she said, "and he got quite white. And then—so like him—he thought of me. 'It's bad news, darling,' he said, 'and we've got to help each other bear it!' "

"So like Peppino," said Georgie. "Mr. Quantock saw

him going to the station. Where is he going to sleep tonight?"

Lucia took a little more fish.

"In Auntie's house in Brompton Square," she said.

"So *that's* where it is!" thought Georgie. If there was a light anywhere in Daisy's house, except in the attics, he would have to go in for a minute, on his return home, and communicate the news.

"Oh, she had a house there, had she?" he said.

"Yes, a charming house," said Lucia, "and full, of course, of dear old memories to Peppino. It will be very trying for him, for he used to go there when he was a boy to see Auntie."

"And has she left it him?" asked Georgie, trying to make his voice sound unconcerned.

"Yes, and it's a freehold," said Lucia. "That makes it easier to dispose of if Peppino settles to sell it. And beautiful Queen Anne furniture."

"My dear, how delicious!" said Georgie. "Probably worth a fortune."

Lucia was certainly rallying from the terrible blow, but she did not allow herself to rally too far, and shook her head sadly.

"Peppino would hate to have to part with Auntie's things," she said. "So many memories. He can recollect her sitting at the walnut bureau (one of those tall ones, you know, which let down in front, and the handles of the drawers all original), doing her accounts in the morning. And a picture of her with her pearls over the fireplace by Sargent; quite an early one. Some fine Chinese Chippendale chairs in the dining room. We must try to keep some of the things."

Georgie longed to ask a hundred questions, but it

would not be wise, for Lucia was so evidently enjoying
letting these sumptuous details leak out mingled with
memories. He was beginning to feel sure that Daisy's
cynical suggestion was correct, and that the stricken
desolation of Peppino and Lucia cloaked a very sub-
stantial inheritance. Bits of exultation kept peeping out,
and Lucia kept poking them back.

"But where will you put all those lovely things, if
you sell the house?" he asked. "Your house here is so
perfect already."

"Nothing is settled yet," said Lucia. "Neither he nor
I can think of anything but dear Auntie. Such a keen
intelligent mind she had when Peppino first remembered her. Very good-looking still in the Sargent picture. And it was all so sudden, when Peppino saw her
last she was so full of vigor."

"That was the time she bit him," thought Georgie.
Aloud he said:

"Of course you must feel it dreadfully. What is the
Sargent? A kit-cat or a full length?"

"Full length, I believe," said Lucia. "I don't know
where we could put it here. And a William III what-
not. But of course it is not possible to think about that
yet. A glass of port?"

"I'm going to give you one," said Georgie. "It's just
what you want after all your worries and griefs."

Lucia pushed her glass toward him.

"Just half a glass," she said. "You are so dear and
understanding, Georgie; I couldn't talk to anyone but
you, and perhaps it does me good to talk. There is
some wonderful port in Auntie's cellar, Peppino says."

She rose.

"Let us go into the music room," she said. "We will

talk a little more, and then play our Mozart if I feel up to it."

"That'll do you good, too," said Georgie.

Lucia felt equal to having more illumination than there had been when she rose out of the shadows before dinner, and they established themselves quite cosily by the fire.

"There will be a terrible lot of business for Peppino," she said. "Luckily his lawyer is the same firm as Auntie's, and quite a family friend. Whatever Auntie had, so he told us, goes to Peppino, though we haven't really any idea what it is. But with death duties and succession duties, I know we shall have to be prepared to be very poor until they are paid off, and the duties increase so iniquitously in proportion to the inheritance. Then everything in Brompton Square has to be valued, and we have to pay on the entire contents, the very carpets and rugs are priced, and some are beautiful Persians. And then there's the valuer to pay, and all the lawyer's charges. And when all that has been paid and finished, there is the higher supertax."

"But there's a bigger income," said Georgie.

"Yes, that's one way of looking at it," said Lucia. "But Peppino says that the charges will be enormous. And there's a beautiful music room."

Lucia gave him one of her rather gimletlike looks.

"Georgino, I suppose everybody in Riseholme is all agog to know what Peppino has been left. That is so dreadfully vulgar, but I suppose it's natural. Is everybody talking about it?"

"Well, I have heard it mentioned," said Georgie. "But I don't see why it's vulgar. I'm interested in it myself. It concerns you and Peppino, and what concerns one's friends must be of interest to one."

"*Caro*, I know that," said Lucia. "But so much more than the actual money is the responsibility it brings. Peppino and I have all we want for our quiet little needs, and now this great increase of wealth is coming to us—great, that is, compared to our modest little income now—and, as I say, it brings its responsibilities. We shall have to use wisely and without extravagance whatever is left after all these immense expenses have been paid. That meadow at the bottom of the garden, of course, we shall buy at once, so that there will no longer be any fear of its being built over and spoiling the garden. And then perhaps a new telescope for Peppino. But what do I want in Riseholme beyond what I've got? Music and friends, and the power to entertain them, my books and my flowers. Perhaps a library, built on at the end of the wing, where Peppino can be undisturbed, and perhaps every now and then a string quartet down from London. That will give a great deal of pleasure, and music is more than pleasure, isn't it?"

Again she turned the gimlet look onto Georgie.

"And then there's the house in Brompton Square," she said, "where Auntie was born. Are we to sell that?"

Georgie guessed exactly what was in her mind. It had been in his too, ever since Lucia had alluded to the beautiful music room. Her voice had lingered over the beautiful music room: she had seemed to underline it, to caress it, to appropriate it.

"I believe you are thinking of keeping the house and partly living there," he said.

Lucia looked round, as if a hundred eavesdroppers had entered unaware.

"Hush, Georgie," she said, "not a word must be said

about that. But it has occurred to both Peppino and me."

"But I thought you hated London," he said. "You're always so glad to get back; you find it so common and garish."

"It is, compared to the exquisite peace and seriousness of our Riseholme," she said, "where there never is a jarring note; at least, hardly ever. But there is in London a certain stir and movement which we lack here. In the swim, Georgie, in the middle of things! Perhaps we get too sensitive here where everything is full of harmony and culture; perhaps we are too much sheltered. If I followed my inclination, I would never leave our dear Riseholme for a single day. Oh, how easy everything would be if one only followed one's inclination! A morning with my books, an afternoon in my garden, my piano after tea, and a friend like you to come in to dine with my Peppino and me and scold me well, as you'll soon be doing for being so bungling over *Mozartino*."

Lucia twirled round the Elizabethan spit that hung in the wide chimney, and again fixed him rather in the style of the Ancient Mariner. Georgie could not choose but hear . . . Lucia's eloquent well-ordered sentences had nothing impromptu about them; what she said was evidently all thought out and probably talked out. If she and Peppino had been talking of nothing else since the terrible blow had shattered them, she could not have been more lucid and crystal clear.

"Georgie, I feel like a leisurely old horse who has been turned out to grass being suddenly bridled and harnessed again. But there is work and energy in me yet, though I thought that I should be permitted to grow old in the delicious peace and leisure of our dear quiet humdrum Riseholme. But I feel that perhaps that is not to be. My conscience is cracking the whip at me, and saying 'You've got to trot again, you lazy old thing.' And I've got to think of Peppino. Dear, contented Peppino would never complain if I refused to budge. He would read his paper, and potter in the garden, and write his dear little poems—such a sweet one, 'Bereavement,' he began it yesterday, a sonnet— and look at the stars. But is it a life for a man?"

Georgie made an uneasy movement in his chair, and Lucia hastened to correct the implied criticism.

"You're different, my dear," she said. "You've got that wonderful power of being interested in everything. Everything. But think what London would give Peppino! His club; the Astronomer-Royal is a member. His other club, political, and politics have lately been quite an obsession with him. The reading room at the British Museum. No, I should be very selfish if I did not see all that. I must and I do think of Peppino. I mustn't be selfish, Georgie."

This idea of Lucia's leaving Riseholme was a live bomb. At the moment of its explosion, Georgie seemed to see Riseholme fly into a thousand disintegrated fragments. And then, faintly, through the smoke he seemed to see Riseholme still intact. Somebody, of course, would have to fill the vacant throne and direct its affairs. And the thought of Beau Nash at Bath flitted across the distant horizon of his mind. It was a naughty thought, but its vagueness absolved it from treason. He shook it off.

"But how on earth are we to get on without you?" he asked.

"Sweet of you to say that, Georgie," said she, giving another twirl to the spit. (There had been a leg of mut-

ton roasted on it last May Day, while they all sat round
in jerkins and stomachers and hose, and all the per-
fumes of Arabia had hardly sufficed to quell the odor of
roast meat which had pervaded the room for weeks afterward.) "Sweet of you to say that, but you mustn't
think that I am deserting Riseholme. We should be in
London perhaps (though, as I say, nothing is settled)
for two or three months in the summer, and always
come here for week-ends, and perhaps from November
till Christmas, and a little while in the spring. And then
Riseholme would always be coming up to us. Five
spare bedrooms, I believe, and one of them quite a
little suite with a bathroom and sitting room attached.
No, dear Georgie, I would never desert my dear Riseholme. If it was a choice between London and Riseholme, I should not hesitate in my choice."

"Then would you keep both houses open?" asked
Georgie, thrilled to the marrow.

"Peppino thought we could manage it," she said, utterly erasing the impression of the shattered nephew.
"He was calculating it out last night, and with board
wages at the other house, if you understand, and vegetables from the country, he thought that with care we
could live well within our means. He got quite excited
about it, and I heard him walking about long after I
had gone to bed. Peppino has such a head for detail.
He intends to keep a complete set of things—clothes
and sponge and everything in London—so that he will
have no luggage. Such a saving of tips and small expenses, in which as he so truly says, money leaks away.
Then there will be no garage expenses in London: we
shall leave the motor here, and rough it with tubes and
taxis in town."

Georgie was fully as excited as Peppino, and could not be discreet any longer.

"Tell me," he said, "how much do you think it will all come to? The money he'll come into, I mean."

Lucia also threw discretion to the winds, and forgot all about the fact that they were to be so terribly poor for a long time.

"About three thousand a year, Peppino imagines, when everything is paid. Our income will be doubled, in fact."

Georgie gave a sigh of pure satisfaction. So much was revealed, not only of the future, but of the past, for no one hitherto had known what their income was. And how clever of Robert Quantock to have made so accurate a guess!

"It's too wonderful for you," he said. "And I know you'll spend it beautifully. I had been thinking over it this afternoon, but I never thought it would be as much as that. And then there are the pearls. I do congratulate you."

Lucia suddenly felt that she had shown too much of the silver (or was it gold?) lining to the cloud of affliction that had overshadowed her.

"Poor Auntie!" she said. "We don't forget her through it all. We hoped she might have been spared us a little longer."

That came out of her note to Daisy Quantock (and perhaps to others as well), but Lucia could not have known that Georgie had already been told about that.

"Now, I've come here to take your mind off these sad things," he said. "You mustn't dwell on them any longer."

She rose briskly.

"You've been ever so good to me," she said. "I should just have moped if I had been alone."

She lapsed into the baby language which they sometimes spoke, varying it with easy Italian.

"Ickle music, Georgie?" she said. "And you must be kindy-kindy to me. No practice all these days. You brought Mozart? Which part is easiest? Lucia wants to take easiest part."

"Lucia shall take which ever part she likes," said Georgie, who had had a good practice at both.

"Treble then," said Lucia. "But oh, how diffy it looks! Hundreds of ickle notes. And me so tupid at reading! Come on then. You begin. *Uno, due, tre.*"

The light by the piano was not very good, but Georgie did not want to put on his spectacles unless he was obliged, for he did not think Lucia knew that he wore them, and somehow spectacles did not seem to "go" with Oxford trousers. But it was no good, and after having made a miserable hash of the first page, he surrendered.

"Me must put on speckies," he said. "Me a blind old man."

Then he had an immense surprise.

"And me a blind old woman," said Lucia. "I've just got speckies, too. Oh, Georgie, aren't we getting *vecchio*? Now we'll start again. *Uno, due—*"

The Mozart went beautifully after that, and each of them inwardly wondered at the accuracy of the other's reading. Lucia suspected that Georgie had been having a try at it, but then, after all, she had had the choice of which part she would take, and if Georgie had practised already, he would have been almost certain to have practised the treble; it never entered her head that he had been so thorough as to practise both. Then they played it through again, changing parts, and again it went excellently. It was late now, and soon Georgie rose to go.

"And what shall I say if anybody who knows I've been dining with you, asks if you've told me anything?" he asked.

Lucia closed the piano and concentrated.

"Say nothing of our plans about the house in Brompton Square," she said, "but there's no reason why people shouldn't know that there is a house there. I hate secretiveness, and after all, when the will comes out, everyone will know. So say there is a house there, full of beautiful things. And similarly they will know about the money. So say what Peppino thinks it will come to."

"I see," said Georgie.

She came with him to the door, and strolled out into the little garden in front where the daffodils were in flower. The night was clear, but moonless, and the company of stars burned brightly.

"Aldebaran!" said Lucia, pointing inclusively to the spangled arch of the sky. "That bright one. Oh, Georgie, how restful it is to look at Aldebaran if one is worried and sad. It lifts one's mind above petty cares and personal sorrows. The patens of bright gold! Wonderful Shakespeare! Look in tomorrow afternoon, won't you, and tell me if there is any news. Naturally, I shan't go out."

"Oh, come and have lunch," said Georgie.

"No, dear Georgie; the funeral is at two. Putney Vale. *Buona notte*."

"*Buona notte*, dear Lucia," he said.

Georgie hurried back to his house, and was disappointed to see that there were no lights in Daisy's drawing room nor in Robert Quantock's study. But when he got up to his bedroom, where Foljambe had forgotten to pull down the blinds, he saw a light in Daisy's bedroom. Even as he looked, the curtains there were drawn back, and he saw her amply clad in a dressing gown, opening windows at top and bottom, for just now the first principle of health consisted in sleeping in a gale. She, too, must have seen his room was lit, and his face at the window, for she made violent signs to him and threw open the casement.

"Well?" she said.

"In Brompton Square," said George. "And three thousand a year!"

"No!" said Daisy.

2

THIS SIMPLE WORD "No" connoted a great deal in the Riseholme vernacular. It was used, of course, as a mere negative, without emphasis, and if you wanted to give weight to your negative, you added "Certainly not." But when you used the word "No" with emphasis, as Daisy had used it from her bedroom window to Georgie, it was not a negative at all, and its signification briefly put was "I never heard anything so marvellous, and it thrills me through and through. Please go on at once, and tell me a great deal more, and then let us talk it all over."

On the occasion Georgie did not go on at once, for having made his climax, he with supreme art shut the window and drew down the blind, leaving Daisy to lie awake half the night and ponder over this remarkable news and wonder what Peppino and Lucia would do with all that money. She arrived at several conclusions:

she guessed that they would buy the meadow beyond the garden, and have a new telescope, but the building of a library did not occur to her. Before she went to sleep, an even more important problem presented itself, and she scribbled a note to Georgie to be taken across in the morning early, in which she wrote, "And did she say anything about the house? What's going to happen to it? And you didn't tell me the number," exactly as she would have continued the conversation if he had not shut his window so quickly and drawn down the blind, ringing down the curtain on his magnificent climax.

Foljambe brought up this note with Georgie's early morning tea and the glass of very hot water which sometimes he drank instead of it, if he suspected an error of diet the night before, and the little glass gallipot of Kruschen salts, which occasionally he added to the hot water or the tea. Georgie was very sleepy, and only half awake, turned round in bed, so that Foljambe should not see the place where he wore the toupée, and smothered a snore, for he would not like her to think that he snored. But when she said, "Telegram for you, sir," Georgie sat up at once in his pink silk pyjamas.

"No!" he said with emphasis.

He tore the envelope open, and a whole sheaf of sheets fell out. The moment he set his eyes on the first words, he knew so well from whom it came that he did not even trouble to look at the last sheet where it would be signed.

BELOVED GEORGIE [*it ran*],

I rang you up till I lost my temper and so send this. Most expensive, but terribly important. I arrived in London yesterday and shall come down for week-end to Riseholme. Shall dine with you Saturday all alone to hear about everything. Come to lunch and dinner Sunday, and ask everybody to one or other, particularly Lucia. Am bringing cook, but order sufficient food for Sunday. Wonderful American and Australian tour, and I'm taking house in London for season. Shall motor down. Bless you.

OLGA

Georgie sprang out of bed, merely glancing through Daisy's pencilled note and throwing it away. There was nothing to be said to it in any case, since he had been told not to divulge the project with regard to the house in Brompton Square, and he didn't know the number. But in Olga's telegram there was enough to make anybody busy for the day, for he had to ask all her friends to lunch or dinner on Sunday, order the necessary food, and arrange a little meal for Olga and himself tomorrow night. He scarcely knew what he was drinking, tea or hot water or Kruschen salts, so excited was he. He foresaw, too, that there would be call for the most skilled diplomacy with regard to Lucia. She must certainly be asked first, and some urging might be required to make her consent to come at all, either to lunch or dinner, even if due regard was paid to her deep mourning, and the festivity limited to one or two guests of her own selection. Yet somehow Georgie felt that she would stretch a point and be persuaded, for everybody else would be going sometime on Sunday to Olga's, and it would be tiresome for her to explain again and again in the days that followed that she had been asked and had not felt up to it. And if she didn't explain carefully every time, Riseholme would be sure to think she hadn't been asked. "A little diplomacy," thought Georgie, as he trotted across to her house after breakfast with no hat, but a fur tippet round his neck.

He was shown into the music room, while her maid went to fetch her. The piano was open, so she had evidently been practising, and there was a copy of the Mozart duet which she had read so skillfully last night on the music rest. For the moment Georgie thought he must have forgotten to take his copy away with him, but then looking at it more carefully he saw that there were pencilled marks for the fingering scribbled over the more difficult passages in the treble, which certainly he had never put there. At the moment he saw Lucia through the window coming up the garden, and he hastily took a chair far away from the piano and buried himself in the *Times*.

They sat close together in front of the fire, and Georgie opened his errand.

"I heard from Olga this morning," he said, "a great long telegram. She is coming down for the week-end."

Lucia gave a wintry smile. She did not care for Olga's coming down. Riseholme was quite silly about Olga.

"That will be nice for you, Georgie," she said.

"She sent you a special message," said he.

"I am grateful for her sympathy," said Lucia. "She might perhaps have written direct to me, but I'm sure she was full of kind intentions. As she sent the message by you verbally, will you verbally thank her? I appreciate it."

Even as she delivered these icy sentiments, Lucia got up rather hastily and passed behind him. Something white on the music rest of the piano had caught her eye.

"Don't move, Georgie," she said. "Sit and warm yourself and light your cigarette. Anything else?"

She walked up the room to the far end where the piano stood, and Georgie, though he was a little deaf, quite distinctly heard the rustle of paper. The most elementary rudiments of politeness forbade him to look round. Besides he knew exactly what was happening. Then there came a second rustle of paper, which he could not interpret.

"Anything else, Georgie?" repeated Lucia, coming back to her chair.

"Yes. But Olga's message wasn't quite that," he said. "She evidently hadn't heard of your bereavement."

"Odd," said Lucia. "I should have thought perhaps that the death of Miss Amy Lucas—however, what was her message then?"

"She wanted you very much—she said 'particularly Lucia'—to go to lunch or dine with her on Sunday. Peppino, too, of course."

"So kind of her, but naturally quite impossible," said Lucia.

"Oh, but you mustn't say that," said Georgie. "She is down for just that day, and she wants to see all her old friends. Particularly Lucia, you know. In fact she asked me to get up two little parties for her at lunch and dinner. So, of course, I came to see you first, to know which you would prefer."

Lucia shook her head.

"A party!" she said. "How do you think I could?"

"But it wouldn't be *that* sort of party," said Georgie. "Just a few of your friends. You and Peppino will have seen nobody tonight and all tomorrow. He will have told you everything by Sunday. And so bad to sit brooding."

The moment Lucia had said it was quite impossible, she had been longing for Georgie to urge her, and had indeed been prepared to encourage him to urge her if he didn't do so of his own accord. His last words had given her an admirable opening.

"I wonder!" she said. "Perhaps Peppino might feel inclined to go, if there really was no party. It doesn't do to brood: you are right, I mustn't let him brood. Selfish of me not to think of that. Who would there be, Georgie?"

"That's really for you to settle," he said.

"You?" she asked.

"Yes," said Georgie, thinking it unnecessary to add that Olga was dining with him on Sunday, and that he would be at lunch and dinner on Sunday. "Yes, she asked me to come."

"Well, then, what if you asked poor Daisy and her husband?" said Lucia. "It would be a treat for them. That would make six. I think six would be enough. I will do my best to persuade Peppino."

"Capital," said Georgie. "And would you prefer lunch or dinner?"

Lucia sighed.

"I think dinner," she said. "One feels more capable of making the necessary effort in the evening. But, of course, it is all conditional on Peppino's feeling."

She glanced at the clock.

"He will just be leaving Brompton Square," she said. "And then, afterward, his lawyer is coming to lunch with him and have a talk. Such a lot of business to see to."

Georgie suddenly remembered that he did not yet know the number of the house.

"Indeed there must be," he said. "Such a delightful square, but rather noisy, I should think, at the lower end."

"Yes, but deliciously quiet at the top end," said Lucia. "A curve you know, and a *cul de sac*. Number twenty-five is just before the beginning of the curve. And no houses at the back. Just the peaceful old churchyard—though sad for Peppino to look out on this morning—and a footpath only up to Ennismore Gardens. My music room looks out at the back."

Lucia rose.

"Well, Georgie, you will be very busy this morning," she said, "getting all the guests for Sunday, and I mustn't keep you. But I should like to play you a morsel of Stravinski which I have been trying over. Terribly modern, of course, and it may sound hideous to you at first, and at best it's a mere little tinkle if you compare it with the immortals. But there is something about it, and one mustn't condemn all modern work unheard. There was a time, no doubt, when even Beethoven's greatest sonatas were thought to be modern and revolutionary."

She led the way to the piano, where on the music rest was the morsel of Stravinski, which explained the second and hitherto unintelligible rustle.

"Sit by me, Georgie," she said, "and turn over quick, when I nod. Something like this."

Lucia got through the first page beautifully, but then everything seemed to go wrong. Georgie had expected it all to be odd and aimless, but surely Stravinski hadn't meant quite what Lucia was playing. Then he suddenly saw that the key had been changed, but in a

very inconspicuous manner, right in the middle of a
bar, and Lucia had not observed this. She went on playing with amazing agility, nodded at the end of the
second page, and then luckily the piece changed back
again into its original clef. Would it be wise to tell her?
He thought not: next time she tried it, or the time after,
she would very likely notice the change of key.

A brilliant roulade, consisting of chromatic scales in
contrary directions, brought this firework to an end,
and Lucia gave a little shiver.

"I must work at it," she said, "before I can judge on
it. . . ."

Her fingers strayed about the piano, and she paused.
Then with the wistful expression Georgie knew so well,
she played the first movement of the "Moonlight
Sonata." Georgie set his face also in the Beethoven expression, and at the end gave the usual little sigh.

"Divine," he said. "You never played it better.
Thank you, Lucia."

She rose.

"You must thank immortal Beethoven," she said.

Georgie's head buzzed with inductive reasoning, as
he hurried about on his vicariously hospitable errands.
Lucia had certainly determined to make a second home
in London, for she had distinctly said, "my music
room" when she referred to the house in Brompton
Square. Also, it was easy to see the significance of her
deigning to touch Stravinski with even the tip of one
finger. She was visualizing herself in the modern world;
she was going to be up to date; the music room in
Brompton Square was not only to echo with the first
movement of the "Moonlight." . . . "It's too thrilling,"

said Georgie, as warmed with this mental activity, he quite forgot to put on his fur tippet.

His first visit, of course, was to Daisy Quantock, but he meant to stay no longer than just to secure her and her husband for dinner on Sunday with Olga, and tell her the number of the house in Brompton Square. He found that she had dug a large trench round her mulberry tree, and was busily pruning the roots with the wood axe by the light of Nature: in fact she had cut off all their ends, and there was a great pile of chunks of mulberry root to be transferred in the wheelbarrow, now empty of manure, to the woodshed.

"Twenty-five, that's easy to remember," she said. "And are they going to sell it?"

"Nothing settled," said Georgie. "My dear, you're being rather drastic, aren't you? Won't it die?"

"Not a bit," said Daisy. "It'll bear twice as many mulberries as before. Last year there was one. You should always prune the roots of a fruit tree that doesn't bear. And the pearls?"

"No news," said Georgie, "except that they come in a portrait of the aunt by Sargent."

"No! By Sargent?" asked Daisy.

"Yes, and Queen Anne furniture and Chinese Chippendale chairs," said Georgie.

"And how many bedrooms?" asked Daisy, wiping her axe on the grass.

"Five spare, so I suppose that means seven," said Georgie, "and one with a sitting room and bathroom attached. And a beautiful music room."

"Georgie, she means to live there," said Daisy, "whether she told you or not. You don't count the bedrooms like that in a house you're going to sell. It isn't done."

"Nothing settled, I told you," said Georgie. "So you'll dine with Olga on Sunday, and now I must fly and get people to lunch with her."

"No! A lunch party too?" asked Daisy.

"Yes. She wants to see everybody."

"And five spare rooms, did you say?" asked Daisy, beginning to fill in her trench.

Georgie hurried out of the front gate, and Daisy shovelled the earth back and hurried indoors to impart all this news to her husband. He had a little rheumatism in his shoulder, and she gave him Coué treatment before she counterordered the chicken which she had bespoken for his dinner on Sunday.

Georgie thought it wise to go first to Olga's house, to make sure that she had told her caretaker that she was coming down for the week-end. That was the kind of thing that prima-donnas sometimes forgot. There was a man sitting on the roof of Old Place with a coil of wire, and another sitting on the chimney. Though listening-in had not yet arrived at Riseholme, Georgie at once conjectured that Olga was installing it, and what would Lucia say? It was utterly un-Elizabethan to begin with, and though she countenanced the telephone, she had expressed herself very strongly on the subject of listening-in. She had had an unfortunate experience of it herself, for on a visit to London not long ago, her hostess had switched it on, and the company was regaled with a vivid lecture on pyorrhea by a hospital nurse. . . . Georgie, however, would see Olga before Lucia came to dinner on Sunday and would explain her abhorrence of the instrument.

Then there was the delightful task of asking everybody to lunch. It was the hour now when Riseholme generally was popping in and out of shops, and finding out the news. It was already known that Georgie had dined with Lucia last night and that Peppino had gone to his aunt's funeral, and everyone was agog to ascertain if anything definite had yet been ascertained about the immense fortune which had certainly come to the Lucases. . . . Mrs. Antrobus spied Georgie going into Olga's house (for the keenness of her eyesight made up for her deafness), and there she was with her eartrumpet adjusted, looking at the view just outside Old Place when Georgie came out. Already the popular estimate had grown like a gourd.

"A quarter of a million, I'm told, Mr. Georgie," said she, "and a house in Grosvenor Square, eh?"

Before Georgie could reply, Mrs. Antrobus's two daughters, Piggy and Goosie, came bounding up hand in hand. Piggy and Goosie never walked like other people: they skipped and gambolled to show how girlish an age is thirty-four and thirty-five.

"Oh, stop, Mr. Georgie," said Piggy. "Let us all hear. And are the pearls worth a queen's ransom?"

"Silly thing," said Goosie. "I don't believe in the pearls."

"Well, I don't believe in Grosvenor Square," said Goosie. "So, silly yourself!"

When this ebullition of high spirits had subsided, and Piggy had slapped Goosie on the back of her hands, they both said, "Hush!" simultaneously.

"Well, I can't say about the pearls," said Georgie.

"Eh, what can't you say?" said Mrs. Antrobus.

"About the pearls," said Georgie, addressing himself to the end of Mrs. Antrobus's trumpet. It was like the trunk of a very short elephant, and she waved it about as if asking for a bun.

"About the pearls, mamma," screamed Goosie and Piggy together. "Don't interrupt Mr. Georgie."

"And the house isn't in Grosvenor Square, but in Brompton Square," said Georgie.

"But that's quite in the slums," said Mrs. Antrobus. "I am disappointed."

"Not at all, a charming neighborhood," said Georgie. This was not at all what he had been looking forward to; he had expected cries of envious surprise at his news. "As for the fortune, about three thousand a year."

"Is that all?" said Piggy with an air of deep disgust.

"A mere pittance to millionaires like Piggy," said Goosie, and they slapped each other again.

"Any more news?" asked Mrs. Antrobus.

"Yes," said Georgie, "Olga Bracely is coming down tomorrow—"

"No!" said all the ladies together.

"And her husband?" asked Piggy.

"No," said Georgie without emphasis. "At least, she didn't say so. But she wants all her friends to come to lunch on Sunday. So you'll all come, will you? She told me to ask everybody."

"Yes," said Piggy. "Oh, how lovely! I adore Olga. Will she let me sit next her?"

"Eh?" said Mrs. Antrobus.

"Lunch on Sunday, Mamma, with Olga Bracely," screamed Goosie.

"But she's not here," said Mrs. Antrobus.

"No, but she's coming, Mamma," shouted Piggy. "Come along, Goosie. There's Mrs. Boucher. We'll tell her about poor Mrs. Lucas."

Mrs. Boucher's Bath chair was stationed opposite the butcher's, where her husband was ordering the joint for Sunday. Piggy and Goosie had poured the tale of Lucia's comparative poverty into her ear, before Georgie got to her. Here, however, it had a different reception, and Georgie found himself the hero of the hour.

"An immense fortune. I call it an immense fortune," said Mrs. Boucher, emphatically, as Georgie approached. "Good morning, Mr. Georgie, I've heard your news, and I hope Mrs. Lucas will use it well. Brompton Square, too! I had an aunt who lived there once, my mother's sister, you understand, not my father's, and she used to say that she would sooner live in Brompton Square than in Buckingham Palace. What will they do with it, do you suppose? It must be worth its weight in gold. What a strange coincidence that Mr. Lucas's aunt and mine should both have lived there! Any more news?"

"Yes," said Georgie. "Olga is coming down tomorrow—"

"Well, that's a bit of news!" said Mrs. Boucher, as her husband came out of the butcher's shop. "Jacob, Olga's coming down tomorrow, so Mr. Georgie says. That'll make you happy! You're madly in love with Olga, Jacob, so don't deny it. You're an old flirt, Jacob; that's what you are. I shan't get much of your attention till Olga goes away again. I should be ashamed at your age, I should. And young enough to be your daughter or mine, either. And three thousand a year, Mr. Georgie says. I call it an immense fortune. That's Mrs. Lucas, you know. I thought perhaps two. I'm astounded. Why, when old Mrs. Toppington—not the wife of the young Mr. Toppington who married the niece of the man who invented laughing gas—but of his father, or perhaps his uncle, I can't be quite sure which, but when old Mr. Toppington died, he left his son or nephew, whichever it was, a sum that brought him in just about that, and he was considered a very rich man. He had the house just beyond the church at Scroby Windham where my father was rector, and he built the new wing with the billiard room—"

Georgie knew he would never get through his morning's work if he listened to everything that Mrs. Boucher had to say about young Mr. Toppington, and broke in.

"And she wants you and the colonel to lunch with her on Sunday," he said. "She told me to ask all her old friends."

"Well, I do call that kind," said Mrs. Boucher, "and of course we'll go. . . . Jacob, the joint. We shan't want the joint. I was going to give you a veal cutlet in the evening, so what's the good of a joint? Just a bit of steak for the servants, a nice piece. Well, that will be a treat, to lunch with dear Olga! Quite a party, I daresay."

Mrs. Quantock's chicken, already countermanded, came in nicely for Georgie's dinner for Olga on Saturday, and by the time all his errands were done, the morning was gone, without any practice at his piano, or work in his garden, or single stitch in his new piece of embroidery. Fresh amazements awaited him when he made his fatigued return to his house. For Foljambe told him that Lucia had sent her maid to borrow his manual on auction bridge. He was too tired to puzzle over that now, but it was strange that Lucia, who despised any form of cards as only fit for those who had not the intelligence to talk or to listen, should have done that. Cards came next to crossword puzzles in Lucia's index of inanities. What did it mean?

Neither Lucia nor Peppino were seen in public at all till Sunday morning, though Daisy Quantock had caught sight of Peppino, on his arrival on Friday afternoon, walking bowed with grief and with a faltering gait through the little paved garden in front of The Hurst to his door. Lucia opened it for him, and they both shook their heads sadly and passed inside. But it was believed that they never came out the whole of Saturday, and their first appearance was at church on Sunday, though indeed Lucia could hardly be said to have appeared, so impenetrable was her black veil. But that, so to speak, was the end of all mourning (besides, everybody knew that she was dining with Olga that night), and at the end of the service, she put up her veil, and held a sort of little reception, standing in the porch and shaking hands with all her friends as they went out. It was generally felt that this signified her re-entry into Riseholme life.

Hardly less conspicuous a figure was Georgie. Though Robert had been so sarcastic about his Oxford trousers, he had made up his mind to get it over, and after church he walked twice round the green quite slowly and talked to everybody, standing a little away so that they should get a complete view. The odious Piggy, it is true, burst into a squeal of laughter and cried, "Oh, Mr. Georgie, I see you've gone into long frocks," and her mother put up her ear-trumpet as she approached as if to give a greater keenness to her general perceptions. But apart from the jarring incident of Piggy, Georgie was pleased with his trousers' reception. They were beautifully cut, too, and fell in charming lines, and the sensation they created was quite a respectful one. But it had been an anxious morning, and he was pleased when it was over.

And such a talk he had had with Olga last night, when she dined alone with him, and sat so long with her elbows on the table that Foljambe looked in three times in order to clear away. Her own adventures, she said, didn't matter; she could tell Georgie about the American tour and the Australian tour, and the coming season in London any time at leisure. What she had to know about with the utmost detail was exactly everything that had happened at Riseholme since she had left it a year ago.

"Good heavens!" she said. "To think that I once thought that it was a quiet backwatery place where I could rest and do nothing but study. But it's a whirl! There's always something wildly exciting going on. Oh, what fools people are not to take an interest in what they call little things. Now go on about Lucia. It's his aunt, isn't it, and mad?"

"Yes, and Peppino's been left her house in Brompton Square," began Georgie.

"No! That's where I've taken a house for the season. What number?"

"Twenty-five," said Georgie.

"Twenty-five?" said Olga. "Why, that's just where the curve begins. And a big—"

"Music room built out at the back," said Georgie.

"I'm almost exactly opposite. But mine's a small one. Just room for my husband and me, and one spare room. Go on quickly."

"And about three thousand a year and some pearls," said Georgie. "And the house is full of beautiful furniture."

"And will they sell it?"

"Nothing settled," said Georgie.

"That means you think they won't. Do you think that they'll settle altogether in London?"

"No, I don't think that," said Georgie very carefully.

"You are tactful. Lucia has told you all about it, but has also said firmly that nothing's settled. So I won't pump you. And I met Colonel Boucher on my way here. Why only one bulldog?"

"Because the other always growled so frightfully at Mrs. Boucher. He gave it away to his brother."

"And Daisy Quantock? Is it still spiritualism?"

"No, that's over, though I rather think it's coming back. After that it was sour milk, and now it's raw vegetables. You'll see tomorrow at dinner. She brings them in a paper bag. Carrots and turnips and celery. Raw. But perhaps she may not. Every now and then she eats like anybody else."

"And Piggy and Goosie?"

"Just the same. But Mrs. Antrobus has got a new ear-trumpet. But what I want to know is, Why did Lucia send across for my manual on auction bridge? She thinks all card games imbecile."

"Oh, Georgie, that's easy!" said Olga. "Why, of course, Brompton Square, though nothing's settled. Parties, you know, when she wants people who like to play bridge."

Georgie became deeply thoughtful.

"It might be that," he said. "But it would be tremendously thorough."

"How else can you account for it? By the way, I've had a listening-in put up at Old Place."

"I know. I saw them at it yesterday. But don't turn it on tomorrow night. Lucia hates it. She only heard it once, and that time it was a lecture on pyorrhea. Now tell me about yourself. And shall we go into the drawing room? Foljambe's getting restless."

Olga allowed herself to be weaned from subjects so much more entrancing to her, and told him of the huge success of the American tour, and spoke of the eight weeks' season which was to begin at Covent Garden in the middle of May. But it all led back to Riseholme.

"I'm singing twice a week," she said. "Brunnhilde and Lucrezia and Salome. Oh, my dear, how I love it! But I shall come down here every single week-end. To go back to Lucia, do you suppose she'll settle in London for the season? I believe that's the idea. Fresh worlds to conquer."

Georgie was silent a moment.

"I think you may be right about the auction bridge," he said at length. "And that would account for Stravinski, too."

"What's that?" said Olga greedily.

"Why, she played me a bit of Stravinski yesterday morning," said Georgie. "And before she never would listen to anything modern. It all fits in."

"Perfect," said Olga.

* * *

Georgie and the Quantocks walked up together the next evening to dine with Olga, and Daisy was carrying a little paper parcel. But that proved to be a disappointment, for it did not contain carrots, but only evening shoes. Lucia and Peppino, as usual, were a little late, for it was Lucia's habit to arrive last at any party, as befitted the Queen of Riseholme, and to make her gracious round of the guests. Everyone, of course, was wondering if she would wear the pearls, but again there was a disappointment, for her only ornaments were two black bangles, and the brooch of entwined sausages of gold containing a lock of Beethoven's hair. (As a matter of fact Beethoven's hair had fallen out some years ago, and she had replaced it with a lock of Peppino's which was the same color. . . . Peppino had never told anybody.) From the first it was evident that though the habiliments of woe still decked her, she had cast off the numb misery of the bereavement.

"So kind of you to invite us," she said to Olga. "And so good," she added in a whisper, "for my poor Peppino. I've been telling him he must face the world again and not mope. Daisy, dear! Sweet to see you, and Mr. Robert. Georgie! Well, I do think this is a delicious little party."

Peppino followed her: it was just like the arrival of royal personages, and Olga had to stiffen her knees so as not to curtsey.

Having greeted those who had the honor to meet her, Lucia became affable rather than gracious. Robert Quantock was between her and Olga at dinner, but then at dinner, everybody left Robert alone, for if disturbed over that function, he was apt to behave rather like a dog with a bone and growl. But if left alone, he was in an extremely good temper afterward.

"And you're only here just for two days, Miss Olga," she said. "At least so Georgie tells me, and he usually knows your movements. And then London, I suppose, and you'll be busy rehearsing for the opera. I must certainly manage to be in London for a week or two this year, and come to *Siegfried*, and *The Valkyrie*, in which, so I see in the papers, you're singing. Georgie, you must take me up to London when the opera comes on. Or perhaps—"

She paused a moment.

"Peppino, shall I tell all our dear friends our little secret?" she said. "If you say no, I shan't. But, please, Peppino—"

Peppino, however, had been instructed to say yes, and accordingly did so.

"You see, dear Miss Olga," said Lucia, "that a little property has come to us through that grievous tragedy last week. A house has been left to Peppino in Brompton Square, all furnished, and with a beautiful music room. So we're thinking, as there is no immediate hurry about selling it, of spending a few weeks there this season, very quietly, of course, but still perhaps entertaining a few friends. Then we shall have time to look about us, and as the house is there, why not use it in the interval? We shall go there at the end of the month."

This little speech had been carefully prepared, for Lucia felt that if she announced the full extent of their plan, Riseholme would suffer a terrible blow. It must be broken to Riseholme by degrees; Riseholme must first be told that they were to be up in town for a week or two, pending the sale of the house. Subsequently Riseholme would hear that they were not going to sell the house.

She looked round to see how this section of Riseholme took it. A chorus of emphatic Noes burst from Georgie, Mrs. Quantock, and Olga, who, of course, had fully discussed this disclosure already; even Robert, very busy with his dinner, said no and went on gobbling.

"So sweet of you all to say no," said Lucia, who knew perfectly well that the emphatic interjection meant only surprise, and the desire to hear more, not the denial that such a thing was possible, "but there it is. Peppino and I have talked it over—*non è vero, carissimo?*—and we feel that there is a sort of call to us to go to London. Dearest Aunt Amy, you know, and all her beautiful furniture! She never would have a stick of it sold, and that seems to point to the fact that she expected Peppino and me not to wholly desert the dear old family home. Aunt Amy was born there, eighty-three years ago."

"My dear! How it takes one back!" said Georgie.

"Doesn't it?" said Olga.

Lucia had now, so to speak, developed her full horsepower. Peppino's presence stoked her, Robert was stoking himself and might be disregarded, while Olga and Georgie were hanging on her words.

"But it isn't the past only that we are thinking of," she said, "but the present and the future. Of course our spiritual home is here—like Lord Haldane and Germany—and, oh, how much we have learned at Riseholme, its lovely seriousness and its gaiety, its culture, its absorption in all that is worthy in art and literature, its old customs, its simplicity."

"Yes," said Olga. (She had meant long ago to tell Lucia that she had taken a house in Brompton Square exactly opposite Lucia's, but who could interrupt the splendor that was pouring out on them?)

Lucia fumbled for a moment at the brooch containing Beethoven's hair. She had a feeling that the pin had come undone. "Dear Miss Olga," she said, "how good of you to take an interest, you with your great mission of melody in the world, in our little affairs! I am encouraged. Well, Peppino and I feel—don't we, *sposo mio?*—that now that this opportunity has come to us, of perhaps having a little salon in London, we ought to

take it. There are modern movements in the world we
really know nothing about. We want to educate ourselves. We want to know what the cosmopolitan mind
is thinking about. Of course we're old, but it is never
too late to learn. How we shall treasure all we are
lucky enough to glean, and bring it back to our dear
Riseholme."

There was a slight and muffled thud on the ground,
and Lucia's fingers went back where the brooch should
have been.

"Georgino, my brooch, the Beethoven brooch," she
said; "it has fallen."

Georgie stooped rather stiffly to pick it up; that work
with the garden roller had found out his lumbar
muscles. Olga rose.

"Too thrilling, Mrs. Lucas!" she said. "You must
tell me much more. Shall we go? And how lovely for
me; I have just taken a house in Brompton Square for
the season."

"No!" said Lucia. "Which?"

"Oh, one of the little ones," said Olga. "Just opposite yours. Forty-two A."

"Such dear little houses!" said Lucia. "I have a
music room. Always yours to practise in."

"Capital good dinner," said Robert, who had not
spoken for a long time.

Lucia put an arm round Daisy Quantock's ample
waist, and thus tactfully avoided the question of precedence. Daisy, of course, was far, far the elder, but then
Lucia was Lucia.

"Delicious indeed," she said. "Georgie, bring the
Beethoven with you."

"And don't be long," said Olga.

Georgie had no use for the society of his own sex

unless they were young, which made him feel young, too, or much older than himself, which had the same result. But Peppino had an unpleasant habit of saying to him "When we come to our age" (which was an unreasonable assumption of juvenility), and Robert of sipping port with the sound of many waters for an indefinite period. So when Georgie had let Robert have two good glasses, he broke up this symposium and trundled them away into the drawing room, only pausing to snatch up his embroidery tambour, on which he was working at what had been originally intended for a bedspread, but was getting so lovely that he now thought of putting it when finished on the top of his piano. He noticed that Lucia had brought a portfolio of music, and peeping inside saw the morsel of Stravinski. . . .

And then, as he came within range of the conversation of the ladies, he nearly fell down from sheer shock.

"Oh, but I adore it," Lucia was saying. "One of the most marvellous inventions of modern times. Were we not saying so last night, Peppino? And Miss Olga is telling me that everyone in London has a listening-in apparatus. Pray turn it on, Miss Olga; it will be a treat to hear it! Ah, the Beethoven brooch. Thank you, Georgie—*mille grazie*."

Olga turned a handle or a screw or something, and there was a short pause; the next item presumably had already been announced. And then, wonder of wonders, there came from the trumpet the first bars of the "Moonlight Sonata."

Now the "Moonlight Sonata" (especially the first movement of it) had an almost sacred significance in Riseholme. It was Lucia's tune, much as "God Save the King" is the King's tune. Whatever musical entertainment had been going on, it was certain that if Lucia was present she would sooner or later be easily induced to play the first movement of the "Moonlight Sonata." Astonished as everybody already was at her not only countenancing but even allowing this mechanism, so lately abhorred by her, to be set to work at all, it was infinitely more amazing that she should permit it to play Her tune. But there she was composing her face to her well-known Beethoven expression, leaning a little forward, with her chin in her hand, and her eyes wearing the far-away look from which the last chord would recall her. At the end of the first movement everybody gave the little sigh which was its due, and the wistful sadness faded from their faces, and Lucia, with a gesture, hushing all attempt at comment or applause, gave a gay little smile to show she knew what was coming next. The smile broadened, as the Scherzo began, into a little ripple of laughter, the hand which had supported her chin once more sought the Beethoven brooch, and she sat eager and joyful and alert, sometimes just shaking her head in wordless criticism, and once saying, "Tut-tut," when the clarity of a run did not come up to her standard, till the sonata was finished.

"A treat," she said at the end, "really most enjoyable. That dear old tune! I thought the first movement was a little hurried; Cortot, I remember, took it a little more slowly, and a little more *legato*, but it was very creditably played."

Olga, at the machine, was out of sight of Lucia, and during the performance Georgie noticed that she had glanced at the Sunday paper. And now when Lucia referred to Cortot, she hurriedly chucked it into a window seat and changed the subject.

"I ought to have stopped it," she said, "because we needn't go to the wireless to hear that. Do show us what you mean, Mrs. Lucas, about the first movement."

Lucia glided to the piano.

"Just a bar or two, shall I?" she said.

Everybody gave a sympathetic murmur, and they had the first movement over again.

"Only just my impression of how Cortot plays it," she said. "It coincides with my own view of it."

"Don't move," said Olga, and everybody murmured, "Don't," or "Please." Robert said, "Please," long after the others, because he was drowsy. But he wanted more music, because he wished to doze a little and not to talk.

"How you all work me!" said Lucia, running her hands up and down the piano with a butterfly touch. "London will be quite a rest after Riseholme. Peppino *mio*, my portfolio on the top of my cloak; would you? . . . Peppino insisted on my bringing some music; he would not let me start without it." (This was a piece of picturesqueness during Peppino's absence; it would have been more accurate to say he was sent back for it, but less picturesque.) "Thank you, *carissimo*. A little morsel of Stravinski; Miss Olga, I am sure, knows it by heart, and I am terrified. Georgie, would you turn over?"

The morsel of Stravinski had improved immensely since Friday; it was still very odd, very modern, but not nearly so odd as when, a few days ago, Lucia had failed to observe the change of key. But it was strange to the true Riseholmite to hear the arch-priestess of

Beethoven and the foe of all modern music, which she used to account sheer Bolshevism, producing these scrannel staccato tinklings that had so often made her wince. And yet it all fitted in with her approbation of the wireless and her borrowing of Georgie's manual on auction bridge. It was not the morsel of Stravinski alone that Lucia was practising (the performance though really improved might still be called practice); it was modern life, modern ideas on which she was engaged preparatory to her descent on London. Though still in harbor at Riseholme, so to speak, it was generally felt that Lucia had cast off her cable, and was preparing to put to sea.

"Very pretty; I call that very pretty. Honk!" said Robert when the morsel was finished. "I call that music."

"Dear Mr. Robert, how sweet of you," said Lucia, wheeling round on the music stool. "Now positively, I will not touch another note. But may we, might we, have another little tune on your wonderful wireless, Miss Olga! Such a treat! I shall certainly have one installed at Brompton Square, and listen to it while Peppino is doing his crossword puzzles. Peppino can think of nothing else now but auction bridge and crossword puzzles, and interrupts me in the middle of my practice to ask for an Athenian sculptor whose name begins with P and is of ten letters."

"Ah, I've got it," said Peppino, "Praxiteles."

Lucia clapped her hands.

"Bravo," she said. "We shall not sit up till morning again."

There was a splendor in the ruthlessness with which Lucia bowled over, like ninepins, every article of her own Riseholme creed, which saw Bolshevism in all modern art, inanity in crossword puzzles and bridge, and aimless vacuity in London. . . . Immediately after the fresh tune on the wireless began, and most unfortunately, they came in for the "Funeral March of a Marionette." A spasm of pain crossed Lucia's face, and Olga abruptly turned off this sad reminder of unavailing woe.

"Go on; I like that tune!" said the drowsy and thoughtless Robert, and a hurried buzz of conversation covered this melancholy coincidence.

It was already late, and Lucia rose to go.

"Delicious evening!" she said. "And lovely to think that we shall so soon be neighbors in London as well, my music room always at your disposal. Are you coming, Georgie?"

"Not this minute," said Georgie firmly.

Lucia was not quite accustomed to this, for Georgie usually left any party when she left. She put her head in the air as she swept by him, but then relented again.

"Dine tomorrow, then? We won't have any music after this feast tonight," said she, forgetting that the feast had been almost completely of her own providing. "But perhaps a little game of cut-throat, you and Peppino and me."

"Delightful," said Georgie.

Olga hurried back after seeing off her other guests.

"Oh, Georgie, what richness," she said. "By the way, of course it *was* Cortot who was playing the 'Moonlight' faster than Cortot plays it."

Georgie put down his tambour.

"I thought it probably would be," he said. "That's the kind of thing that happens to Lucia. And now we know where we are. She's going to make a circle in

London and be its center. Too thrilling! It's all as clear as it can be. All we don't know about yet is the pearls."

"I doubt the pearls," said Olga.

"No, I think there are pearls," said Georgie, after a moment's intense concentration. "Otherwise she wouldn't have told me they appeared in the Sargent portrait of the aunt."

Olga suddenly gave a wild hoot of laughter.

"Oh, why does one ever spend a single hour away from Riseholme?" she said.

"I wish you wouldn't," said Georgie. "But you go off tomorrow?"

"Yes, to Paris. My excuse is to meet my Georgie—"

"Here he is," said Georgie.

"Yes, bless him. But the one who happens to be my husband. Georgie, I think I'm going to change my name and become what I really am, Mrs. George Shuttleworth. Why should singers and actresses call themselves Madame Macaroni or Signora Semolina? Yes, that's my excuse, as I said when you interrupted me, and my reason is gowns. I'm going to have lots of new gowns."

"Tell me about them," said Georgie. He loved hearing about dress.

"I don't know about them yet; I'm going to Paris to find out. Georgie, you'll have to come and stay with me when I'm settled in London. And when I go to practise in Lucia's music room you shall play my accompaniments. And shall I be shingled?"

Georgie's face was suddenly immersed in concentration.

"I wouldn't mind betting—" he began.

Olga again shouted with laughter.

"If you'll give me three to one that I don't know what you were going to say, I'll take it," she said.

"But you can't know," said Georgie.

"Yes I do. You wouldn't mind betting that Lucia will be shingled."

"Well, you are quick," said Georgie admiringly.

It was known, of course, next morning, that Lucia and Peppino were intending to spend a few weeks in London before selling the house, and who knew what *that* was going to mean? Already it was time to begin rehearsing for the next May Day revels, and Foljambe, that paragon of all parlormaids, had been overhauling Georgie's jerkin and hose and dainty little hunting boots with turn-down flaps in order to be ready. But when Georgie, dining at The Hurst next evening, said something about May Day revels (Lucia, of course, would be Queen again) as they played cut-throat with the *Manual on Auction Bridge* handy for the settlement of such small disputes as might arise over the value of the different suits, she only said:

"Those dear old customs! So quaint! And fifty to me above, Peppino, or is it a hundred? I will turn it up while you deal, Georgie!"

This complete apathy of Lucia to May Day revels indicated one of two things: that either mourning would prevent her being Queen, or absence. In consequence of which, Georgie had his jerkin folded up again and put away, for he was determined that nobody except Lucia should drive him out to partake in such a day of purgatory as had been his last year. . . . Still, there was nothing conclusive about that; it might be mourning. But the evidence accumulated that Lucia meant to make a pretty solid stay in London, for she certainly had some cards printed at "Ye Signe of ye Daffodille" on the village green where Peppino's poems were on sale, with the inscription:

> *Mr. and Mrs. Philip Lucas*
> *request the pleasure of the company of*
> . . . .
> *at* . . . . *on* . . . .

25 Brompton Square.   R.S.V.P.

Daisy Quantock had found that out, for she saw the engraved copper plate lying on the counter, and while the shopman's back was turned, had very cleverly read it, though it was printed the wrong way round, and was very confusing. Still she managed to do so, and the purport was plain enough: that Lucia contemplated formally asking somebody to something sometime at 25 Brompton Square. "And would she," demanded Daisy with bitter irony, "have had cards printed like that, if they were only meaning to go up for a week or two?" And if that was not enough, Georgie saw a postcard on Lucia's writing table with "From Mrs. Philip Lucas, 25 Brompton Square, S.W.3" plainly printed on the top.

It was getting very clear then (and during this week, Riseholme naturally thought of nothing else) that Lucia designed a longer residence in the garish metropolis than she had admitted. Since she chose to give no information on the subject, mere pride and scorn of vulgar curiosity forebade anyone to ask her, though of course it was quite proper (indeed a matter of duty) to probe the matter to the bottom by every other means in your power, and as these bits of evidence pieced themselves together, Riseholme began to take a very gloomy view of Lucia's real nature. On the whole, it was felt that Mrs. Boucher, when she paused in her

Bath chair as it was being wheeled round the green, nodding her head very emphatically, and bawling into Mrs. Antrobus's ear-trumpet, reflected public opinion.

"She's deserting Riseholme and all her friends," said Mrs. Boucher; "that's what she's doing. She means to cut a dash in London, and lead London by the nose. There'll be fashionable parties, you'll see; there'll be paragraphs; and then when the season's over, she'll come back and swagger about them. For my part I shall take no interest in them. Perhaps she'll bring down some of her smart friends for a Saturday till Monday. There'll be dukes and duchesses at The Hurst. That's what she's meaning to do, I tell you, and I don't care who hears it."

That was lucky, as anyone within the radius of a quarter of a mile could have heard it.

"Well, never mind, my dear," said Colonel Boucher, who was pushing his wife's chair.

"Mind? I should hope not, Jacob," said Mrs. Boucher. "And now let us go home, or we'll be late for lunch and that would never do, for I expect the Prince of Wales and the Lord Chancellor, and we'll play bridge and crossword puzzles all afternoon."

Such fury and withering sarcasm, though possibly excessive, had, it was felt, a certain justification, for had not Lucia for years given little indulgent smiles when anyone referred to the cheap delights and restless apish chatterings of London? She had always come back from her visits to that truly provincial place which thought itself a center, wearied with its false and foolish activity, its veneer of culture, its pseudo-Athenian rage for any new thing. They were all busy enough at Riseholme, but busy over worthy objects, over Beethoven and Shakespeare, over high thinking, over study of the true masterpieces. And now, the moment that Aunt Amy's death gave her and Peppino the means to live in the fiddling little anthill by the Thames, they were turning their backs on all that hitherto had made existence so splendid and serious a reality, and were training, positively training for frivolity, by exercises in Stravinski, auction bridge, and crossword puzzles. Only the day before the fatal influx of fortune had come to them, Lucia, dropping in on Colonel and Mrs. Boucher about teatime, had found them very cosily puzzling out a Children's Crossword in the evening paper, having given up the adult conundrum as too difficult, had pretended that even this was far beyond her poor wits, and had gone home the moment she had swallowed her tea in order to finish a canto of Dante's *Purgatorio.* . . . And it was no use Lucia's saying that they intended only to spend a week or two in Brompton Square before the house was sold: Daisy's quickness and cleverness about the copper-plate at "Ye Signe of ye Daffodille" had made short work of that. Lucia was evidently the prey of a guilty conscience, too: she meant, so Mrs. Boucher was firmly convinced, to steal away, leaving the impression she was soon coming back.

Vigorous reflections like these came in fits and spurts from Mrs. Boucher as her husband wheeled her home for lunch.

"And as for the pearls, Jacob," she said as she got out, hot with indignation, "if you asked me, actually asked me what I think about the pearls, I should have to tell you that I don't believe in the pearls. There may be half a dozen seed pearls in an old pillbox; I don't say there are not. But that's all the pearls we shall see. Pearls!"

3

GEORGIE HAD only just come down to breakfast and had not yet opened his *Times* one morning at the end of this hectic week, when the telephone bell rang. Lucia had not been seen at all the day before, and he had a distinct premonition, though he had not time to write it down, that this was she. It was; and her voice sounded very brisk and playful.

"Is that, Georgino?" she said. "Zat oo, Georgie?"

Georgie had another premonition, stronger than the first.

"Yes, it's me," he said.

"Georgie, is oo coming round to say Ta-ta to poor Lucia and Peppino?" she said.

("I knew it," thought Georgie.)

"What, are you going away?" he asked.

"Yes, I told you the other night," said Lucia in a great hurry, "when you were doing crosswords, you and Peppino. Sure I did. Perhaps you weren't attending. But—"

"No, you never told me," said Georgie firmly.

"How cwoss oo sounds. But come round, Georgie, about eleven and have 'ickle chat. We're going to be very stravvy and motor up, and perhaps keep the motor for a day or two."

"And when are you coming back?" asked Georgie.

"Not quite settled," said Lucia brightly. "There's a lot of bizz-bizz for poor Peppino. Can't quite tell how long it will take. Eleven, then?"

Georgie had hardly replaced the receiver when there came a series of bangs and rings at his front door, and Foljambe coming from the kitchen with his dish of bacon in one hand, turned to open it. It was only de Vere with a copy of the *Times* in her hand.

"With Mrs. Quantock's compliments," said de Vere, "and would Mr. Pillson look at the paragraph she has marked, and send it back? Mrs. Quantock will see him whenever he comes round."

"That all?" said Foljambe rather crossly. "What did you want to knock the house down for then?"

De Vere vouchsafed no reply, but turned slowly in her high-heeled shoes and regarded the prospect.

Georgie also had come into the hall at this battering summons, and Foljambe gave him the paper. There were a large blue pencil mark and several notes of exclamation opposite a short paragraph:

"Mr. and Mrs. Philip Lucas will arrive today from The Hurst, Riseholme, at 25 Brompton Square."

"No!" said Georgie. "Tell Mrs. Quantock I'll look in after breakfast." And he hurried back and opened his copy of the *Times* to see if it were the same there. It was; there was no misprint, nor could any other interpretation be attached to it. Though he knew the fact already, print seemed to bring it home. Print also disclosed the further fact that Lucia must have settled everything at least before the morning post yesterday, or this paragraph could never have appeared today. He gobbled up his breakfast, burning his tongue terribly with his tea. . . .

"It isn't only deception," said Daisy the moment he appeared without even greeting him, "for that we knew already, but it's funk as well. She didn't dare tell us."

"She's going to motor up," said Georgie, "starting soon after eleven. She's just asked me to come and say good-bye."

"That's more deception then," said Daisy, "for naturally, having read that, we should have imagined she was going up by the afternoon train, and gone round to say good-by after lunch, and found her gone. If I were you, I shouldn't dream of going to say good-by to her after this. She's shaking the dust of Riseholme off her London shoes. . . . But we'll have no May Day revels if I've got anything to do with it."

"Nor me," said Georgie. "But it's no use being cross with her. Besides, it's so terribly interesting. I shouldn't wonder if she was writing some invitations on the cards you saw—"

"No, I never saw the cards," said Daisy scrupulously. "Only the plate."

"It's the same thing. She may be writing invitations now, to post in London."

"Go a little before eleven then, and see," said Daisy. "Even if she's not writing them then, there'll be envelopes lying about perhaps."

"Come, too," said Georgie.

"Certainly not," said Daisy. "If Lucia doesn't choose

to tell me she's going away, the only dignified thing to do is to behave as if I knew nothing whatever about it. I'm sure I hope she'll have a very pleasant drive. That's all I can say about it; I take no further interest in her movements. Besides, I'm very busy: I've got to finish weeding my garden, for I've not been able to touch it these last days, and then my planchette arrived this morning. And a Ouija board."

"What's that?" said Georgie.

"A sort of planchette, but much more—much more powerful. Only it takes longer, as it points at letters instead of writing," said Daisy. "I shall begin with planchette and take it up seriously, because I know I'm very psychic, and there'll be a little time for it now that we shan't be trapesing round all day in ruffs and stomachers over those May Day revels. Perhaps there'll be May Day revels in Brompton Square for a change. I shouldn't wonder: nothing would surprise me about Lucia now. And it's my opinion we shall get on very well without her."

Georgie felt he must stick up for her: she was catching it so frightfully hot all round.

"After all, it isn't criminal to spend a few weeks in London," he observed.

"Whoever said it was?" said Daisy. "I'm all for everybody doing exactly as they like. I just shrug my shoulders."

She heaved up her round little shoulders with an effort.

"Georgie, how do you think she'll begin up there?" she said. "There's that cousin of hers with whom she stayed sometimes, Aggie Sandeman, and then, of course, there's Olga Bracely. Will she just pick up acquaintances, and pick up more from them, like one of those charity snowballs? Will she be presented? Not that I take the slightest interest in it."

Georgie looked at his watch and rose.

"I do," he said. "I'm thrilled about it. I expect she'll manage. After all, we none of us wanted to have May Day revels last year but she got us to. She's got drive."

"I should call it push," said Daisy. "Come back and tell me exactly what's happened."

"Any message?" asked Georgie.

"Certainly not," said Daisy again, and began untying the string of the parcel that held the instruments of divination.

Georgie went quickly down the road (for he saw Lucia's motor already at the door) and up the paved walk that led past the sundial, round which was the circular flower border known as Perdita's border, for it contained only the flowers that Perdita gathered. To-day it was all a-bloom with daffodils and violets and primroses, and it was strange to think that Lucia would not go gassing on about Perdita's border, as she always did at this time of the year, but would have to be content with whatever flowers there happened to be in Brompton Square: a few sooty crocuses perhaps and a periwinkle. . . . She was waiting for him, kissed her hand through the window, and opened the door.

"Now for a little chat," she said, adjusting a very smart hat, which Georgie was sure he had never seen before. There was no trace of mourning about it: it looked in the highest spirits. So, too, did Lucia.

"Sit down, Georgie," she said, "and cheer me up. Poor Lucia feels ever so sad at going away."

"It is rather sudden," he said. "Nobody dreamed you were off today, at least until they saw the *Times* this morning."

Lucia gave a little sigh.

"I know," she said, "but Peppino thought that was the best plan. He said that if Riseholme knew when I was going, you'd all have had little dinners and lunches for us, and I should have been completely worn out with your kindness and hospitality. And there was so much to do, and we weren't feeling much like gaiety. Seen anybody this morning? Any news?"

"I saw Daisy," said Georgie.

"And told her?"

"No, it was she who saw it in the *Times* first, and sent it round to me," said Georgie. "She's got a Ouija board, by the way. It came this morning."

"That's nice," said Lucia. "I shall think of Riseholme as being ever so busy. And everybody must come up and stay with me, and you first of all. When will you be able to come?"

"Whenever you ask me," said Georgie.

"Then you must give me a day or two to settle down, and I'll write to you. You'll be popping across though every moment of the day to see Olga."

"She's in Paris," said Georgie.

"No! What a disappointment! I had already written her a card, asking her to dine with us the day after tomorrow, which I was taking up to London to post there."

"She may be back by then," said Georgie.

Lucia rose and went to her writing table, on which, as Georgie was thrilled to observe, was a whole pile of stamped and directed envelopes.

"I think I won't chance it," said Lucia, "for I had enclosed another card for Signor Cortese which I wanted her to forward, asking him for the same night. He composed *Lucrezia* you know, which I see is coming out in London in the first week of the opera season, with her, of course, in the name part. But it will be safer to ask them when I know she is back."

Georgie longed to know to whom all the other invitations were addressed. He saw that the top one was directed to an M.P., and guessed that it was for the member for the Riseholme district, who had lunched at The Hurst during the last election.

"And what are you going to do tonight?" he asked.

"Dining with dear Aggie Sandeman. I threw myself on her mercy, for the servants won't have settled in, and I hoped we should have just a little quiet evening with her. But it seems that she's got a large dinner party on. Not what I should have chosen, but there's no help for it now. Oh, Georgie, to think of you in dear old quiet Riseholme and poor Peppino and me gabbling and gobbling at a huge dinner party."

She looked wistfully round the room.

"Good-by, dear music room," she said, kissing her hand in all directions. "How glad I shall be to get back! Oh, Georgie, your *Manual on Auction Bridge* got packed by mistake. So sorry. I'll send it back. Come in and play the piano sometimes, and then it won't feel lonely. We must be off, or Peppino will get fussing. Say good-by to everyone for us, and explain. And Perdita's border! Will sweet Perdita forgive me for leaving all her lovely flowers and running away to London? After all, Georgie, Shakespeare wrote *The Winter's Tale* in London, did he not? Lovely daffies! And violets dim. Let me give you 'ickle violet, Georgie, to remind you of poor Lucia tramping about in long unlovely streets, as Tennyson said."

Lucia, so Georgie felt, wanted no more comments or questions about her departure, and went on drivelling

like this till she was safely in the motor. She had expected Peppino to be waiting for her and beginning to
fuss, but so far from his fussing, he was not there at
all. So she got in a fuss instead.

"Georgino, will you run back and shout for Peppino?" she said. "We shall be so late, and tell him that
I am sitting in the motor waiting. Ah, there he is! Peppino, where have you been? Do get in and let us start,
for there are Piggy and Goosie running across the
green, and we shall never get off if we have to begin
kissing everybody. Give them my love, Georgie, and
say how sorry we were just to miss them. Shut the door
quickly, Peppino, and tell him to drive on."

The motor purred and started. Lucia was gone. "She
had a bad conscience, too," thought Georgie, as Piggy
and Goosie gambolled up rather out of breath with
pretty playful cries, "and I'm sure I don't wonder."

The news that she had gone of course now spread
rapidly, and by lunchtime Riseholme had made up its
mind what to do, and that was hermetically to close its
lips forever on the subject of Lucia. You might think
what you pleased, for it was a free country, but silence
was best. But this counsel of perfection was not easy to
practise next day when the evening paper came. There,
for all the world to read were two quite long paragraphs, in "Five O'clock Chit-Chat," over the renowned
signature of Hermione, entirely about Lucia and 25
Brompton Square, and there for all the world to see
was the reproduction of one of her most elegant photographs, in which she gazed dreamily outward and a
little upward, with her fingers still pressed on the last
chord of (probably) the "Moonlight Sonata." . . . She
had come up, so Hermione told countless readers, from
her Elizabethan country seat at Riseholme (where she

was a neighbor of Miss Olga Bracely) and was settling
for the season in the beautiful little house in Brompton
Square, which was the freehold property of her husband, and had just come to him on the death of his
aunt. It was a veritable treasure house of exquisite furniture, with a charming music room where Lucia had
given Hermione a cup of tea from her marvellous Wor-
cester tea service. . . . (At this point Daisy, whose
hands were trembling with passion, exclaimed in a loud
and injured voice, "The very day she arrived!") Mrs.
Lucas (one of the Warwickshire Smythes by birth)
was, as all the world knew, a most accomplished musi-
cian and Shakespearean scholar, and had made Riseholme a center of culture and art. But nobody would
suspect the blue stocking in the brilliant, beautiful, and
witty hostess whose presence would lend an added gaiety to the London season.

Daisy was beginning to feel physically unwell. She
hurried over the few remaining lines, and then ejaculat-
ing, "Witty! Beautiful!" sent de Vere across to Georgie's with the paper, bidding him to return it, as she
hadn't finished with it. But she thought he ought to
know. . . . Georgie read it through, and with admirable self-restraint, sent Foljambe back with it and a
message of thanks—nothing more—to Mrs. Quantock
for the loan of it. Daisy, by this time feeling better,
memorized the whole of it.

Life under the new conditions was not easy, for a
mere glance at the paper might send any true Riseholmite into a paroxysm of chattering rage or a deep disgusted melancholy. The *Times* again recorded the fact
that Mr. and Mrs. Philip Lucas had arrived at 25
Brompton Square; there was another terrible paragraph
headed "Dinner," stating that Mrs. Sandeman enter-

tained the following at dinner. There were an ambassador, a marquis, a countess (dowager), two viscounts
with wives, a baronet, a quantity of honorables and
knights, and Mr. and Mrs. Philip Lucas. Every single
person except Mr. and Mrs. Philip Lucas had a title.
The list was too much for Mrs. Boucher, who, reading
it at breakfast, suddenly exclaimed:

"I didn't think it of them. And it's a poor consola-
tion to know that they must have gone in last."

Then she hermetically sealed her lips again on this
painful subject, and when she had finished her breakfast (her appetite had quite gone), she looked up every
member of that degrading party in Colonel Boucher's
Who's Who.

The announcement that Mr. and Mrs. Philip Lucas
had arrived at 25 Brompton Square was repeated once
more, in case anybody had missed it (Riseholme had
not), and Robert Quantock observed that at this rate
the three thousand pounds a year would soon be gone,
with nothing to show for it except a few press cuttings.
That was very clever and very withering, but anyone
could be withering over such a subject. It roused, it is
true, a faint and unexpressed hope that the arrival of
Lucia in London had not spontaneously produced the
desired effect, or why should she cause it to be repeated so often? But that brought no real comfort, and
a few days afterward, there fell a further staggering
blow. There was a Court, and Mrs. Agnes Sandeman
presented Mrs. Philip Lucas. Worse yet, her gown was
minutely described, and her ornaments were diamonds
and pearls.

The vow of silence could no longer be observed; human nature was human nature, and Riseholme would

have burst unless it had spoken. Georgie sitting in his little back parlor overlooking the garden, and lost in exasperated meditation, was roused by his name being loudly called from Daisy's garden next door, and looking out, saw the unprecedented sight of Mrs. Boucher's Bath chair planted on Daisy's lawn.

"She must have come in along the gravel path by the back door," he thought to himself. "I shouldn't have thought it was wide enough." He looked to see if his tie was straight, and then leaned out to answer.

"Georgie, come round a minute," called Daisy. "Have you seen it?"

"Yes," said Georgie, "I have. And I'll come."

Mrs. Boucher was talking in her loud emphatic voice, when he arrived.

"As for pearls," she said, "I can't say anything about them, not having seen them. But as for diamonds, the only diamonds she ever had were two or three little chips on the back of her wristwatch. That, I'll swear to."

The two ladies took no notice of him: Daisy referred to the description of Lucia's dress again.

"I believe it was her last dinner gown with a train added," she said. "It was a sort of brocade."

"Yes, and plush is a sort of velvet," said Mrs. Boucher. "I've a good mind to write to the *Times*, and say they're mistaken. Brocade! Bunkum! It's pushing and shoving, instead of diamonds and pearls. But I've had my say, and that's all. I shouldn't a bit wonder if we saw the King and Queen had gone to lunch quite quietly at Brompton Square."

"That's all very well," said Daisy, "but what are we to do?"

"Do?" said Mrs. Boucher. "There's plenty to do in

Riseholme, isn't there? I'm sure I never suffered from
lack of employment, and I should be sorry to think
that I had less interests now than I had before last
Wednesday week. Wednesday, or was it Thursday,
when they slipped away like that? Whichever it was, it
makes no difference to me, and if you're both disengaged this evening, you and Mr. Georgie, the Colonel
and I would be very glad if you would come and take
your bit of dinner with us. And Mr. Quantock, too, of
course. But as for diamonds and pearls, well, let's leave
that alone. I shall wear my emerald tiara tonight and
my ruby necklace. My sapphires have gone to be
cleaned."

But though Riseholme was justifiably incensed over
Lucia's worldliness and all this pushing and shoving
and this self-advertising publicity, it had seldom been
so wildly interested. Also, after the first pangs of shame
had lost their fierceness, a very different sort of emotion began to soothe the wounded hearts: it was possible to see Lucia in another light. She had stepped
straight from the sheltered and cultured life of Riseholme into the great busy feverish world, and already
she was making her splendid mark there. Though it
might have been she who had told Hermione what to
say in those fashionable paragraphs of hers (and those
who knew Lucia best were surely best competent to
form just conclusions about that), still Hermione had
said it, and the public now knew how witty and beautiful Lucia was, and what a wonderful house she had.
Then on the very night of her arrival she had been a
guest at an obviously superb dinner party, and had
since been presented at court. All this, to look at it
fairly, reflected glory on Riseholme, and if it was impossible in one mood not to be ashamed of her, it was

even more impossible in other moods not to be proud
of her. She had come, and almost before she had seen,
she was conquering. She could be viewed as a sort of
ambassadress, and her conquests in that light were
Riseholme's conquests. But pride did not oust shame,
nor shame pride, and shuddering anticipations as to
what new enormity the daily papers might reveal were
mingled with secret and delighted conjectures as to
what Riseholme's next triumph would be.

It was not till the day after her presentation that any
news came to Riseholme direct from the ambassadress's headquarters. Every day Georgie had been expecting to hear, and in anticipation of her summons to
come up and stay in the bedroom with the bathroom
and sitting room attached, had been carefully through
his wardrobe, and was satisfied that he would present a creditable appearance. His small portmanteau,
Foljambe declared, would be ample to hold all that he
wanted, including the suit with the Oxford trousers,
and his cloth-topped boots. When the long expected
letter came, he therefore felt prepared to start that very
afternoon, and tore it open with the most eager haste
and propped it against his teapot.

GEORGINO MIO,
    Such a whirl ever since we left, that I haven't had
a moment. But tonight (oh, such a relief) Peppino
and I have dined alone, quite à la Riseholme, and
for the first time I have had half an hour's quiet practice in my music room, and now sit down to write to
you. (You'd have scolded me if you'd heard me
play, so stiff and rusty have I become.)
    Well, now for my little chronicles. The very first
evening we were here, we went out to a big dinner at

dearest Aggie's. Some interesting people: I enjoyed
a pleasant talk with the Italian Ambassador, and
called on them the day after, but I had no long conversation with anyone, for Aggie kept bringing up
fresh people to introduce me to, and your poor Lucia got quite confused with so many, till Peppino
and I sorted them out afterward. Everyone seemed
to have heard of our coming up to town, and I assure you that ever since, the tiresome telephone has
been a perfect nuisance, though all so kind. Would
we go to lunch one day, or would we go to dinner
another, and there was a private view here, and a
little music in the afternoon there: I assure you I
have never been so petted and made so much of.

We have done a little entertaining, too, already—
just a few old friends like our member of Parliament, Mr. Garroby-Ashton. ["She met him once,"
thought Georgie in parenthesis.] He insisted also on
our going to tea with him at the House of Commons.
I knew that would interest Peppino, for he's becoming quite a politician, and so we went. Tea on the
terrace, and a pleasant little chat with the Prime
Minister, who came and sat at our table for ever so
long. How I wanted you to be there and make a
sketch of the Thames; just the sort of view you do
so beautifully! Wonderful river, and I repeated to
myself, "Sweet Thames, run softly, till I end my
song." Then such a scurry to get back to dine somewhere or other and go to a play. Then dearest Aggie
(such a good soul) had set her heart on presenting
me and I couldn't disappoint her. Did you see the
description of my dress? How annoyed I was that it
appeared in the papers! So vulgar all that sort of

thing, and you know how I hate publicity, but they tell me I must just put up with it and not mind.

The house is getting into order, but there are lots of little changes and furbishings up to be done before I venture to show it to anyone as critical as you, Georgino. How you would scream at the carpet in the dining room! I know it would give you indigestion. But when I get the house straight, I shall insist on your coming, whatever your engagements are, and staying a long, long time. We will fix a date when I come down for some week-end.

Your beloved Olga is back, but I haven't seen her yet. I asked Signor Cortese to dine and meet her one night, and I asked her to meet him. I thought that would make a pleasant little party, but they were both engaged. I hope they have not quarrelled. Her house, just opposite mine, looks very tiny, but I daresay it is quite large enough for her and her husband. She sings at the opening night of the Opera next week, in *Lucrezia*. I must manage to go even if I can only look in for an act or two. Peppino (so extravagant of him) has taken a box for two nights in the week. It is his birthday present to me, so I couldn't scold the dear! And after all, we shall give a great deal of pleasure to friends, by letting them have it when we do not want it ourselves.

Love to everybody at dear Riseholme. I feel quite like an exile, and sometimes I long for its sweet peace and quietness. But there is no doubt that London suits Peppino very well, and I must make the best of this incessant hustle. I had hoped to get down for next Sunday, but Mrs. Garroby-Ashton (I hear he will certainly be raised to the peerage when the birthday honors come out) has made a point of

our spending it with them. . . . Good night, dear
Georgino. Me so, so sleepy.

LUCIA

Georgie swallowed this letter at a gulp, and then, beginning again, took it in sips. At first it gave him an
impression of someone wholly unlike her, but when
sipped, every sentence seemed wonderfully characteristic. She was not adapting herself to new circumstances;
she was adapting new circumstances to herself with all
her old ingenuity and success, and with all her invinci-
ble energy. True, you had sometimes to read between
the lines, and divide everything by about three in order
to allow for exaggerations, and when Lucia spoke of
not disappointing dearest Aggie, who had set her heart
on presenting her at court, or of Mrs. Garroby-Ashton
making a point of her going down for the week-end
which she had intended to spend at Riseholme, Georgie only had to remember how she had been forced (so
she said) to be Queen at those May Day revels. By
sheer power of will, she had made each of them become
a Robin Hood or a Maid Marian, or whatever it was,
and then, when she had got them all at work she said it
was she who was being worked to death over *their*
May Day revels. They had forced her to organize
them, they had insisted that she should be Queen, and
lead the dances and sing louder than anybody, and be
crowned and curtsied to. They had been wax in her
hands, and now in new circumstances, Georgie felt sure
that dearest Aggie had been positively forced to
present her, and no doubt, Mrs. Garroby-Ashton, cor-
nered on that terrace of the House of Commons, while
sweet Thames flowed softly, had had no choice but to
ask her down for a Sunday. Willpower, indomitable

perseverance now, as always, was getting her just precisely what she had wanted: by it she had become Queen of Riseholme, and by it she was firmly climbing away in London, and already she was saying that everybody was insisting on her dining and lunching with them, whereas it was her moral force that made them powerless in her grip. Riseholme, she had no use for now: she was busy with something else; she did not care to be bothered with Georgie, and so she said it was the dining-room carpet.

"Very well," said Georgie bitterly. "And if she doesn't want me, I won't want her. So that's that."

He briskly put the letter away, and began to consider what he should do with himself all day. It was warm enough to sit out and paint: in fact, he had already begun a sketch of the front of his house from the green opposite; there was his piano if he settled to have a morning of music; there was the paper to read; there was news to collect; there was Daisy Quantock next door who would be delighted to have a sitting with the planchette, which was really beginning to write whole words instead of making meaningless dashes and scribbles; and yet none of these things which, together with plenty of conversation and a little housekeeping and manicuring, had long made life such a busy and strenuous performance, seemed to offer an adequate stimulus. And he knew well enough what rendered them devoid of tonic: it was that Lucia was not here, and however much he told himself he did not want her, he like all the rest of Riseholme was beginning to miss her dreadfully. She aggravated and exasperated them: she was a hypocrite (all that pretence of not having read the Mozart duet, and desolation at Auntie's death), a poseuse, a sham, and a snob, but there was

something about her that stirred you into violent
though protesting activity, and though she might infuri-
ate you, she prevented your being dull. Georgie enjoyed painting, but he knew that the fact that he would
show his sketch to Lucia gave spice to his enjoyment,
and that she, though knowing no more about it than a
rhinoceros, would hold it at arm's length, with her
head a little on one side and her eyes slightly closed,
and say:

"Yes, Georgie, very nice, very nice. But have you
got the value of your middle distance quite right? And
a little more depth in your distance, do you think?"

Or if he played his piano, he knew that what inspired his nimbleness would be the prospect of playing
his piece to her, and if he was practising on the sly a
duet for performance with her, the knowledge that he
was stealing a march on her and would astonish her
(though she might suspect the cause of his facility).
And as for conversation, it was useless to deny that
conversation languished in Riseholme if the subject of
Lucia, her feats and her frailties, was tabooed.

"We've got to pull ourselves together," thought
Georgie, "and start again. We must get going and learn
to do without her, as she's getting on so nicely without
us. I shall go and see how the planchette is pro-
gressing."

Daisy was already at it, and the pencil was getting
up steam. A day or two ago it had written not once
only but many times a strange sort of hieroglyphic,
which might easily be interpreted to be the mystic word
Abfou. Daisy had therefore settled (what could be
more obvious?) that the name of the control who
guided these strange gyrations was Abfou, which
sounded very Egyptian and antique. Therefore, she

powerfully reasoned, the scribbles which could not be made to fit any known configuration of English letters might easily be Arabic. Why Abfou should write his name in English characters and his communications in Arabic was not Daisy's concern, for who knew what were the conditions on the other side? A sheet was finished just as Georgie came in, and though it presented nothing but Arabic script, the movements of the planchette had been so swift and eager that Daisy quite forgot to ask if there was any news.

"Abfou is getting in more direct touch with me every time I sit," said Daisy. "I feel sure we shall have something of great importance before long. Put your hand on the planchette, too, Georgie, for I have always believed that you have mediumistic powers. Concentrate first; that means you must put everything else out of your head. Let us sit for a minute or two with our eyes shut. Breathe deeply. Relax. Sometimes slight hypnosis comes on, so the book says, which means you get very drowsy."

There was silence for a few moments; Georgie wanted to tell Daisy about Lucia's letter, but that would certainly interrupt Abfou, so he drew up a chair, and after laying his hand on Daisy's, closed his eyes and breathed deeply. And then suddenly the most extraordinary things began to happen.

The planchette trembled: it vibrated like a kettle on the boil, and began to skate about the paper. He had no idea what its antic motions meant; he only knew that it was writing something, Arabic perhaps, but something firm and decided. It seemed to him that so far from aiding its movement, he almost, to be on the safe side, checked it. He opened his eyes, for it was impossible not to want to watch this manifestation of psychic force, and also he wished to be sure (though he had no real suspicions on the subject) that his collaborator was not, to put it coarsely, pushing. Exactly the same train of thought was passing in Daisy's mind, and she opened her eyes, too.

"Georgie, my hand is positively being dragged about," she said excitedly. "If anything, I try to resist."

"Mine, too; so do I," said Georgie. "It's too wonderful. Do you suppose it's Arabic still?"

The pencil gave a great dash, and stopped.

"It is Arabic," said Daisy as she examined the message; "at least, there's heaps of English, too."

"No!" said Georgie, putting on his spectacles in his excitement, and not caring whether Daisy knew he wore them or not. "I can see it looks like English, but what a difficult handwriting! Look, that's 'Abfou,' isn't it? And that is 'Abfou' again there."

They bent their heads over the script.

"There's an 'L,' " cried Daisy, "and there it is again. And then there's 'L from L.' And then there's 'dead' repeated twice. It can't mean that Abfou is dead, because this is positive proof that he's alive. And then I can see 'mouse'?"

"Where?" said Georgie eagerly. "And what would 'dead mouse' mean?"

"There!" said Daisy pointing. "No: it isn't 'dead mouse.' It's 'dead' and then a lot of Arabic, and then 'mouse.' "

"I don't believe it is 'mouse,' " said Georgie, "though of course, you know Abfou's handwriting much better than I do. It looks to me far more like 'Museum.' "

"Perhaps he wants me to send all the Arabic he's written up to the British Museum," said Daisy with a flash of genius, "so that they can read it and say what it means."

"But, then there's 'Museum' or 'mouse' again there," said Georgie, "and surely that word in front of it— It is! It's Riseholme! Riseholme mouse or Riseholme Museum! I don't know what either would mean."

"You may depend upon it that it means something," said Daisy, "and there's another capital 'L.' Does it mean Lucia, do you think? But 'dead' . . ."

"No: dead's got nothing to do with the 'L,'" said Georgie. "'Museum' comes in between, and quantities of Arabic."

"I think I'll just record the exact time; it would be more scientific," said Daisy. "A quarter to eleven. No, that clock's three minutes fast by the church time."

"No, the church time is slow," said Georgie.

Suddenly he jumped up.

"I've got it," he said. "Look! 'L from L.' That means a letter from Lucia. And it's quite true. I heard this morning, and it's in my pocket now."

"No!" said Daisy, "that's just a sign Abfou is giving us, that he really is with us, and knows what is going on. Very evidential."

The absorption of them both in this script may be faintly appreciated by the fact that neither Daisy evinced the slightest curiosity as to what Lucia said, nor Georgie the least desire to communicate it.

"And then there's 'dead,'" said Georgie, looking out of the window. "I wonder what that means."

"I'm sure I hope it's not Lucia," said Daisy with stoical calmness, "but I can't think of anybody else."

Georgie's eyes wandered over the green; Mrs. Boucher was speeding round in her Bath chair, pushed by her husband, and there was the Vicar walking very

fast, and Mrs. Antrobus and Piggy and Goosie. . . .
nobody else seemed to be dead. Then his eye came
back to the foreground of Daisy's front garden.

"What has happened to your mulberry tree?" he
said parenthetically. "Its leaves are all drooping. You
ought never to have pruned its roots without knowing
how to do it."

Daisy jumped up.

"Georgie, you've got it!" she said. "It's the mulberry
tree that's dead. Isn't that wonderful?"

Georgie was suitably impressed.

"That's very curious: very curious, indeed," he said.
"Letter from Lucia, and the dead mulberry tree. I do
believe there's something in it. But let's go on studying
the script. Now I look at it again I feel certain it is
Riseholme Museum, not Riseholme mouse. The only
difficulty is that there isn't a museum in Riseholme."

"There are plenty of mice," observed Daisy, who
had had some trouble with these little creatures.
"Abfou may be wanting to give me advice about some
kind of ancient Egyptian trap. . . . But if you aren't
very busy this morning, Georgie, we might have another sitting and see if we get anything more definite.
Let us attain collectedness as the directions advise."

"What's collectedness?" asked Georgie.

Daisy gave him the directions: Collectedness seemed
to be a sort of mixture of intense concentration and
complete vacuity of mind.

"You seem to have to concentrate your mind upon
nothing at all," said he after reading it.

"That's just it," said Daisy. "You put all thoughts
out of your head, and then focus your mind. We have
to be only the instrument through which Abfou func-
tions."

They sat down again after a little deep breathing and relaxation, and almost immediately the planchette began to move across the paper with a firm and steady progression. It stopped sometimes for a few minutes, which was proof of the authenticity of the controlling force, for in spite of all efforts at collectedness, both Daisy's and Georgie's minds were full of things which they longed for Abfou to communicate, and if either of them was consciously directing those movements, there could have been no pause at all. When finally it gave that great dash across the paper again, indicating that the communication was finished, they found the most remarkable results.

Abfou had written two pages of foolscap in a tall upright hand, which was quite unlike either Daisy's or Georgie's ordinary script, and this was another proof (if proof were wanted) of authenticity. It was comparatively easy to read, and, except for a long passage at the end in Arabic, was written almost entirely in English.

"Look, there's Lucia written out in full four times," said Daisy eagerly. "And 'Pepper.' What's Pepper?"

Georgie gasped.

"Why Peppino, of course," he said. "I do call that odd. And see how it goes on—'Muck company,' no 'Much company, much grand company, higher and higher.' "

"Poor Lucia!" said Daisy. "How sarcastic! That's what Abfou thinks about it all. By the way, you haven't told me what she says yet; never mind, this is far more interesting. . . . Then there's a little Arabic; at least I think it's Arabic, for I can't make anything out of it, and then—why, I believe those next words are 'From Olga.' Have you heard from Olga?"

"No," said Georgie, "but there's something about her in Lucia's letter. Perhaps that's it."

"Very likely. And then I can make out Riseholme, and it isn't 'mouse,' it's quite clearly 'museum,' and then—I can't read that, but it looks English, and then 'opera,' that's Olga again, and 'dead,' which is the mulberry tree. And then 'It is better to work than to be idle. Think not—' something—"

" 'Bark,' " said Georgie. "No, 'hard.' "

"Yes. 'Think not hard thoughts of any, but turn thy mind to improving work.'—Georgie, isn't that wonderful?—and then it goes off into Arabic. What a pity! It might have been more about the museum. I shall certainly send all the first Arabic scripts to the British Museum."

Georgie considered this.

"Somehow I don't believe that is what Abfou means," said he. "He says Riseholme Museum, not British Museum. You can't possibly get 'British' out of that word."

Georgie left Daisy still attempting to detect more English among Arabic passages and engaged himself to come in again after tea for fresh investigation. Within a minute of his departure Daisy's telephone rang.

"How tiresome these interruptions are," said Daisy to herself as she hurried to the instrument. "Yes, yes. Who is it?"

Georgie's voice had the composure of terrific excitement.

"It's me," he said. "The second post has just come in, and a letter from Olga. 'From Olga,' you remember."

"No!" said Daisy. "Do tell me if she says anything about—"

But Georgie had already rung off. He wanted to read his letter from Olga, and Daisy sat down again quite awestruck at this further revelation. The future clearly was known to Abfou as well as the past, for Georgie knew nothing about Olga's letter when the words "From Olga" occurred in the script. And if in it she said anything about "opera" (which really was on the cards), it would be more wonderful still.

The morning was nearly over, so Daisy observed to her prodigious surprise, for it had really gone like a flash (a flash of the highest illuminative power), and she hurried out with a trowel and a rake to get half an hour in the garden before lunch. It was rather disconcerting to find that though she spent the entire day in the garden, often not sitting down to her planchette till dusk rendered it impossible to see the mazes of cotton threads she had stretched over newly-sown beds, to keep off sparrows (she had on one occasion shattered with a couple of hasty steps the whole of those defensive fortifications), she seemed, in spite of blistered hands and aching back, to be falling more and more into arrears over her horticulture. Whereas that ruffian Simkinson, whom she had dismissed for laziness when she found him smoking a pipe in the potting shed and doing a crossword puzzle when he ought to have been working, really kept her garden in very good order by slouching about it for three half days in the week. To be sure, she had pruned the roots of the mulberry tree, which had taken a whole day (and so incidentally had killed the mulberry tree), and though the death of that antique vegetable had given Abfou a fine opportunity for proving himself, evidence now was getting so abundant that Daisy almost wished it hadn't happened. Then, too, she was beginning to have secret qualms that she had torn up as weeds a quantity of seedlings which the indolent Simkinson had just pricked out, for though the beds were now certainly weedless, there was no sign of any other growth there. And either Daisy's little wooden labels had got mixed, or she had sown Brussels sprouts in the circular bed just outside the dining-room window instead of Phlox Drummondi. She thought she had attached the appropriate label to the seed she had sown, but it was very dark at the time, and in the morning the label certainly said "Brussels sprouts." In which case there would be a bed of phlox at the far end of the little strip of kitchen garden. The seeds in both places were sprouting now, so she would know the worst or the best before long.

Then, again, there was the rockery she had told Simkinson to build, which he had neglected for crossword puzzles, and though Daisy had been working six or eight hours a day in her garden ever since, she had not found time to touch a stone of it, and the fragments lying like a moraine on the path by the potting shed still rendered any approach to the latter a mountaineering feat. They consisted of fragments of mediaeval masonry, from the site of the ancient abbey, finials and crockets and pieces of mullioned windows which had been turned up when a new siding of the railway had been made, and everyone almost had got some with the exception of Mrs. Boucher, who called them rubbish. Then there were some fossils, ammonites and spar and curious flints with holes in them and bits of talc, for Lucia one year had commandeered them all into the study of geology and they had got hammers and whacked away at the face of an old quarry, detaching these petrified relics and hitting themselves over the fingers in the process. It was that year that the

Roman camp outside the village had been put under the plough, and Riseholme had followed it like a bevy of rooks, and Georgie had got several trays full of fragments of iridescent glass, and Colonel Boucher had collected bits of Samian ware, and Mrs. Antrobus had found a bronze fibula, or safety pin. Daisy had got some chunks of Roman brickwork, and a section of Roman drainpipe, which now figured among the materials for her rockery; and she had bought, for about their weight in gold, quite a dozen bronze coins. These, of course, would not be placed in the rockery, but she had put them somewhere very carefully, and had subsequently forgotten where that was. Now as these archaeological associations came into her mind from the contemplation of the materials for the rockery, she suddenly thought she remembered that she had put them at the back of the drawer in her card table.

The sight of these antique fragments disgusted Daisy; they littered the path, and she could not imagine them built up into a rockery that should have the smallest claim to be an attractive object. How could the juxtaposition of a stone mullion, a drainpipe, and an ammonite present a pleasant appearance? Besides, who was to juxtapose them? She could not keep pace with the other needs of the garden, let alone a rockery, and where, after all, was the rockery to stand? The asparagus bed seemed the only place, and she preferred asparagus.

Robert was bawling out from the dining-room window that lunch was ready, and as she retraced her steps to the house, she thought that perhaps it would be better to eat humble pie and get Simkinson to return. It was clear to Daisy that if she was to do her duty as medium between ancient Egypt and the world of today, the garden would deteriorate even more rapidly than it was doing already, and no doubt Robert would consent to eat the humble pie for her, and tell Simkinson that they couldn't get on without him, and that when she had said he was lazy, she had meant industrious, or whatever else was necessary.

Robert was in a very good temper that day because Roumanian oils, which were the main source of his fortunes, had announced a higher dividend than usual, and he promised to seek out Simkinson and explain what lazy meant, and if he didn't understand to soothe his injured feelings with a small tip.

"And tell him he needn't make a rockery at all," said Daisy. "He always hated the idea of a rockery. He can dig a pit and bury the fossils and the architectural fragments and everything. That will be the easiest way of disposing of them."

"And what is he to do with the earth he takes out of the pit, my dear?" asked Robert.

"Put it back, I suppose," said Daisy rather sharply. Robert was so pleased at having "caught" her, that he did not even explain that she had been caught. . . .

After lunch Daisy found the coins; it was odd that, having forgotten where she had put them for so long, she should suddenly remember, and she was inclined to attribute this inspiration to Abfou. The difficulty was to know what, having found them, to do with them next. Some of them obviously bore signs of once having had profiles of Roman emperors stamped on them, and she was sure she had heard that some Roman coins were of great value, and probably these were the ones. Perhaps when she sent the Arabic script to the

British Museum, she might send these, too, for identification. . . . And then she dropped them all on the floor as the great idea struck her.

She flew into the garden, calling to Georgie, who was putting up croquet hoops.

"Georgie, I've got it!" she said. "It's as plain as plain. What Abfou wants us to do is to start a Riseholme Museum. He wrote Riseholme Museum quite distinctly. Think how it would pay, too, when we're overrun with American tourists in the summer! They would all come to see it. A shilling admission, I should put it at, and sixpence for the catalogue."

"I wonder if Abfou meant that," said Georgie.

"He said it," said Daisy. "You can't deny that!"

"But what should we put in the Museum?" asked he.

"My dear, we should fill it with antiquities and things which none of us want in our houses. There are those beautiful fragments of the Abbey which I've got, and which are simply wasted in my garden with no one to see them, and my drainpipe. I would present them all to the Museum, and the fossils, and perhaps some of my coins. And my Roman brickwork."

Georgie paused with a hoop in his hand.

"That is an idea," he said. "And I've got all those lovely pieces of iridescent glass, which are always tumbling about. I would give them."

"And Colonel Boucher's Samian ware," cried Daisy. "He was saying only the other day how he hated it, but didn't quite want to throw it away. It will be a question of what we leave out, not of what we put in. Besides, I'm sure that's what Abfou meant. We must form a committee at once. You and Mrs. Boucher and I, I should think, would be enough. Large committees are a great mistake."

"Not Lucia?" asked Georgie, with lingering loyalty.

"No. Certainly not," said Daisy. "She would only send us orders from London, as to what we were to do and want us to undo all we had done when she came back, besides saying she had thought of it, and making herself president!"

"There's something in that," said Georgie.

"Of course there is; there's sense," said Daisy. "Now I shall go straight and see Mrs. Boucher."

Georgie dealt a few smart blows with his mallet to the hoop he was putting in place.

"I shall come, too," he said. "Riseholme Museum! I believe Abfou did mean that. We *shall* be busy again."

4

THE COMMITTEE met that very afternoon, and the next morning and the next afternoon, and the scheme quickly took shape. Robert, rolling in golden billows of Roumanian oil, was called in as financial advisor, and after calculation, the scheme strongly recommended itself to him. All the summer the town was thronged with visitors, and inquiring American minds would hardly leave unvisited the Museum at so Elizabethan a place.

"I don't know what you'll have in your Museum," he said, "but I expect they'll go to look, and even if they don't find much, they'll have paid their shillings. And if Mrs. Boucher thinks her husband will let you have that big tithe barn of his, at a small rent, I daresay you'll have a paying proposition."

The question of funds therefore in order to convert the tithe barn into a museum was instantly gone into.

Robert professed himself perfectly ready to equip the tithe barn with all necessary furniture and decoration, if he might collar the whole of the receipts, but his willingness to take all financial responsibilities made the committee think that they would like to have a share in them, since so shrewd a businessman clearly saw the probability of making something out of it. Up till then, the sordid question of money had not really occurred to them: there was to be a museum which would make them busy again, and the committee was to run it. They were quite willing to devote practically the whole of their time to it, for Riseholme was one of those happy places where the proverb that Time is Money was a flat fallacy, for nobody had ever earned a penny with it. But since Robert's financial judgment argued that the Museum would be a profitable investment, the committee naturally wished to have a hand in it, and the three members each subscribed fifty pounds, and co-opted Robert to join the board and supply the rest. Profits (if any) would be divided up between the members of the committee in proportion to their subscriptions. The financial Robert would see to all that, and the rest of them could turn their attention to the provision of curiosities.

There was evidently to be no lack of them, for everyone in Riseholme had stores of miscellaneous antiquities and "specimens" of various kinds, which encumbered their houses and required a deal of dusting, but which couldn't quite be thrown away. A very few striking objects were only lent: among these were Daisy's box of coins, and Mrs. Antrobus's fibula, but the most of them, like Georgie's glass and Colonel Boucher's pieces of Samian ware, were fervently bestowed. Objects of all sorts poured in: the greater portion of a spinning wheel, an Elizabethan pestle and mortar, no end of Roman tiles, a large wooden post unhesitatingly called a whipping post, some indecipherable documents on parchment with seals attached, belonging to the Vicar, an ordnance map of the district, numerous collections of fossils and of carved stones from the site of the Abbey, ancient quilts, a baby's cradle, worm-eaten enough to be Anglo-Saxon, queershaped bottles, a tigerware jug, fire irons too ponderous for use, and (by special vote of the Parish Council) the stocks which had hitherto stood at the edge of the pond on the green. All Riseholme was busy again, for fossils had to be sorted out (it was early realized that even a museum could have too many ammonites), curtains had to be stitched for the windows, labels to be written, Samian ware to be pieced together, cases arranged, a catalogue prepared. The period of flatness consequent on Lucia's desertion had passed off, and what had certainly added zest to industry was the thought that Lucia had nothing to do with the Museum. When next she deigned to visit her discarded kingdom, she would find how busily and successfully and originally they had got on without her, and that there was no place for her on the committee, and probably none in the Museum for the Elizabethan turnspit which so often made the chimney of her music room smoke.

Riseholme, indeed, was busier than ever, for not only had it the Museum feverishly to occupy it so that it might be open for the tourist season this year, and, if possible, before Lucia came down for one of her promised week-ends, but it was immersed in a wave of psychical experiments. Daisy Quantock had been perfectly honest in acknowledging that the idea of the

Museum was not hers at all, but Abfou's, her Egyptian
guide. She had, it is true, been as ingenious as Joseph in
interpreting Abfou's directions, but it was Abfou to
whom all credit was due, and who evidently took such
a deep interest in the affairs of Riseholme. She even offered to present the Museum with the sheet of foolscap
on which the words "Riseholme Museum" (not
"mouse") were written, but the general feeling of the
committee, while thanking her for her munificence, was
that it would not be tactful to display it, since the same
Sibylline sheet contained those sarcastic remarks about
Lucia. It was proved also that Abfou had meant the
Museum to be started, for subsequently he several
times said, "Much pleased with your plans for the
Museum. Abfou approves." So everybody else wanted
to get into touch with Abfou, too, and no less than
four planchettes or Ouija boards were immediately ordered by various members of Riseholme society. At
present Abfou did not manifest himself to any of them,
except in what was possibly Arabic script (for it certainly bore a strong resemblance to his earlier efforts of
communication with Daisy), and while she encouraged
the scribes to persevere in the hope that he might soon
regale them with English, she was not really very anxious that he should. With her he was getting Englisher
and Englisher every day, and had not Simkinson, after
having had the true meaning of the word "lazy" carefully explained to him, consented to manage her garden
again, it certainly would have degenerated into prime-
val jungle, for she absolutely had not a minute to attend to it.

Simkinson, however, was quite genial.

"Oh, yes, ma'am, very pleased to come back," he
said. "I knew you wouldn't be able to get on long with-

out me, and I want no explanations. Now let's have a look round and see what you've been doing. Why, whatever's happened to my mulberry tree?"

That was Simkinson's way: he always talked of "my flowers" and "my asparagus" when he meant hers.

"I've been pruning its roots," she said.

"Well, ma'am, you've done your best to do it in," said Simkinson. "I don't think it's dead though, I daresay it'll pull round."

Abfou had been understood to say it was dead, but perhaps he meant something else, thought Daisy, and they went on to the small circular bed below the dining-room windows.

"Phlox," said Daisy hopefully.

"Broccoli," said Simkinson examining the young green sprouts. "And the long bed there. I sowed a lot of annuals there, and I don't see a sign of anything coming up."

He fixed her with a merry eye.

"I believe you've been weeding, ma'am," he said. "I shall have to get you a lot of young plants if you want a bit of color there. It's too late for me to put my seeds in again."

Daisy rather wished she hadn't come out with him, and changed the subject to something more cheerful.

"Well, I shan't want the rockery," she said. "You needn't bother about that. All these stones will be carted away in a day or two."

"Glad of that, ma'am. I'll be able to get to my potting shed again. Well, I'll try to put you to rights. I'd best pull up the broccoli first; you won't want it under your windows, will you? You stick to rolling the lawn, ma'am, if you want to garden. You won't do any harm then."

It was rather dreadful being put in one's place like this, but Daisy did not dare risk a second quarrel, and the sight of Georgie at the dining-room window (he had come across to "weedj," as the psychical processes, whether Ouija or planchette, were now called) was rather a relief. Weeding, after all, was unimportant compared to weedjing.

"And I don't believe I ever told you what Olga wrote about," said Georgie as soon as she was within range. "We've talked of nothing but Museum. Oh, and Mrs. Boucher's planchette has come. But it broke in the post, and she's gumming it together."

"I doubt if it will act," said Daisy. "But what did Olga say? It quite went out of my head to ask you."

"It's too heavenly of her," said he. "She's asked me to go up and stay with her for the first night of the opera. She's singing *Lucrezia*, and has got a stall for me."

"No!" said Daisy, making a trial trip over the blotting paper to see if the pencil was sharp. "That will be an event! I suppose you're going."

"Just about," said Georgie. "It's going to be broadcasted, too, and I shall be listening to the original."

"How interesting!" said Daisy. "And there you'll be in Brompton Square, just opposite Lucia. Oh, you heard from her? What did she say?"

"Apparently she's getting on marvellously," said Georgie. "Not a moment to spare. Just what she likes."

Daisy pushed the planchette aside. There would be time for that when she had had a little talk about Lucia.

"And are you going to stay with her, too?" she asked.

Georgie was quite determined not to be ill-natured. He had taken no part (or very little) in this trampling on Lucia's majesty, which had been so merrily going on.

"I should love to, if she would ask me," he observed. "She only says she's going to. Of course, I shall go to see her."

"I wouldn't," said Daisy savagely. "If she asked me fifty times I should say 'No' fifty times. What's happened is that she's dropped us. I wouldn't have her on our museum committee if—if she gave her pearls to it and said they belonged to Queen Elizabeth. I wonder you haven't got more spirit."

"I've got plenty of spirit," said Georgie, "and I allow I did feel rather hurt at her letter. But then, after all, what does it matter?"

"Of course it doesn't if you're going to stay with Olga," said Daisy. "How she'll hate you for that!"

"Well, I can't help it," he said. "Lucia hasn't asked me, and Olga has. She's twice reminded Olga that she may use her music room to practise in whenever she likes. Isn't that kind? She would love to be able to say that Olga's always practising in her music room. But aren't we ill-natured? Let's weedj instead."

Georgie found, when he arrived next afternoon in Brompton Square, that Olga had already had her early dinner, and that he was to dine alone at seven and follow her to the opera house.

"I'm on the point of collapse from sheer nerves," she said. "I always am before I sing, and then out of desperation I pull myself together. If—I say 'if'—I survive till midnight, we're going to have a little party here. Cortese is coming, and Princess Isabel, and one or two other people. Georgie, it's very daring of you to come here, you know, because my husband's away,

and I'm an unprotected female alone with Don Juan.
How's Riseholme? Talk to me about Riseholme. Are
you engaged to Piggy yet? And is it broccoli or phlox
in Daisy's round bed? Your letter was so mysterious,
too. I know nothing about the museum yet. What
museum? Are you going to kill and stuff Lucia and put
her in the hall? You simply alluded to the museum as
if I knew all about it. If you don't talk to me, I shall
scream."

Georgie flung himself into the task, delighted to be
thought capable of doing anything for Olga. He
described at great length and with much emphasis the
whole of the history of Riseholme from the first
epiphany of Arabic and Abfou on the planchette board
down to the return of Simkinson. Olga lost herself in
these chronicles, and when her maid came in to tell her
it was time to start, she got up quite cheerfully.

"And so it was broccoli," she said. "I was afraid it
was going to be phlox after all. You're an angel, Georgie, for getting me through my bad hour. I'll give you
anything you like for the Museum. Wait for me afterward at the stage door. We'll drive back together."

From the moment Olga appeared, the success of the
opera was secure. Cortese, who was conducting, had
made his music well; it thoroughly suited her, and she
was singing and looking and acting her best. Again and
again after the first act, the curtain had to go up, and
not until the house was satisfied could Georgie turn his
glances this way and that to observe the audience.
Then in the twilight of a small box on the second tier
he espied a woman who was kissing her hand somewhere in his direction, and a man waving a program,
and then he suddenly focussed them and saw who they
were. He ran upstairs to visit them, and there was

Lucia in an extraordinarily short skirt with her hair shingled, and round her neck three short rows of seed pearls.

"*Georgino mio!*" she cried. "This is a surprise! You came up to see our dear Olga's triumph. I do call that loyalty. Why did you not tell me you were coming?"

"I thought I would call tomorrow," said Georgie, with his eyes still going backward and forward between the shingle and the pearls and the legs.

"Ah, you are staying the night in town?" she asked. "Not going back by the midnight train? The dear old midnight train, and waking in Riseholme! At your club?"

"No, I'm staying with Olga," said Georgie.

Lucia seemed to become slightly cataleptic for a moment, but recovered.

"No! Are you really?" she said. "I think that is unkind of you, Georgie. You might have told me you were coming."

"But you said that the house wasn't ready," said he. "And she asked me."

Lucia put on a bright smile.

"Well, you're forgiven," she said. "We're all at sixes and sevens yet. And we've seen nothing of dearest Olga—or Mrs. Shuttleworth, I should say, for that's on the bills. Of course we'll drive you home, and you must come in for a chat, before Mrs. Shuttleworth gets home, and then no doubt she will be very tired and want to go to bed."

Lucia as she spoke had been surveying the house with occasional little smiles and wagglings of her hand in vague directions.

"Ah, there's Elsie Garroby-Ashton," she said, "and who is that with her, Peppino? Lord Shrivenham, surely. So come back with me and have 'ickle talk, Georgie. Oh, there's the Italian Ambassadress. Dearest Gioconda! Such a sweet. And look at the royal box; what a gathering! That's the royal box, Georgie, away to the left—that large one—in the tier below. Too near the stage for my taste: so little illusion—"

Lucia suddenly rose and made a profound curtsey.

"I think she saw us, Peppino," she said, "perhaps you had better bow. No, she's looking somewhere else now: you did not bow quick enough. And what a party in dearest Aggie's box. Who can that be? Oh, yes, it's Tony Limpsfield. We met him at Aggie's, do you remember, on the first night we were up. So join us at the grand entrance, Georgie, and drive back with us. We shall be giving a lift to somebody else, I'll be bound, but if you have your motor, it is so ill-natured not to pick up friends. I always do it: they will be calling us the 'Lifts of London,' as Marcia Whitby said."

"I'm afraid I can't do that," said Georgie. "I'm waiting for Olga, and she's having a little party, I believe."

"No! Is she really?" asked Lucia, with all the old Riseholme vivacity. "Who is coming?"

"Cortese, I believe," said Georgie, thinking it might be too much for Lucia if he mentioned a princess, "and one or two of the singers."

Lucia's mouth watered, and she swallowed rapidly. That was the kind of party she longed to be asked to, for it would be so wonderful and glorious to be able casually to allude to Olga's tiny, tiny little party after the first night of the opera, not a party at all really, just a few *intimes*, herself and Cortese and so on. How could she manage it, she wondered? Could she pretend not to know that there was a party, and just drop in for a moment in neighborly fashion with enthusiastic congratulations? Or should she pretend her motor had not come, and hang about the stage door with Georgie— Peppino could go home in the motor—and get a lift? Or should she hint very violently to Georgie how she would like to come in just for a minute? Or should she, now that she knew there was to be a party, merely assert that she had been to it? Perhaps a hint to Georgie was the best plan. . . .

Her momentary indecision was put an end to by the appearance of Cortese, threading his way among the orchestra, and the lowering of the lights. Georgie, without giving her any further opportunity, hurried back to his stall, feeling that he had had an escape, for Lucia's beady eye had been fixing him, just in the way it always used to do when she wanted something and, in consequence, meant to get it. He felt he had been quite wrong in ever supposing that Lucia had changed. She was just precisely the same, translated into a larger sphere. She had expanded: strange though it seemed, she had only been in bud at Riseholme. "I wonder what she'll do?" thought Georgie as he settled himself into his stall. "She wants dreadfully to come."

The opera came to an end in a blaze of bouquets and triumph and recalls, and curtseys. It was something of an occasion, for it was the first night of the opera, and the first performance of *Lucrezia* in London, and it was late when Olga came florally out. The party, which was originally meant to be no party at all, but just a little supper with Cortese and one or two of the singers, had marvellously increased during the evening, for friends had sent round messages and congratulations, and Olga had asked them to drop in, and when she and Georgie arrived at Brompton Square, the whole of the curve at the top was packed with motors.

"Heavens, what a lot of people I seem to have asked," she said, "but it will be great fun. There won't be nearly enough chairs, but we'll sit on the floor, and there won't be nearly enough supper, but I know there's a ham, and what can be better than a ham? Oh, Georgie, I am happy."

Now from opposite, across the narrow space of the square, Lucia had seen the arrival of all these cars. In order to see them better, she had gone on to the balcony of her drawing room and noted their occupants with her opera glasses. There was Lord Limpsfield, and the Italian Ambassadress, and Mr. Garroby-Ashton, and Cortese, and some woman to whom Mr. Garroby-Ashton bowed and Mrs. Garroby-Ashton curtsied. Up they streamed. And there was the Duchess of Whitby (Marcia, for Lucia had heard her called that), coming up the steps, and curtseying, too, but as yet Olga and Georgie quite certainly had not come. It seemed strange that so many brilliant guests should arrive before their hostess, but Lucia saw at once that this was the most chic informality that it was possible to conceive. No doubt Mr. Shuttleworth was there to receive them, but how wonderful it all was! . . . And then the thought occurred to her that Olga would arrive, and with her would be Georgie, and she felt herself turning bright green all over with impotent jealousy. Georgie in that crowd! It was impossible that Georgie should be there, and not she, but that was certainly what would happen unless she thought of something. Georgie would go back to Riseholme and describe this gathering, and he would say that Lucia was not there: he supposed she had not been asked.

Lucia thought of something; she hurried downstairs and let herself out. Motors were still arriving, but perhaps she was not too late. She took up her stand in the central shadow of a gas lamp close to Olga's door and waited.

Up the square came yet another car, and she could see it was full of flowers. Olga stepped out, and she darted forward.

"Oh, Mrs. Shuttleworth," she said. "Splendid! Glorious! Marvellous! If only Beethoven was alive! I could not think of going to bed, without just popping across to thank you for a revelation! Georgie, dear! Just to shake your hand: that is all. All! I won't detain you. I see you have a party! You wonderful Queen of Song."

Olga at all times was good-natured. Her eye met Georgie's for a moment.

"Oh, but come in," she said. "Do come in. It isn't a party: it's just anybody. Georgie, be a dear, and help to carry all those flowers in. How nice of you to come across, Mrs. Lucas! I know you'll excuse my running on ahead, because all—at least I hope all—my guests have come, and there's no one to look after them."

Lucia, following closely in her wake, and taking no further notice of Georgie, slipped into the little front drawing room behind her. It was crammed, and it was such a little room. Why had she not foreseen this? Why had she not sent a note across to Olga earlier in the day, asking her to treat Lucia's house precisely as her own, and have her party in the spacious music room? It would have been only neighborly. But the bitterness of such regrets soon vanished in the extraordinary sweetness of the present, and she was soon in conversation with Mrs. Garroby-Ashton, and distributing little smiles and nods to all the folk with whom she had the slightest acquaintance. By the fireplace was standing the royal lady, and that for the moment was the only chagrin, for Lucia had not the vaguest idea who she was. Then Georgie came in, looking like a flower stall, and then came a slight second chagrin, for Olga led him up to the royal lady, and introduced him. But that would be all right, for she could easily get Georgie to tell her who she was, without exactly asking him, and then poor Georgie made a very awkward sort of bow, and dropped a large quantity of flowers, and said "tarsome."

Lucia glided away from Mrs. Garroby-Ashton and stood near the Duchess of Whitby. Marcia did not seem to recognize her at first, but that was quickly remedied, and after a little pleasant talk, Lucia asked her to lunch to meet Olga, and fixed in her mind that she must ask Olga to lunch on the same day to meet the Duchess of Whitby. Then edging a little nearer to the center of attraction, she secured Lord Limpsfield by angling for him with the bait of dearest Aggie, to whom she must remember to telephone early next morning, to ask her to come and meet Lord Limpsfield.

That would do for the present, and Lucia abandoned herself to the joys of the moment. A move was made downstairs to supper, and Lucia, sticking like a limpet to Lord Limpsfield, was wafted in azure to Olga's little tiny dining room, and saw at once that there were not nearly enough seats for everybody. There were two small round tables, and that was absolutely all: the rest would have to stand and forage at the narrow buffet which ran along the wall.

"It's musical chairs," said Olga cheerfully, "those who are quick get seats, and the others don't. Tony, go and sit next the princess; and Cortese, you go the other side. We shall all get something to eat sometime. Georgie, go and stand by the buffet—there's a dear—and make yourself wonderfully useful, and oh, rush upstairs first, and bring the cigarettes; they stay the pangs of hunger. Now we're getting on beautifully. Darling Marcia, there's just one chair left. Slip into it."

Lucia had lingered for a moment at the door to ask Olga to lunch the day after tomorrow, and Olga said she would be delighted, so there was a wonderful little party arranged for. To complete her content, it was only needful to be presented to the hitherto anonymous princess and learn her name. By dexterously picking up her fan for her and much admiring it, as she made a low curtsey, she secured a few precious words with her, but the name was still denied her. To ask anybody what it was would faintly indicate that she didn't know it, and that was not to be thought of.

Georgie popped in, as they all said at Riseholme, to see Lucia next morning when Olga had gone to a rehearsal at Covent Garden, and found her in her music room, busy over Stravinski. Olga's party had not been in the *Times*, which was annoying, and Lucia was still unaware what the princess's name was. Though the previous evening had been far the most rewarding she had yet spent, it was wiser to let Georgie suppose that such an affair was a very ordinary occurrence, and not to allude to it for some time.

"Ah, Georgino!" she said. "How nice of you to pop in. By *buona fortuna* I have got a spare hour this morning, before Sophy Alingsby—dear Sophy, such a brain—fetches me to go to some private view or other, so we can have a good chat. Yes, this is the music room, and before you go, I must trot you round to see the rest of our little establishment. Not a bad room—

those are the famous Chippendale chairs—as soon as we get a little more settled, I shall give an evening party or two with some music. You must come."

"Should love to," said Georgie.

"Such a whirl it has been, and it gets worse every day," went on Lucia. "Sometimes Peppino and I go out together, but often he dines at one house and I at another—they do that in London, you know—and sometimes I hardly set eyes on him all day. I haven't seen him this morning, but just now they told me he had gone out. He enjoys it so much that I do not mind how tired I get. Ah! that telephone, it never ceases ringing. Sometimes I think I will have it taken out of the house altogether, for I get no peace. Somebody always seems to be wanting Peppino or me."

She hurried, all the same, with considerable alacrity to the machine, and really there was no thought in her mind of having the telephone taken out, for it had only just been installed. The call, however, was rather a disappointment, for it only concerned a pair of walking shoes. There was no need, however, to tell Georgie that, and pressing her finger to her forehead, she said, "Yes, I can manage three thirty" (which meant nothing), and quickly rang off.

"Not a moment's peace," said Lucia. "Ting-a-ting-a-ting from morning till night. Now tell me all about Riseholme, Georgie; that will give me such a delicious feeling of tranquillity. Dear me, who is this coming to interrupt us now?"

It was only Peppino. He seemed leisurely enough, and rather unnecessarily explained that he had only been out to get a toothbrush from the chemist's in Brompton Road. This he carried in a small paper parcel.

"And there's the man coming about the telephone this morning, Lucia," he said. "You want the extension to your bedroom, don't you?"

"Yes, dear, as we have got it in the house, we may as well have it conveniently placed," she said. "I'm sure the miles I walk up and down stairs, as I was telling Georgie—"

Peppino chuckled.

"She woke them up, Georgie," he said. "None of their leisurely London ways for Lucia. She had the telephone put into the house in record time. Gave them no peace till she got it done."

"Very wise," said Georgie tactfully. "That's the way to get things. Well, about Riseholme. We've really been very busy indeed."

"Dear old place!" said Lucia. "Tell me all about it."

Georgie rapidly considered with himself whether he should mention the Museum. He decided against it, for, put it as you might, the Museum, apart from the convenience of getting rid of interesting rubbish, was of a conspiratorial nature, a policy of revenge against Lucia for her desertion, and a demonstration of how wonderfully well and truly they all got on without her. It was then the mark of a highly injudicious conspirator to give information to her against whom this plot was directed.

"Well, Daisy has been having some most remarkable experiences," he said. "She got a Ouija board and a planchette—we use the planchette most—and very soon it was quite clear that messages were coming through from a guide."

Lucia laughed with a shrill metallic note of rather hostile timbre.

"Dear Daisy," she said. "If only she would take

common sense as her guide. I suppose the guide is a Chaldean astrologer or King Nebuchadnezzar."

"Not at all," said Georgie. "It's an Egyptian called Abfou."

A momentary pang of envy shot through Lucia. She could well imagine the quality of excitement which thrilled Riseholme, how Georgie would have popped in to tell her about it, and how she would have got a Ouija board too, and obtained twice as many messages as Daisy. She hated the thought of Daisy having Abfou all her own way, and gave another little shrill laugh.

"Daisy is priceless," she said. "And what has Abfou told her?"

"Well, it was very odd," said Georgie. "The morning I got your letter Abfou wrote 'L from L,' and if that doesn't mean 'Letter from Lucia,' I don't know what else it could be."

"It might just as well mean 'Lozengers from Leamington,'" said Lucia witheringly. "And what else?"

Georgie felt the conversation was beginning to border rather dangerously on the Museum, and tried a lighthearted sortie into another subject.

"Oh, just things of that sort," he said. "And then she had a terrible time over her garden. She dismissed Simkinson for doing crossword puzzles instead of the lawn, and determined to do it all herself. She sowed sprouts in that round bed under the dining-room window."

"No!" said Peppino, who was listening with qualms of homesickness to these chronicles.

"Yes, and the phlox in the kitchen garden," said Georgie.

He looked at Lucia, and became aware that her gimlet eye was on him, and was afraid he had made the transition from Abfou to horticulture rather too eagerly. He went volubly on.

"And she dug up all the seeds that Simkinson had planted, and pruned the roots of her mulberry tree and probably killed it," he said. "Then in that warm weather last week—no, the week before—I got out my painting things again, and am doing a sketch of my house from the green. Foljambe is very well, and, and . . ." He could think of nothing else except the Museum.

Lucia waited till he had quite run down.

"And what more did Abfou say?" she asked. "His message of 'L from L' would not have made you busy for very long."

Georgie had to reconsider the wisdom of silence. Lucia clearly suspected something, and when she came down for her weekend, and found the affairs of the Museum entirely engrossing the whole of Riseholme, his reticence, if he persisted in it, would wear a very suspicious aspect.

"Oh, yes, the Museum," he said with feigned lightness. "Abfou told us to start a Museum, and it's getting on splendidly in that tithe barn of Colonel Boucher's. And Daisy's given all the things she was going to make into a rockery, and I'm giving my Roman glass and two sketches, and Colonel Boucher his Samian ware and an ordnance map, and there are lots of fossils and some coins."

"And a committee?" asked Lucia.

"Yes. Daisy and Mrs. Boucher and I, and we co-opted Robert," he said with affected carelessness.

Again some nameless pang shot through Lucia. Absent or present, she ought to have been the chairman of the committee and told them exactly what to do and

how to do it. But she felt no doubt that she could
remedy all that when she came down to Riseholme for
a weekend. In the meantime, it was sufficient to have
pulled his secret out of Georgie, like a cork, with a
loud pop, and an effusion of contents.

"Most interesting," she said. "I must think what I
can give you for your museum. Well, that's a nice little
gossip."

Georgie could not bring himself to tell her that the
stocks had already been moved from the village green
to the tithe barn, for he seemed to remember that Lucia and Peppino had presented them to the Parish
Council. Now the Parish Council had presented them
to the Museum, but that was a reason the more why
the Parish Council and not he should face the donors.

"A nice little gossip," said Lucia. "And what a
pleasant party last night. I just popped over, to congratulate dear Olga on the favorable, indeed the very
favorable reception of *Lucrezia*, for I thought she would
be hurt—artists are so sensitive—if I did not add my
little tribute; and then you saw how she refused to let
me go, but insisted that I should come in. And I found
it all most pleasant; one met many friends, and I was
very glad to be able to look in."

This expressed very properly what Lucia meant to
convey. She did not in the least want to put Olga in her
place, but to put herself, in Georgie's eyes, in her own
place. She had just, out of kindness, stepped across to
congratulate Olga, and then had been dragged in. Unfortunately Georgie did not believe a single word of it;
he had already made up his mind that Lucia had laid
an ambush for Olga, so swiftly and punctually had she
come out of the shadow of the gas lamp on her arrival.
He answered her therefore precisely in the spirit in

which she had spoken. Lucia would know very
well. . . .

"It was good of you," he said enthusiastically. "I'm
sure Olga appreciated your coming immensely. How
forgetful of her not to have asked you at first! And as
for *Lucrezia* just having a favorable reception, I
thought it was the most brilliant success it is possible to
imagine."

Lucia felt that her attitude hadn't quite produced the
impression she had intended. Though she did not want
Georgie (and Riseholme) to think *she* joined in the
uncritical adulation of Olga, she certainly did not want
Georgie to tell Olga that she didn't. And she still
wanted to hear the princess's name.

"No doubt, dear Georgie," she said, "it was a great
success. And she was in wonderful voice, and looked
most charming. As you know, I am terribly critical, but
I can certainly say that. Yes. And her party delicious.
So many pleasant people. I saw you having great jokes
with the princess."

Peppino having been asleep when Lucia came back
last night, and not having seen her this morning, had
not heard about the princess.

"Indeed, who was that?" he asked Lucia.

Very tiresome of Peppino. But Lucia's guide (better
than poor Daisy's Abfou) must have been very atten-
tive to her needs that morning, for Peppino had hardly
uttered these awkward words, when the telephone
rang. She could easily therefore trip across to it, protesting at these tiresome interruptions, and leaving
Georgie to answer.

"Yes, Mrs. Lucas," said Lucia. "Covent Garden?
Yes. Then please put me through. . . . Dearest Olga is

ringing up. No doubt about *The Valkyrie* next week. . . ."

Georgie had a brain wave. He felt sure Lucia would have answered Peppino's question instantly if she had known what the princess's name was. He had noticed that Lucia in spite of her hangings about had not been presented to the illustrious lady last night, and the brain wave that she did not know the illustrious lady's name swept over him. He also saw that Lucia was anxiously listening not to the telephone only, but to him. If Lucia (and there could be no doubt about that) wanted to know, she must eat her humble pie and ask him. . . .

"Yes, dear Diva, it's me," said Lucia. "Couldn't sleep a wink. *Lucrezia* running in my head all night. Marvellous. You rang me up?"

Her face fell.

"Oh, I am disappointed you can't come," she said. "You are naughty. I shall have to give you a little engagement book to put things down in. . . ."

Lucia's guide befriended her again, and her face brightened. It grew almost to an unearthly brightness as she listened to Olga's apologies and a further proposal.

"Sunday evening?" she said. "Now let me think a moment; yes, I am free on Sunday. So glad you said Sunday, because all other nights are full. Delightful. And how nice to see Princess Isabel again. Good-by."

She snapped the receiver back in triumph.

"What was it you asked me, Peppino?" she said. "Oh, yes: it was Princess Isabel. Dear Olga insists on my dining with her on Sunday to meet her again. Such a nice woman."

"I thought we were going down to Riseholme for the Sunday," said Peppino.

Lucia made a little despairing gesture.

"My poor head!" she said. "It is I who ought to have an engagement book chained to me. What am I to do? I hardly like to disappoint dear Olga. But you go down, Peppino, just the same. I know you are longing to get a breath of country air. Georgie will give you dinner one night, I am sure, and the other he will dine with you. Won't you, Georgie? So dear of you. Now who shall I get to fill my Olga's place at lunch tomorrow? Mrs. Garroby-Ashton, I think. Dear me, it is close on twelve, and Sophy will scold me if I keep her waiting. How the morning flashes by! I had hardly begun my practice, when Georgie came, and I've hardly had a word with him before it is time to go out. What will happen to my morning's post I'm sure I don't know. But I insist on your getting your breath of country air on Sunday, Peppino. I shall have plenty to do here, with all my arrears."

There was one note Lucia found she had to write before she went out, and she sent Peppino to show Georgie the house while she scribbled it, and addressing it to Mr. Stephen Merriall at the office of the *Evening Gazette*, sent it off by hand. This was hardly done when Mrs. Alingsby arrived, and they went off together to the private view of the post-cubists, and revelled in the works of those remarkable artists. Some were portraits and some landscapes, and it was usually easy to tell which was which, because a careful scrutiny revealed an eye or a stray mouth in some, and a tree or a house in others. Lucia was specially enthusiastic over a picture of Waterloo Bridge, but she had mistaken the number in the catalogue, and it proved to be a por-

trait of the artist's wife. Luckily she had not actually
read out to Sophy that it was Waterloo Bridge, though
she had said something about the river, but this was
easily covered up in appreciation.

"Too wonderful," she said. "How they get to the
very soul of things! What is it that Wordsworth says?
'The very pulse of the machine.' Pulsating, is it not?"

Mrs. Alingsby was tall and weird and intense,
dressed rather like a bird-of-paradise that had been out
in a high gale, but very well connected. She had long
straight hair which fell over her forehead, and sometimes got in her eyes, and she wore on her head a scar-
let jockey cap with an immense cameo in front of it.
She hated all art that was earlier than 1923, and a considerable lot of what was later. In music, on the other
hand, she was primitive, and thought Bach decadent:
in literature her taste was for stories without a story,
and poems without meter or meaning. But she had collected round her a group of interesting outlaws, of
whom the men looked like women, and the women like
nothing at all, and though nobody ever knew what they
were talking about, they themselves were talked about.
Lucia had been to a party of hers, where they all sat in
a room with black walls, and listened to early Italian
music on a spinet while a charcoal brazier on a blue
hearth was fed with incense. . . . Lucia's general opinion of her was that she might be useful up to a point,
for she certainly excited interest.

"Wordsworth?" she asked. "Oh, yes. I remember
who you mean. About the Westmorland Lakes. Such a
kill-joy."

She put on her large horn spectacles to look at the
picture of the artist's wife, and her body began to sway
with a lithe circular motion.

"Marvellous! What a rhythm!" she said. "Sigismund is the most rhythmical of them all. You ought to be painted by him. He would make something wonderful of you. Something *andante*, *adagio* almost. He's coming to see me on Sunday. Come and meet him. Breakfast about half past twelve. Vegetarian with cocktails."

Lucia accepted this remarkable invitation with avidity; it would be an interesting and progressive meal. In these first weeks, she was designedly experimental; she intended to sweep into her net all there was which could conceivably harbor distinction, and sort it out by degrees. She was no snob in the narrow sense of the word; she would have been very discontented if she had only the highborn on her visiting list. The highborn, of course, were safe—you could not make a mistake in having a duchess to tea, because in her own line a duchess had distinction—but it would not have been enough to have all the duchesses there were: it might even have been a disappointing tea party if the whole room was packed with them. What she wanted was the foam of the wave, the topmost, the most sunlit of the billows that rode the sea. Anything that had proved itself billowish was her game, and anything which showed signs of being a billow, even if it entailed a vegetarian lunch with cocktails and the possible necessity of being painted like the artist's wife with an eyebrow in one corner of the picture and a substance like desiccated cauliflower in the center. That had always been her way: whatever those dear funny folk at Riseholme had thought of, a juggler, a professor of Yoga, a geologist, a psychoanalyst had been snapped up by her and exploited till he exploded.

But Peppino was not as nimble as she. The incense at Sophy's had made him sneeze, and the primitive tunes on the spinet had made him snore—that had been all the uplift they had held for him. Thus, though she did not mind tiring herself to death, because Peppino was having such an interesting time, she didn't mind his going down to Riseholme for the Sunday to rest, while she had a vegetarian lunch with post-cubists, and a dinner with a princess. Literally, she could scarcely tell which of the two she looked forward to most; the princess was safe, but the post-cubists might prove more perilously paying. It was impossible to make a corner in princesses, for they were too independent, but already, in case of post-cubism turning out to be the rage, she could visualize her music room and even the famous Chippendale chairs being painted black, and the Sargent picture of Auntie being banished to the attic. She could not make them the rage, for she was not (as yet) the supreme arbiter here that she had been at Riseholme, but should they become the rage, there was no one surely more capable than herself of giving the impression that she had discovered them.

Lucia spent a strenuous afternoon with correspondence and telephonings, and dropped into Mrs. Sandeman's for a cup of tea, of which she stood sorely in need. She found there was no need to tell dearest Aggie about the party last night at Olga's, for the *Evening Gazette* had come in, and there was an account of it, described in Hermione's matchless style. Hermione had found the bijou residence of the prima donna in Brompton Square full of friends—*très intimes*—who had been invited to celebrate the huge success of *Lucrezia* and to congratulate Mrs. Shuttleworth. There was Princess Isabel, wearing her wonderful turquoises, chatting with the composer, Signor Cortese (Princess

Isabel spoke Italian perfectly), and among other friends Hermione had noticed the Duchess of Whitby, Lord Limpsfield, Mrs. Garroby-Ashton, and Mrs. Philip Lucas.

5

THE MYSTERY of that Friday evening in the last week in June became portentous on the ensuing Saturday morning. . . .

A cab had certainly driven from the station to The Hurst late on Friday evening, but owing to the darkness it was not known who got out of it. Previously the windows of The Hurst had been very diligently cleaned all Friday afternoon. Of course the latter might be accounted for by the mere fact that they needed cleaning, but if it had been Peppino or Lucia herself who had arrived by the cab (if both of them, they would almost certainly have come by their motor), surely some sign of their presence would have manifested itself either to Riseholme's collective eye or to Riseholme's ear. But the piano, Daisy felt certain, had not been heard, nor had the telephone tinkled for anybody. Also, when she looked out about half past

ten in the evening, and again when she went upstairs to
bed, there were no lights in the house. But somebody
had come, and as the servants' rooms looked out onto
the back, it was probably a servant or servants. Daisy
had felt so terribly interested in this that she came rest-
lessly down, and had a quarter of an hour's weedjing to
see if Abfou could tell her. She had been quite unable
to form any satisfactory conjecture herself, and Abfou,
after writing "Museum" once or twice, had relapsed
into rapid and unintelligible Arabic. She did not ring
up Georgie to ask help in solving this conundrum, because she hoped to solve it unaided and be able to tell
him the answer.

She went upstairs again, and after a little deep
breathing and bathing her feet in alternate applica-
tions of hot and cold water in order to produce somno-
lence, found herself more widely awake than ever. Her
well-trained mind cantered about on scents that led
nowhere, and she was unable to find any that seemed
likely to lead anywhere. Of Lucia, nothing whatever
was known except what was accessible to anybody who
spent a penny on the *Evening Gazette*. She had written
to nobody, she had given no sign of any sort, and but
for the *Evening Gazette*, she might, as far as Riseholme was concerned, be dead. But the *Evening
Gazette* showed that she was alive, painfully alive in
fact, if Hermione could be trusted. She had been seen
here, there, and everywhere in London: Hermione had
observed her chatting in the park with friends, sitting
with friends in her box at the opera, shopping in Bond
Street, watching polo (why, she did not know a horse
from a cow!) at Hurlingham, and even in a punt at
Henley. She had been entertaining in her own house,
too: there had been dinner parties and musical parties,

and she had dined at so many houses that Daisy had
added them all up, hoping to prove that she had spent
more evenings than there had been evenings to spend,
but to her great regret they came out exactly right.
Now she was having her portrait painted by Sigismund,
and not a word had she written, not a glimpse of herself had she vouchsafed, to Riseholme. . . . Of course
Georgie had seen her when he went up to stay with
Olga, but his account of her had been far from reassur-
ing. She had said that she did not care how tired she
got while Peppino was enjoying London so tremendously. Why then, thought Daisy with a sense of in-
credulous indignation, had Peppino come down a few
Sundays ago, all by himself, and looking a perfect
wreck? . . . "Very odd, *I* call it," muttered Daisy,
turning over to her other side.

It was odd, and Peppino had been odd. He had
dined with Georgie one night, and on the other, Georgie had dined with him, but he had said nothing about
Lucia that Hermione had not trumpeted to the world.
Otherwise, Peppino had not been seen at all on that
Sunday except when Mrs. Antrobus, not feeling very
well in the middle of the Psalms on Sunday morning,
had come out, and observed him standing on tiptoe and
peering into the window of the Museum that looked onto the Roman Antiquities. Mrs. Antrobus (feeling much
better as soon as she got into the air) had come quite
close up to him before he perceived her, and then with
only the curtest word of greeting, just as if she was the
Museum Committee, he had walked away so fast that
she could not but conclude that he wished to be alone.
It was odd, too, and scarcely honorable, that he should
have looked into the window like that, and clearly it was
for that purpose that he had absented himself from

church, thinking that he would be unobserved. Daisy
had not the smallest doubt that he was spying for Lucia,
and had been told merely to collect information and to
say nothing, for though he knew that Georgie was on the
committee, he had carefully kept off the subject of the
Museum on both their tête-à-tête dinners. Probably he
had begun his spying the moment church began, and if
Mrs. Antrobus had not so providentially felt faint, no
one would have known anything about it. As it was, it
was quite likely that he had looked into every window
by the time she saw him, and knew all that the
Museum contained. Since then, the Museum had been
formally opened by Lady Ambermere, who had lent
(not presented) some mittens which she said belonged
to Queen Charlotte (it was impossible to prove that
they hadn't), and the committee had put up some very
baffling casement curtains which would make an end to
spying for ever.

Now this degrading espionage had happened three
weeks ago (come Sunday), and therefore for three
weeks (come Monday), Lucia must have known all
about the Museum. But not a word had she transmitted
on that or any other subject; she had not demanded a
place on the committee, nor presented the Elizabethan
spit which so often made the chimney of her music
room smoke, nor written to say that they must arrange
it all quite differently. That she had a plan, a policy
about the Museum, no one who knew Lucia could possibly doubt, but her policy (which thus at present was
wrapped in mystery) might be her complete and eter-
nal ignoring of it. It would indeed be dreadful if she intended to remain unaware of it, but Daisy doubted if
anyone in her position and of her domineering character could be capable of such inhuman self-control. No,

she meant to do something when she came back, but nobody could guess what it was or when she was coming.

Daisy tossed and turned as she revolved these knotty points. She was sure Lucia would punish them all for making a museum while she was away, and not asking her advice and begging her to be president, and she would be ill with chagrin when she learned how successful it was proving. The tourist season, when char-à-bancs passed through Riseholme in endless procession, had begun, and whole parties after lunching at the Ambermere Arms went to see it. In the first week alone, there had been a hundred and twenty-six visitors, and that meant a corresponding tale of shillings without reckoning sixpenny catalogues. Even the committee paid their shillings when they went in to look at their own exhibits, and there had been quite a scene when Lady Ambermere with a party from The Hall tried to get in without paying for any of them on the ground that she had lent the Museum Queen Charlotte's mittens. Georgie, who was hanging up another picture of his, had heard it all and hidden behind a curtain. The small boy in charge of the turnstile (bought from a bankrupt circus for a mere song) had, though trembling with fright, absolutely refused to let the turnstile turn until the requisite number of shillings had been paid, and didn't care whose mittens they were which Lady Ambermere had lent, and when, snatching up a catalogue without paying for it, she had threatened to report him to the committee, this intrepid lad had followed her, continuing to say, "Sixpence, please, my lady," till one of the party, in order to save brawling in a public place, had produced the insignificant sum. And if Lucia tried to get in without paying,

on the ground that she and Peppino had given the
stocks to the Parish Council, which had lent them to
the Museum, she would find her mistake. At length, in
the effort to calculate what would be the total receipts
of the year if a hundred and twenty-six people per
week paid their shillings, Daisy lapsed into an uneasy
arithmetical slumber.

Next morning (Saturday), the mystery of that arrival at The Hurst the evening before grew infinitely
more intense. It was believed that only one person had
come, and yet there was no doubt that several pounds
of salmon, dozens ("Literally dozens," said Mrs.
Boucher, "for I saw the basket") of eggs, two chickens, a leg of lamb, as well as countless other provisions
unidentified were delivered at the back door of The
Hurst; a positive frieze of tradesmen's boys was strung
across the green. Even if the mysterious arrival was
Lucia herself, she could not, unless the whirl and
worldliness of her London life had strangely increased
her appetite, eat all that before Monday. And besides,
why had she not rung up Georgie, or somebody, or
opened her bedroom window on this hot morning? Or
could it be Peppino again, sent down here for a rest
cure and a stuffing of his emaciated frame? But then he
would not have come down without some sort of at-
tendant to look after him. . . . Riseholme was completely baffled; never had its powers of inductive
reasoning been so nonplussed, for though so much
went into The Hurst, nobody but the tradesmen's boys
with empty baskets came out. Georgie and Daisy
stared at each other in blankness over the garden
paling, and when, in despair of arriving at any solution,
they sought the oracles of Abfou, he would give them
nothing but hesitating Arabic.

"Which shows," said Daisy, as she put the planchette away in disgust, "that even he doesn't know, or doesn't wish to tell us." Lunchtime arrived, and there were very poor appetites in Riseholme (with the exception of that Gargantuan of whom nothing was known). But as for going to The Hurst and ringing the bell and asking if Mrs. Lucas was at home, all Riseholme would sooner have died lingering and painful deaths rather than let Lucia know that they took the smallest interest in anything she had done, was doing, or would do.

About three o'clock Georgie was sitting on the green opposite his house, finishing his sketch, which the affairs of the Museum had caused him sadly to neglect. He had got it upside down on his easel and was washing some more blue into the sky, when he heard the hoot of a motor. He just looked up, and what he saw caused his hand to twitch so violently that he put a large dab of cobalt on the middle of his red-brick house. For the motor had stopped at The Hurst, not a hundred yards away, and out of it got Lucia and Peppino. She gave some orders to her chauffeur, and then without noticing him (*perhaps* without seeing him), she followed Peppino into the house. Hardly waiting to wash the worst of the cobalt off his house, Georgie hurried into Daisy's, and told her exactly what had happened.

"No!" said Daisy, and out they came again, and stood in the shadow of her mulberry tree to see what would happen next. The mulberry tree had recovered from the pruning of its roots (so it wasn't it which Abfou had said was dead), and gave them good shelter.

Nothing happened next.

"But it's impossible," said Daisy, speaking in a sort

of conspiratorial whisper. "It's queer enough her coming without telling any of us, but now she's here, she surely must ring somebody up."

Georgie was thinking intently.

"The next thing that will happen," he said, "will be that servants and luggage will arrive from the station. They'll be here any minute; I heard the three-twenty whistle just now. She and Peppino have driven down."

"I shouldn't wonder," said Daisy. "But even now, what about the chickens and all those eggs? Georgie, it must have been her cook who came last night—she and Peppino were dining out in London—and ordered all those provisions this morning. But there was enough to last them a week. And three pints of cream, so I've heard since, and enough ice for a skating rink and—"

It was then that Georgie had the flash of intuition that was for ever memorable. It soared above inductive reasoning.

"She's having a weekend party of some of her smart friends from London," he said slowly. "And she doesn't want any of us."

Daisy blinked at this amazing light. Then she cast one withering glance in the direction of The Hurst.

"She!" she said. "And her shingles. And her seed pearls! That's all."

A minute afterward, the station cab arrived pyramidal with luggage. Four figures disembarked; three female and one male.

"The major-domo," said Daisy, and without another word marched back into her house to ask Abfou about it all. He came through at once, and wrote "Snob" all over the paper.

There was no reason why Georgie should not finish his sketch, and he sat down again and began by taking

out the rest of the misplaced cobalt. He felt so certain
of the truth of his prophecy that he just let it alone to
fulfill itself, and for the next hour he never worked
with more absorbed attention. He knew that Daisy
came out of her house, walking very fast, and he supposed she was on her way to spread the news and fore-
cast the sequel. But beyond the fact that he was
perfectly sure that a party from London was coming
down for the weekend, he could form no idea of what
would be the result of that. It might be that Lucia
would ask him or Daisy, or some of her old friends to
dine, but if she had intended to do that, she would
probably have done it already. The only alternative
seemed to be that she meant to ignore Riseholme altogether. But shortly before the arrival of the fast train
from London at 4:30, his prophetical calm began (for
he was but human) to be violently agitated, and he
took his tea in the window of his drawing room, which
commanded a good view of the front garden of The
Hurst, and put his opera glasses ready to hand. The
window was a big bow, and he distinctly saw the end
of Robert's brass telescope projecting from the corresponding window next door.

Once more a motor horn sounded, and the Lucases'
car drew up at the gate of The Hurst. There stepped
out Mrs. Garroby-Ashton, followed by the weird bright
thing which had called to take Lucia to the private
view of the post-cubists. Georgie had not time for the
moment to rack his brain as to the name he had forgotten, for observation was his primary concern, and
next he saw Lord Limpsfield, whom he had met at
Olga's party. Finally there emerged a tall, slim,
middle-aged man in Oxford trousers, for whom Georgie
instantly conceived a deep distrust. He had thick au-

burn hair, for he wore no hat, and he waved his hands about in a silly manner as he talked. Over his shoulder was a little cape. Then Lucia came tripping out of the house with her short skirts and her shingles, and they all chattered together, and kissed and squealed, and pointed in different directions, and moved up the garden into the house. The door was shut, and the end of Robert's brass telescope withdrawn.

Hardly had these shameful events occurred when Georgie's telephone bell rang. It might be Daisy wanting to compare notes, but it might be Lucia asking him to tea. He felt torn in half at the idea: carnal curiosity urged him with clamor to go; dignity dissuaded him. Still halting between two opinions, he went toward the instrument, which continued ringing. He felt sure now that it was Lucia, and what on earth was he to say? He stood there so long that Foljambe came hurrying into the room, in case he had gone out.

"See who it is, Foljambe," he said.

Foljambe with amazing calm took off the receiver.

"Trunk call," she said.

He glued himself to the instrument, and soon there came a voice he knew.

"No! Is it you?" he asked. "What is it?"

"I'm motoring down tomorrow morning," said Olga, "and Princess Isabel is probably coming with me, though she is not absolutely certain. But expect her, unless I telephone tomorrow. Be a darling and give us lunch, as we shall be late, and come and dine. Terrible hurry: good-by."

"No, you must wait a minute," screamed Georgie. "Of course I'll do that, but I must tell you, Lucia's just come with a party from London and hasn't asked any of us."

"No!" said Olga. "Then don't tell her I'm coming. She's become such a bore. She asks me to lunch and dinner every day. How thrilling though, Georgie! Whom has she got?"

Suddenly the name of the weird bright female came back to Georgie.

"Mrs. Alingsby," he said.

"Lor!" said Olga. "Who else?"

"Mrs. Garroby-Ashton—"

"What?"

"Garr-o-by Ash-ton," said Georgie very distinctly; "and Lord Limpsfield. And a tall man in Oxford trousers with auburn hair."

"It sounds like your double, Georgie," said Olga. "And a little cape like yours?"

"Yes," said Georgie rather coldly.

"I think it must be Stephen Merriall," said Olga after a pause.

"And who's that?" asked he.

"Lucia's lover," said Olga quite distinctly.

"No!" said Georgie.

"Of course he isn't. I only meant he was always there. But I believe he's Hermione. I'm not sure, but I think so. Georgie, we shall have a hectic Sunday. Good-by, tomorrow about two or three for lunch, and two or three *for* lunch. What a gossip you are."

He heard that delicious laugh, and the click of her receiver.

Georgie was far too thrilled to gasp. He sat quite quiet, breathing gently. For the honor of Riseholme he was glad that a princess was perhaps coming to lunch with him, but apart from that he would really have

much preferred that Olga should be alone. The "affaire
Lucia" was so much more thrilling than anything else,
but Princess Isabel might feel no interest in it, and instead they would talk about all sorts of dull things like
kings and courts. . . . Then suddenly he sprang from
his chair: there was a leg of lamb for Sunday lunch,
and an apple tart, and nothing else at all. What was to
be done? The shops by now would be shut.

He rang for Foljambe.

"Miss Olga's coming to lunch and possibly—possibly a friend of hers," he said. "What are we to do?"

"A leg of lamb and an apple tart's good enough for
anybody, isn't it?" said Foljambe severely.

This really seemed true as soon as it was pointed
out, and Georgie made an effort to dismiss the matter
from his mind. But he could not stop still: it was all so
exciting, and after having changed his Oxford trousers
in order to minimize the likeness between him and that
odious Mr. Merriall, he went out for a constitutional,
round the green, from all points of which he could see
any important development at The Hurst. Riseholme
generally was doing the same, and his stroll was interrupted by many agreeable stoppages. It was already
known that Lucia and Peppino had arrived, and that
servants and luggage had come by the 3:20, and that
Lucia's motor had met the 4:30 and returned laden
with exciting people. Georgie therefore was in high demand, for he might supply the names of the exiting
people, and he had the further information to divulge
that Olga was arriving tomorrow, and was lunching
with him and dining at her own house. He said nothing
about a possible princess; she might not come, and in
that case he knew there would be a faint suspicion in
everybody's mind that he had invented it; whereas if

she did, she would no doubt sign his visitors' book for everyone to see.

Feeling ran stormy high against Lucia, and as usual when Riseholme felt a thing deeply, there was little said by way of public comment, though couples might have been observed with set and angry faces and gabbling mouths. But higher yet ran curiosity and surmise as to what Lucia would do, and what Olga would do. Not a sign had come from anyone from The Hurst, not a soul had been asked to lunch, dinner, or even tea, and if Lucia seemed to be ashamed of Riseholme society before her grand friends, there was no doubt that Riseholme society was ashamed of Lucia. . . .

And then suddenly a deadly hush fell on these discussions, and even those who were walking fastest in their indignation came to a halt, for out of the front door of The Hurst streamed the "exciting people" and their hosts. There was Lucia, hatless and shingled and short-skirted, and the Bird-of-Paradise and Mrs. Garroby-Ashton, and Peppino and Lord Limpsfield and Mr. Merriall all talking shrilly together, with shrieks of hollow laughter. They came slowly across the green toward the little pond round which Riseholme stood, and passed within fifty yards of it, and if Lucia had been the Gorgon, Riseholme could not more effectually have been turned into stone. She, too, appeared not to notice them, so absorbed was she in conversation, and on they went straight toward the Museum. Just as they passed Colonel Boucher's house, Mrs. Boucher came out in her Bath chair, and without pause was wheeled straight through the middle of them. She then drew up by the side of the green below the large elm.

The party passed into the Museum. The windows were open, and from inside, there came shrieks of laughter. This continued for about ten minutes, and then . . . they all came out again. Several of them carried catalogues, and Mr. Merriall was reading out of one in a loud voice.

"Pair of worsted mittens," he announced, "belonging to Queen Charlotte and presented by the Lady Ambermere."

"Don't," said Lucia. "Don't make fun of our dear little Museum, Stephen."

As they retraced their way along the edge of the green, movement came back to Riseholme again. Lucia's policy with regard to the Museum had declared itself. Georgie strolled up to Mrs. Boucher's Bath chair. Mrs. Boucher was extremely red in the face, and her hands were trembling.

"Good evening, Mr. Georgie," she said. "Another party of strangers, I see, visiting the Museum. They looked very odd people, and I hope we shan't find anything missing. Any news?"

That was a very dignified way of taking it, and Georgie responded in the same spirit.

"Not a scrap that I know of," he said, "except that Olga's coming down tomorrow."

"That will be nice," said Mrs. Boucher. "Riseholme is always glad to see *her*."

Daisy joined them.

"Good evening, Mrs. Quantock," said Mrs. Boucher. "Any news?"

"Yes, indeed," said Daisy rather breathlessly. "Didn't you see them? Lucia and her party?"

"No," said Mrs. Boucher firmly. "She is in London surely. Anything else?"

Daisy took the cue. Complete ignorance that Lucia was in Riseholme at all was a noble maneuver.

"It must have been my mistake," she said. "Oh, my mulberry tree has quite come round."

"No!" said Mrs. Boucher in the Riseholme voice. "I am pleased. I daresay the pruning did it good. And Mr. Georgie's just told me that our dear Olga, or I should say Mrs. Shuttleworth, is coming down tomorrow, but he hasn't told me what time yet."

"Two or three, she said," answered Georgie. "She's motoring down, and is going to have lunch with me whenever she gets here."

"Indeed! Then I should advise you to have something cold that won't spoil by waiting. A bit of cold lamb, for instance. Nothing so good on a hot day."

"What an excellent idea!" said Georgie. "I was thinking of hot lamb. But the other's much better. I'll have it cooked tonight."

"And a nice tomato salad," said Mrs. Boucher, "and if you haven't got any, I can give you some. Send your Foljambe round, and she'll come back with half a dozen ripe tomatoes."

Georgie hurried off to see to these new arrangements, and Colonel Boucher having strolled away with Piggy, his wife could talk freely to Mrs. Quantock. . . . She did.

Lucia waking rather early next morning found she had rather an uneasy conscience as her bedfellow, and she used what seemed very reasonable arguments to quiet it. There would have been no point in writing to Georgie or any of them to say that she was bringing down some friends for the weekend and would be occupied with them all Sunday. She could not with all these guests play duets with Georgie, or get poor Daisy to give an exhibition of Ouija, or have Mrs. Boucher in her Bath chair to tea, for she would give them all long histories of purely local interest, which could not conceivably amuse people like Lord Limpsfield or weird Sophy. She had been quite wise to keep Riseholme and Brompton Square apart, for they would not mix. Besides, her guests would go away on Monday morning, and she had determined to stop over till Tuesday and be extremely kind, and not the least condescending. She would have one or two of them to lunch, and one or two more to dinner, and give Georgie a full hour of duets as well. Naturally if Olga had been here, she would have asked Olga on Sunday, but Olga had been singing last night at the opera. Lucia had talked a good deal about her at dinner, and given the impression that they were never out of each other's houses either in town or here, and had lamented her absence.

"Such a pity," she had said. "For dearest Olga loves singing in my music room. I shall never forget how she dropped in for some little garden party and sang the Awakening of Brunnhilde. Even you, dear Sophy, with your passion for the primitive, would have enjoyed that. She sang *Lucrezia* here, too, before anyone had heard it. Cortese brought the score down the moment he had finished it—ah, I think that was in her house—there was just Peppino and me, and perhaps one or two others. We would have had dearest Olga here all day tomorrow if only she had been here. . . ."

So Lucia felt fairly easy, having planned these treats for Riseholme on Monday, as to her aloofness today, and then her conscience brought up the question of the Museum. Here she stoutly defended herself; she knew nothing about the Museum (except what Peppino had seen through the window a few Sundays before); she

had not been consulted about the Museum; she was
not on the committee; and it was perfectly proper for
her to take her party to see it. She could not prevent
them bursting into shrieks of laughter at Queen Charlotte's mittens and Daisy's drainpipes, nor could she
possibly prevent herself from joining in those shrieks of
laughter herself, for surely this was the most ridiculous
collection of rubbish ever brought together. A glass
case for Queen Charlotte's mittens, a heap of fossils
such as she had chipped out by the score from the old
quarry, some fragments of glass (Georgie ought to
have known better), some quilts, a dozen coins, lent,
only lent, by poor Daisy! In fact the only object of the
slightest interest was the pair of stocks which she and
Peppino had bought and set up on the village green.
She would see about that when she came down in August, and back they should go on to the village green.
Then there was the catalogue; who could help laughing
at the catalogue which described in most pompous language the contents of this dustbin? There was nothing
to be uneasy about over that. And as for Mrs. Boucher
having driven right through her party without a glance
of recognition, what did that matter? On her own side,
also, Lucia had given no glance of recognition to Mrs.
Boucher; if she had, Mrs. Boucher would have told
them all about her asparagus or how her Elizabeth had
broken a plate. It was odd, perhaps, that Mrs. Boucher
hadn't stopped . . . and was it rather odd also that,
though from the corner of her eye she had seen all
Riseholme standing about on the green, no one had
made the smallest sign of welcome? It was true that
she had practically cut them (if a process conducted at
the distance of fifty yards can be called a cut), but she
was not quite sure that she enjoyed the same process

herself. Probably it meant nothing; they saw she was engaged with her friends, and very properly had not thrust themselves forward.

Her guests mostly breakfasted upstairs, but by the middle of the morning they had all straggled down. Lucia had brought with her yesterday her portrait by Sigismund, which Sophy declared was a masterpiece of *adagio*. She was advising her to clear all other pictures out of the music room and hang it there alone, like a wonderful slow movement, when Mr. Merriall came in with the Sunday paper.

"Ah, the paper has come," said Lucia. "Is not that Riseholmish of us? We never get the Sunday paper till midday."

"Better late than never," said Mr. Merriall, who was rather addicted to quoting proverbial sayings. "I see that Mrs. Shuttleworth's coming down here today. Do ask her to dine and perhaps she'll sing to us."

Lucia paused for a single second, then clapped her hands.

"Oh, what fun that would be!" she said. "But I don't think it can be true. Dearest Olga popped in—or did I pop in—yesterday morning in town, and she said nothing about it. No doubt, she had not made up her mind then whether she was coming or not. Of course I'll ring her up at once and scold her for not telling me."

Lucia found from Olga's caretaker that she and a friend were expected, but she knew they couldn't come to lunch with her, as they were lunching with Mr. Pillson. She "couldn't say, I'm sure" who the friend was, but promised to give the message that Mrs. Lucas hoped they would both come and dine. . . . The next thing was to ring up Georgie and be wonderfully cordial.

"*Georgino mio*, is it 'oo?" she asked.

"Yes," said Georgie. He did not have to ask who it was, nor did he feel inclined for baby talk.

"Georgino, I never caught a glimpse of you yesterday," she said. "Why didn't 'oo come round and see me?"

"Because you never asked me," said Georgie firmly, "and because you never told me you were coming."

"Me so sorry," said Lucia. "But me was so fussed and busy in town. Delicious to be in Riseholme again."

"Delicious," said Georgie.

Lucia paused a moment.

"Is Georgino cross with me?" she asked.

"Not a bit," said Georgie brightly. "Why?"

"I didn't know. And I hear my Olga and a friend are lunching with you. I am hoping they will come and dine with me tonight. And do come in afterward. We shall be eight already, or of course I should ask you."

"Thanks so much, but I'm dining with her," said Georgie.

A pause.

"Well, all of you come and dine here," said Lucia. "Such amusing people, and I'll squeeze you in."

"I'm afraid I can't accept for Olga," said Georgie. "And I'm dining with her, you see."

"Well, will you come across after lunch and bring them?" said Lucia. "Or tea?"

"I don't know what they will feel inclined to do," said Georgie. "But I'll tell them."

"Do, and I'll ring up at lunchtime again, and have ickle talk to my Olga. Who is her friend?"

Georgie hesitated: he thought he would not give that away just yet. Lucia would know in heaps of time.

"Oh, just somebody whom she's possibly bringing down," he said, and rang off.

Lucia began to suspect a slight mystery, and she disliked mysteries, except when she made them herself. Olga's caretaker was "sure she couldn't say," and Georgie (Lucia was sure) wouldn't. So she went back to her guests, and very prudently said that Olga had not arrived at present, and then gave them a wonderful account of her little *intime* dinner with Olga and Princess Isabel. Such a delightful amusing woman; they must all come and meet Princess Isabel some day soon in town.

Lucia and her guests, with the exception of Sophy Alingsby who continued to play primitive tunes with one finger on the piano, went for a stroll on the green before lunch. Mrs. Quantock hurried by with averted face, and naturally everybody wanted to know how the Red Queen from Alice in Wonderland was. Lucia amused them by a bright version of poor Daisy's Ouija board and the story of the mulberry tree.

"Such dears they all are," she said. "But too killing. And then she planted broccoli instead of phlox. It's only in Riseholme that such things happen. You must all come and stay with me in August, and we'll enter into the life of the place. I adore it, simply adore it. We are always wildly excited about something. . . . And next door is Georgie Pillson's house. A lamb! I'm devoted to him. He does embroidery, and gave those broken bits of glass to the Museum. And that's dear Olga's house at the end of the road. . . ."

Just as Lucia was kissing her hand to Olga's house, her eagle eye had seen a motor approaching, and it drew up at Georgie's house. Two women got out, and there was no doubt whatever who either of them were.

They went in at the gate, and he came out of his front door like the cuckoo out of a clock and made a low bow. All this Lucia saw, and though for the moment petrified, she quickly recovered, and turned sharply round.

"Well, we must be getting home again," she said, in a rather strangled voice. "It is lunchtime."

Mr. Merriall did not turn so quickly, but watched the three figures at Georgie's door.

"Appearances are deceptive," he said. "But isn't that Olga Shuttleworth and Princess Isabel?"

"No! Where?" said Lucia looking in the opposite direction.

"Just gone into that house; Georgie Pillson's, didn't you say?"

"No, really?" said Lucia. "How stupid of me not to have seen them. Shall I pop in now? No, I think I will ring them up presently, unless we find that they have already rung me up."

Lucia was putting a brave face on it, but she was far from easy. It looked like a plot; it did indeed, for Olga had never told her she was coming to Riseholme, and Georgie had never told her that Princess Isabel was the friend she was bringing with her. However, there was lunchtime in which to think over what was to be done. But though she talked incessantly and rather satirically about Riseholme, she said no more about the prima donna and the princess. . . .

Lucia might have been gratified (or again she might not) if she had known how vivacious a subject of conversation she afforded at Georgie's select little luncheon party. Princess Isabel (with her mouth now full of Mrs. Boucher's tomatoes) had been subjected during this last week to an incessant bombardment from Lucia, and had heard on quite good authority that she alluded to her as "Isabel, dear Princess Isabel."

"And I will not go to her house," she said. "It is a free country, and I do not choose to go to her kind house. No doubt she is a very good woman. But I want to hear more of her, for she thrills me. So does your Riseholme. You were talking of the Museum."

"Georgie, go on about the Museum," said Olga.

"Well," said Georgie, "there it was. They all went in, and then they all came out again, and one of them was reading my catalogue—I made it—aloud, and they all screamed with laughter."

"But I daresay it was a very funny catalogue, Georgie," said Olga.

"I don't think so. Mr. Merriall read out about Queen Charlotte's mittens, presented by Lady Ambermere."

"No!" said Olga.

"Most interesting!" said the Princess. "She was my aunt, big-aunt, is it? No, great-aunt—that is it. Afterward we will go to the Museum and see her mittens. Also, I must see the lady who kills mulberry trees. Olga, can't you ask her to bring her planchette and prophesy?"

"Georgie, ring up Daisy, and ask her to come to tea with me," said Olga. "We must have a weedj."

"And I must go for a drive, and I must walk on the green, and I must have some more delicious apple pie," began the Princess.

Georgie had just risen to ring up Daisy, when Foljambe entered with the news that Mrs. Lucas was on the telephone and would like to speak to Olga.

"Oh, say we're still at lunch, please, Foljambe," said

she. "Can she send a message? And you say Stephen Merriall is there, Georgie?"

"No, you said he was there," said Georgie. "I only described him."

"Well, I'm pretty sure it is he, but you will have to go sometime this afternoon and find out. If it is, he's Hermione, who's always writing about Lucia in the *Evening Gazette*. Priceless! So you must go across for a few minutes, Georgie, and make certain."

Foljambe came back to ask if Mrs. Lucas might pop in to pay her respects to Princess Isabel.

"So kind of her, but she must not dream of troubling herself," said the Princess.

Foljambe retired and appeared for the third time with a faint, firm smile.

"Mrs. Lucas will ring up Mrs. Shuttleworth in a quarter of an hour," she said.

The Princess finished her apple tart.

"And now let us go and see the Museum," she said.

• • •

Georgie remained behind to ring up Daisy, to explain when Lucia telephoned next that Olga had gone out, and to pay his visit to The Hurst. To pretend that he did not enjoy that, would be to misunderstand him altogether. Lucia had come down here with her smart party and had taken no notice of Riseholme, and now two people a million times smarter had by a clearly providential dealing come down at the same time and were taking no notice of her. Instead they were hobnobbing with people like himself and Daisy whom Lucia had slighted. Then she had laughed at the Museum, and especially at the catalogue and the mittens, and now the great-niece of the owner of the mittens had gone to see them. That was a stinger, in fact it was all a stinger, and well Lucia deserved it.

He was shown into the music room, and he had just time to observe that there was a printed envelope on the writing table addressed to the *Evening Gazette*, when Lucia and Mr. Merriall came hurrying in.

"*Georgino mio*," said Lucia effusively. "How nice of you to come in. But you've not brought your ladies? Oh, this is Mr. Merriall."

(Hermione, of the *Evening Gazette*, it's proved, thought Georgie.)

"They thought they wouldn't add to your big party," said Georgie sumptuously. (That was another stinger.)

"And was it Princess Isabel I saw at your door?" asked Mr. Merriall with an involuntary glance at the writing table. (Lucia had not mentioned her since.)

"Oh, yes. They just motored down and took potluck with me."

"What did you give them?" asked Lucia, forgetting her anxieties for a moment.

"Oh, just cold lamb and apple tart," said Georgie.

"No!" said Lucia. "You ought to have brought them to lunch here. Oh, Georgie, my picture, look. By Sigismund."

"Oh, yes," said Georgie. "What's it of?"

"*Cattivo!*" said Lucia. "Why, it's a portrait of me. Sigismund, you know, he's the greatest rage in London just now. Everybody is crazy to be painted by him."

"And they look crazy when they are. It's a mad world, my masters," said Mr. Merriall.

"Naughty," said Lucia. "Is it not wonderful, Georgie?"

"Yes. I expect it's very clever," said Georgie. "Very clever indeed."

"I should so like to show it dearest Olga," said Lucia, "and I'm sure the Princess would be interested in it. She was talking about modern art the other day when I dined with Olga. I wonder if they would look in at teatime, or indeed any other time."

"Not very likely, I'm afraid," said Georgie, "for Daisy Quantock's coming to tea, I know. We're going to weedj. And they're going out for a drive sometime."

"And where are they now?" asked Lucia. It was terrible to have to get news of her intimate friends from Georgie, but how else was she to find out?

"They went across to see the Museum," said he. "They were most interested in it."

Mr. Merriall waved his hands, just in the same way as Georgie did.

"Ah, that Museum!" he said. "Those mittens! Shall I ever get over those mittens? Lucia said she would give it the next shoelace she broke."

"Yes," said Georgie. "The Princess wanted to see those mittens. Queen Charlotte was her great-aunt. I told them how amused you all were at the mittens."

Lucia had been pressing her finger to her forehead, a sign of concentration. She rose as if going back to her other guests.

"Coming into the garden presently?" she asked, and glided from the room.

"And so you're going to have a sitting with the Ouija board," said Mr. Merriall. "I am intensely interested in Ouija. Very odd phenomena certainly occur. Strange but true."

A fresh idea had come into Georgie's head. Lucia certainly had not appeared outside the window that looked into the garden, and so he walked across to the other one which commanded a view of the green. There she was heading straight for the Museum.

"It is marvellous," he said to Mr. Merriall. "We have had some curious results here, too."

Mr. Merriall was moving daintily about the room, and Georgie wondered if it would be possible to convert Oxford trousers into an ordinary pair. It was dreadful to think that Olga, even in fun, had suggested that such a man was his double. There was the little cape as well.

"I have quite fallen in love with your Riseholme," said Mr. Merriall.

"We all adore it," said Georgie, not attending very much because his whole mind was fixed on the progress of Lucia across the green. Would she catch them in the Museum, or had they already gone? Smaller and smaller grew her figure and her twinkling legs, and at last she crossed the road and vanished behind the belt of shrubs in front of the tithe barn.

"All so homey and intimate. 'Home, Sweet Home,' in fact," said Mr. Merriall. "We have been hearing how Mrs. Shuttleworth loves singing in this room."

Georgie was instantly on his guard again. It was quite right and proper that Lucia should be punished, and of course Riseholme would know all about it, for indeed Riseholme was administering the punishment. But it was a very different thing to let her down before those who were not Riseholme.

"Oh, yes, she sings here constantly," he said. "We are all in and out of each other's houses. But I must be getting back to mine now."

Mr. Merriall longed to be asked to this little Ouija party at Olga's, and at present his hostess had been quite unsuccessful in capturing either of the two great stars. There was no harm in trying. . . .

"You couldn't perhaps take me to Mrs. Shuttleworth's for tea?" he asked.

"No, I'm afraid I could hardly do that," said Georgie. "Good-by. I hope we shall meet again."

Nemesis meantime had been dogging Lucia's footsteps, with more success than Lucia was having in dogging Olga's. She had arrived, as Georgie had seen, at the Museum, and again paid a shilling to enter that despised exhibition. It was rather full, for visitors who had lunched at the Ambermere Arms had come in, and there was quite a crowd round Queen Charlotte's mittens, among whom was Lady Ambermere herself who had driven over from the Hall with two depressed guests whom she had forced to come with her. She put up her glasses and stared at Lucia.

"Ah, Mrs. Lucas!" she said with the singular directness for which she was famous. "For the moment I did not recognize you with your hair like that. It is a fashion that does not commend itself to me. You have come in, of course, to look at her late Majesty's mittens, for really there is very little else to see."

As a rule, Lucia shamelessly truckled to Lady Ambermere, and schemed to get her to lunch or dinner. But today she didn't care two straws about her, and while these rather severe remarks were being addressed to her, her eyes darted eagerly round the room in search of those for whom she would have dropped Lady Ambermere without the smallest hesitation.

"Yes, dear Lady Ambermere," she said. "So interesting to think that Queen Charlotte wore them. Most good of you to have presented them to our little Museum."

"Lent," said Lady Ambermere. "They are heirlooms in my family. But I am glad to let others enjoy the sight of them. And by a remarkable coincidence I have just had the privilege of showing them to a relative of their late owner. Princess Isabel. I offered to have the case opened for her, and let her try them on. She said, most graciously, that it was not necessary."

"Yes, dear Princess Isabel," said Lucia, "I heard she had come down. Is she here still?"

"No. She and Mrs. Shuttleworth have just gone. A motor drive, I understand, before tea. I suggested, of course, a visit to The Hall, where I would have been delighted to entertain them. Where did they lunch?"

"At Georgie Pillson's," said Lucia bitterly.

"Indeed. I wonder why Mr. Pillson did not let me know. Did you lunch there, too?"

"No. I have a party in my own house. Some friends from London, Lord Limpsfield, Mrs. Garroby-Ashton—"

"Indeed!" said Lady Ambermere. "I had meant to return to The Hall for tea, but I will change my plans and have a cup of tea with you, Mrs. Lucas. Perhaps you would ask Mrs. Shuttleworth and her distinguished guest to drop in. I will present you to her. You have a pretty little garden, I remember. Quaint. You are at liberty to say that I am taking tea with you. But stay! If they have gone out for a drive, they will not be back quite yet. It does not matter; we will sit in your garden."

Now in the ordinary way this would have been a most honorable event, but today, though Lady Ambermere had not changed, her value had. If only Olga had not come down bringing her whom Lucia could almost refer to as that infernal Princess, it would have been rich, it would have been glorious, to have Lady Ambermere dropping in to tea. Even now she would be better than nothing, thought Lucia, and after inspecting the visitors' book of the Museum, where Olga and the Princess had inscribed their names, and where now Lady Ambermere wrote hers, very close to the last one, so as to convey the impression that they were one party, they left the place.

Outside was drawn up Lady Ambermere's car, with her companion, the meek Miss Lyall, sitting on the front seat nursing Lady Ambermere's stertorous pug.

"Let me see," said she. "How had we best arrange? A walk would be good for Pug before he has his tea. Pug takes lukewarm milk with a biscuit broken up into it. Please put Pug on his leash, Miss Lyall, and we will all walk across the green to Mrs. Lucas's little house. The motor shall go round by the road and wait for us there. That is Mrs. Shuttleworth's little house, is it not? So you might kindly step in there, Mrs. Lucas, and leave a message for them about tea, stating that I shall be there. We will walk slowly and you will soon catch us up."

The speech was thoroughly Ambermerian: everybody in Riseholme had a "little house" compared with The Hall: everybody had a "little garden." Equally Ambermerian was her complete confidence that her wish was everybody else's pleasure, and Lucia dismally reflected that she, for her part, had never failed to indicate that it was. But just now, though Lady Ambermere was so conspicuously second-best, and though she was like a small luggage engine with a Roman nose and a fat dog, the wretched Lucia badly wanted somebody to "drop in," and by so doing give her some sort of status—alas, that one so lately the Queen of Riseholme should desire it—in the sight of her guests. She could say what a bore Lady Ambermere was the moment she had gone.

Wretched also was her errand: she knew that Olga and the infernal Princess were to have a Ouija with Daisy and Georgie, and that her invitation would be futile, and as for that foolish old woman's suggestion that her presence at The Hurst would prove an attraction to Olga, she was aware that if anything was needful to make Olga refuse to come, it would be that Lady Ambermere was there. Olga had dined at The Hall once, and had been induced to sing, while her hostess played Patience and talked to Pug.

Lucia had a thought; not a very bright one, but comparatively so. She might write her name in the Princess's book: that would be something. So, when her ring was answered, and she ascertained, as she already knew, that Olga was out, and left the hopeless invitation that she and her guest would come to tea, where they would meet Lady Ambermere, she asked for the Princess's book.

Olga's parlormaid looked puzzled.

"Would that be the book of crossword puzzles, ma'am?" she asked. "I don't think her Highness brought any other book, and that she's taken with her for her drive."

Lucia trudged sadly away. Halfway across the green she saw Georgie and Daisy Quantock with a large sort of drawing board under arm coming briskly in her direction. She knew where they were going, and she pulled her shattered forces together.

"Dearest Daisy, not set eyes on you!" she said. "A

few friends from London, how it ties one! But I shall
pop in tomorrow, for I stop till Tuesday. Going to have
a Ouija party with dear Piggy and Goosie? Wish I
could come, but Lady Ambermere has quartered herself on me for tea, and I must run on and catch her up.
Just been to your delicious Museum. Wonderful mittens! Wonderful everything. Peppino and I will look
out something for it!"

"Very kind," said Daisy. It was as if the North Pole
had spoken.

Pug and Miss Lyall and Lady Ambermere and her
two depressed guests had been admitted to The Hurst
before Lucia caught them up, and she found them all
seated stonily in the music room, where Stephen Merriall had been finishing his official correspondence. Well
Lucia knew what he had been writing about: there
might perhaps be a line or two about The Hurst, and
the party weekending there, but that, she was afraid,
would form a mere little postscript to more exalted
paragraphs. She hastily introduced him to Lady Ambermere and Miss Lyall, but she had no idea who Lady
Ambermere's guests were, and suspected they were
poor relations for Lady Ambermere introduced them to
nobody.

Pug gave a series of wheezy barks.

"Clever little man," said Lady Ambermere. "He is
asking for his tea. He barks four times like that for his
tea."

"And he shall have it," said Lucia. "Where are the
others, Stephen?"

Mr. Merriall exerted himself a little on hearing Lady
Ambermere's name: he would put in a sentence about
her. . . .

"Lord Limpsfield and Mrs. Garroby-Ashton have

gone to play golf," he said. "Barbarously energetic of
them, is it not, Lady Ambermere? What a sweet little
dog."

"Pug does not like strangers," said Lady Amber-
mere. "And I am disappointed not to see Lord
Limpsfield. Do we expect Mrs. Shuttleworth and the
Princess?"

"I left the message," said Lucia.

Lady Ambermere's eyes finished looking at Mr.
Merriall and proceeded slowly round the room.

"What is that curious picture?" she said. "I am completely puzzled."

Lucia gave her bright laugh: it was being an awful
afternoon, but she had to keep her flag flying.

"Striking, is it not?" she said. "Dear Benjy
Sigismund insisted on painting me. Such a lot of sit-
tings."

Lady Ambermere looked from one to the other.

"I do not see any resemblance," she said. "It ap-
pears to me to resemble nothing. Ah, here is tea. A
little lukewarm milk for Pug, Miss Lyall. Mix a little
hot water with it; it does not suit him to have it quite
cold. And I should like to see Mr. Georgie Pillson. No
doubt he could be told that I am here."

This was really rather desperate: Lucia could not
produce Olga or the Princess or Lord Limpsfield or
Mrs. Garroby-Ashton for Lady Ambermere, and she
knew she could not produce Georgie, for by that time
he would be at Olga's. All that was left for her was to
be able to tell Lord Limpsfield and Mrs. Garroby-Ashton when they returned that they had missed Lady
Ambermere. As for Riseholme . . . but it was better
not to think how she stood with regard to Riseholme,
which yesterday she had settled to be of no account at

all. If only, before coming down, she had asked them all to lunch and tea and dinner. . . .

The message came back that Mr. Pillson had gone to tea with Mrs. Shuttleworth. Five minutes later came regrets from Olga that she had friends with her, and could not come to tea. Lady Ambermere ate seed cake in silence. Mrs. Alingsby meantime had been spending the afternoon in her bedroom, and she now appeared in a chintz wrapper and morocco slippers. Her hair fell over her eyes like that of an Aberdeen terrier, and she gave a shrill scream when she saw Pug.

"I can't bear dogs," she said. "Take that dog away, dear Lucia. Burn it, drown it! You told me you hadn't got any dogs."

Lady Ambermere turned on her a face that should have instantly petrified her, if she had had any proper feeling. Never had Pug been so blasphemed. She rose as she swallowed the last mouthful of seed cake.

"We are inconveniencing your guests, Mrs. Lucas," she said. "Pug and I will be off. Miss Lyall, Pug's leash. We must be getting back to The Hall. I shall look in at Mrs. Shuttleworth's, and sign my name in the Princess's book. Good-by, Mrs. Lucas. Thank you for my tea."

She pointedly ignored Mrs. Alingsby, and headed the gloomy frieze that defiled through the door. The sole bright spot was that she would find only a book of crossword puzzles to write her name in.

6

LUCIA'S GUESTS went off by the early train next morning, and she was left like Marius among the ruins of Carthage. But, unlike that weak-hearted senator, she had no intention of mourning; her first function was to rebuild, and presently she became aware that the work of rebuilding had to begin from its very foundations. There was as background the fact that her weekend party had not been a triumphant success, for she had been speaking in London of Riseholme being such a queer dear old-fashioned little place, where everybody adored her, and where Olga kept incessantly running in to sing acts and acts of the most renowned operas in her music room; she had also represented Princess Isabel as being a dear and intimate friend, and these two cronies of hers had politely but firmly refused all invitations to pop in. Lady Ambermere, it is true, had popped in, but nobody had seemed the least impressed

with her, and Lucia had really been very glad when after Sophy's painful remarks about Pug, she had popped
out, leaving that astonished post-cubist free to inquire
who that crashing old hag was. Of course all this could
be quickly lived down again when she got to London,
but it certainly did require obliteration.

What gave her more pause for thought was the effect
that her weekend had produced on Riseholme. Lucia
knew that all Riseholme knew that Olga and the
Princess had lunched off cold lamb with Georgie, and
had never been near The Hurst, and Riseholme, if she
knew Riseholme at all, would have something to talk
about there. Riseholme knew also that Lucia and her
party had shrieked with laughter at the Museum, while
the Princess had politely signed her name in the visitors' book after reverently viewing her great-aunt's mittens. But what else had been happening, whether Olga
was here still, what Daisy and her Ouija board had
been up to, who had dined (if anyone except Georgie)
at Olga's last night, Lucia was at present ignorant, and
all that she had to find out, for she had a presentiment
that nobody would pop in and tell her. Above all, what
was Riseholme saying about her? How were they taking it all?

Lucia had determined to devote this day to her old
friends, and she rang up Daisy and asked her and
Robert to lunch. Daisy regretted that she was engaged,
and rang off with such precipitation that (so it was
easy to guess) she dropped the receiver on the floor,
said "Drat," and replaced it. Lucia then rang up Mrs.
Boucher and asked her and the colonel to lunch. Mrs.
Boucher with great emphasis said that she had got
friends to lunch. Of course that might mean that Daisy
Quantock was lunching there; indeed it seemed a very

natural explanation, but somehow it was far from satisfying Lucia.

She sat down to think, and the unwelcome result of thought was a faint suspicion that just as she had decided to ignore Riseholme while her smart party from London was with her, Riseholme was malignant enough to retaliate. It was very base, it was very childish, but there was that possibility. She resolved to put a playful face on it and rang up Georgie. From the extraordinary celerity with which he answered, she wondered whether he was expecting a call from her or another.

"*Georgino mio!*" she said.

The eagerness with which Georgie had said, "Yes. Who is it?" seemed to die out of his voice.

"Oh, it's you, is it?" he said. "Good morning."

Lucia was not discouraged.

"Me coming round to have a good long chat," she said. "All my tiresome guests have gone, Georgie, and I'm staying till *domani*. So lovely to be here again."

"*Si*," said Georgie—just "*si*."

The faint suspicion became a shade more definite.

"Coming at once then," said Lucia.

Lucia set forth and emerging on to the green, was in time to see Daisy Quantock hurry out of Georgie's house and bolt into her own like a plump little red-faced rabbit. Somehow that was slightly disconcerting: it required very little inductive reasoning to form the theory that Daisy had popped in to tell Georgie that Lucia had asked her to lunch, and that she had refused. Daisy must have been present also when Lucia rang Georgie up and instead of waiting to join in the good long chat had scuttled home again. A slight effort therefore was needed to keep herself up to the gay, playful level and be quite unconscious that anything unpropitious could possibly have occurred. She found Georgie with his sewing in the little room which he called his study because he did his embroidery there. He seemed somehow to Lucia to be encased in a thin covering of ice, and she directed her full effulgence to the task of melting it.

"Now that is nice!" she said. "And we'll have a good gossip. So lovely to be in Riseholme again. And isn't it naughty of me? I was almost glad when I saw the last of my guests off this morning, and promised myself a real Riseholme day. Such dears all of them, too, and tremendously in the movement; such arguments and discussions as we had! All day yesterday I was occupied, talks with one, strolls with another, and all the time I was longing to trot round and see you and Daisy and all the rest. Any news, Georgie? What did you do with yourself yesterday?"

"Well, I was very busy, too," said Georgie. "Quite a rush. I had two guests at lunch, and then I had tea at Olga's—"

"Is she here still?" asked Lucia. She did not intend to ask that, but she simply could not help it.

"Oh, yes. She's going to stop here two or three days, as she doesn't sing in London again till Thursday."

Lucia longed to ask if the Princess was remaining as well, but she had self-control enough not to. Perhaps it would come out some other way. . . .

"Dear Olga," said Lucia effusively. "I reckon her quite a Riseholmite."

"Oh, quite," said Georgie, who was determined not to let his ice melt. "Yes; I had tea at Olga's, and we had the most wonderful weedj. Just she and the Princess and Daisy and I."

Lucia gave her silvery peal of laughter. It sounded as if it had "turned" a little in this hot weather, or got a little tarnished.

"Dear Daisy!" she said. "Is she not priceless? How she adores her conjuring tricks and hocus-pocuses! Tell me all about it. An Egyptian guide: Abfou, was it not?"

Georgie thought it might be wiser not to tell Lucia all that Abfou had vouchsafed, unless she really insisted, for Abfou had written the most sarcastic things about her in perfect English at top speed. He had called her a snob again, and said she was too grand now for her old friends, and had been really rude about her shingled hair.

"Yes, Abfou," he said. "Abfou was in great form, and Olga has telegraphed for a planchette. Abfou said she was most psychical, and had great mediumistic gifts. Well, that went on a long time."

"What else did Abfou say?" asked Lucia, fixing Georgie with her penetrating eye.

"Oh, he talked about Riseholme affairs," said Georgie. "He knew the Princess had been to the Museum, for he had seen her there. It was he, you know, who suggested the Museum. He kept writing Museum, though we thought it was 'mouse' at first."

Lucia felt perfectly certain in her own mind that Abfou had been saying things about her. But perhaps, as it was Daisy who had been operating, it was better not to ask what they were. Ignorance was not bliss, but knowledge might be even less blissful. And Georgie was not thawing: he was polite, he was reserved, but so far from chatting, he was talking with great care. She must get him in a more confidential mood.

"That reminds me," she said. "Peppino and I

haven't given you anything for the Museum yet. I must
send you the Elizabethan spit from my music room.
They say it is the most perfect spit in existence. I don't
know what Peppino didn't pay for it."

"How kind of you," said Georgie. "I will tell the
committee of your offer. Olga gave us a most magnificent present yesterday: the manuscript of *Lucrezia,*
which Cortese had given her. I took it to the Museum
directly after breakfast, and put it in the glass case opposite the door."

Again Lucia longed to be as sarcastic as Abfou and
ask whether a committee meeting had been held to
settle if this should be accepted. Probably Georgie had
some perception of that, for he went on in a great
hurry.

"Well, the weedj lasted so long that I had only just
time to get home to dress for dinner and go back to
Olga's," he said.

"Who was there?" asked Lucia.

"Colonel and Mrs. Boucher, that's all," said Georgie. "And after dinner Olga sang too divinely. I played
her accompaniments. A lot of Schubert songs."

Lucia was beginning to feel sick with envy. She pictured to herself the glory of having taken her party
across to Olga's after dinner last night, of having
played the accompaniments instead of Georgie (who
was a miserable accompanist), of having been persuaded afterward to give them the little morsel of Stravinski, which she had got by heart. How brilliant it
would all have been; what a sumptuous paragraph
Hermione would have written about her weekend! Instead of which Olga had sung to those old Bouchers,
neither of whom knew one note from another, nor
cared the least for the distinction of hearing the prima

donna sing in her own house. The bitterness of it could not be suppressed.

"Dear old Schubert songs!" she said with extraordinary acidity. "Such sweet old-fashioned things. '*Wiedmung*,' I suppose."

"No, that's by Schumann," said Georgie, who was nettled by her tone, though he guessed what she was suffering.

Lucia knew he was right, but had to uphold her own unfortunate mistake.

"Schubert, I think," she said. "Not that it matters. And so, as dear old Pepys said, and so to bed?"

Georgie was certainly enjoying himself.

"Oh, no, we didn't go to bed till terribly late," he said. "But you would have hated to be there, for what we did next. We turned on the gramophone—"

Lucia gave a little wince. Her views about gramophones, as being a profane parody of music, were well known.

"Yes, I should have run away then," she said.

"We turned on the gramophone and danced!" said Georgie firmly.

This was the worst she had heard yet. Again she pictured what yesterday evening might have been. The idea of having popped in with her party after dinner, to hear Olga sing, and then dance impromptu with a prima donna and a princess. . . . It was agonizing: it was intolerable.

She gave a dreadful little titter.

"How very droll!" she said. "I can hardly imagine it. Mrs. Boucher in her Bath chair must have been an unwieldy partner, Georgie. Are you not very stiff this morning?"

"No, Mrs. Boucher didn't dance," said Georgie with

fearful literalness. "She looked on and wound up the gramophone. Just we four danced: Olga and the Princess and Colonel Boucher and I."

Lucia made a great effort with herself. She knew quite well that Georgie knew how she would have given anything to have brought her party across, and it only made matters worse (if they could be made worse) to be sarcastic about it and pretend to find it all ridiculous. Olga certainly had left her and her friends alone, just as she herself had left Riseholme alone, in this matter of her weekend party. Yet it was unwise to be withering about Colonel Boucher's dancing. She had made it clear that she was busy with her party, and but for this unfortunate accident of Olga's coming down, nothing else could have happened in Riseholme that day except by her dispensing. It was unfortunate, but it must be lived down, and if dear old Riseholme was offended with her, Riseholme must be propitiated.

"Great fun it must have been," she said. "How delicious a little impromptu thing like that is! And singing, too: well, you had a nice evening, Georgie. And now let us make some delicious little plan for today. Pop in presently and have 'ickle music and bit of lunch."

"I'm afraid I've just promised to lunch with Daisy," said he.

This again was rather ominous, for there could be no doubt that Daisy, having said she was engaged, had popped in here to effect an engagement.

"How gay!" said Lucia. "Come and dine this evening then! Really, Georgie, you are busier than any of us in London."

"Too tarsome," said Georgie, "because Olga's coming in here."

"And the Princess?" asked Lucia before she could stop herself.

"No, she went away this morning," said Georgie.

That was something, anyhow, thought Lucia. One distinguished person had gone away from Riseholme. She waited, in slowly diminishing confidence, for Georgie to ask her to dine with him instead. Perhaps he would ask Peppino too, but if not, Peppino would be quite happy with his telescope and his crosswords all by himself. But it was odd and distasteful to wait to be asked to dinner by anybody in Riseholme instead of everyone wanting to be asked by her.

"She went away by the ten thirty," said Georgie, after an awful pause.

Lucia had already learned certain lessons in London. If you get a snub—and this seemed very like a snub—the only possible course was to be unaware of it. So though the thought of being snubbed by Georgie nearly made her swoon, she was unaware of it.

"Such a good train," she said, magnificently disregarding the well-known fact that it stopped at every station, and crawled in between.

"Excellent," said Georgie with conviction. He had not the slightest intention of asking Lucia to dine, for he wanted his tête-à-tête with Olga. There would be such a lot to talk over, and besides it would be tiresome to have Lucia there, for she would be sure to gabble away about her wonderful life in London, and her music room and her Chippendale chairs, and generally to lay down the law. She must be punished, too, for her loathsome conduct in disregarding her old friends when she had her party from London, and be made to learn that her old friends were being much smarter than she was.

Lucia kept her end up nobly.

"Well, Georgie, I must trot away," she said. "Such a lot of people to see. Look in, if you've got a spare minute. I'm off again tomorrow. Such a whirl of things in London this week."

Lucia, instead of proceeding to see lots of people, went back to her house and saw Peppino. He was sitting in the garden in very old clothes, smoking a pipe, and thoroughly enjoying the complete absence of anything to do. He was aware that officially he loved the bustle of London, but it was extremely pleasant to sit in his garden and smoke a pipe, and above all to be rid of those rather hectic people who had talked quite incessantly from morning till night all Sunday. He had given up the crossword, and was thinking over the material for a sonnet on Tranquillity, when Lucia came out to him.

"I was wondering, Peppino," she said. "if it would not be pleasanter to go up to town this afternoon. We should get the cool of the evening for our drive, and really, now all our guests have gone, and we are going tomorrow, these hours will be rather tedious. We are spoilt, *caro*, you and I, by our full life up there, where any moment the telephone bell may ring with some delightful invitation. Of course in August we will be here, and settle down to our quaint old life again, but these little odds and ends of time, you know."

Peppino was reasonably astonished. Half an hour ago Lucia had set out, burning with enthusiasm to pick up the "old threads," and now all she seemed to want to do was to drop the old threads as quickly as possible. Though he knew himself to be incapable of following the swift and antic movements of Lucia's mind, he was capable of putting two and two together. He had been faintly conscious all yesterday that matters were not going precisely as Lucia wished, and knew that her efforts to entice Olga and her guest to the house had been as barren as a fig tree, but there must have been something more than that. Though not an imaginative man (except in thinking that words rhymed when they did not), it occurred to him that Riseholme was irritated with Lucia, and was indicating it in some unusual manner.

"Why, my dear, I thought you were going to have people to lunch and dinner," he said, "and see about sending the spit to the Museum, and be tremendously busy all day."

Lucia pulled herself together. She had a momentary impulse to confide in Peppino and tell him all the ominous happenings of the last hour, how Daisy had said she was engaged for lunch and Mrs. Boucher had friends to lunch, and Georgie had Olga to dinner and had not asked her, and how the munificent gift of the spit was to be considered by the Museum committee before they accepted it. But to have done that would be to acknowledge not one snub but many snubs, which was contrary to the whole principle of successful attainment. Never must she confess, even to Peppino, that the wheels of her chariot seemed to drive heavily, or that Riseholme was not at the moment agape to receive the signs of her favor. She must not even confess it to herself, and she made a rapid and complete *volte face*.

"It shall be as you like, *caro*," she said. "You would prefer to spend a quiet day here, so you shall. As for me, you've never known me yet otherwise than busy, have you? I have a stack of letters to write, and there's my piano looking, oh, so reproachfully at me, for I haven't touched the dear keys since I came, and I must just glance through *Henry VIII*, as we're going to see it tomorrow. I shall be busy enough, and you will have your day in the sun and the air. I only thought you might prefer to run up to town today, instead of waiting till tomorrow. Now don't keep me chatting here any longer."

Lucia proved her quality on that dismal day. She played her piano with all her usual concentration; she read *Henry VIII*; she wrote her letters; and it was not till the *Evening Gazette* came in that she allowed herself a moment's relaxation. Hurriedly she turned the pages, stopping neither for crossword nor record of international interests, till she came to Hermione's column. She had feared (and with a gasp of relief she saw how unfounded her fears had been) that Hermione would have devoted his picturesque pen to Olga and the Princess, and given her and her party only the fag end of his last paragraph, but she had disquieted herself in vain. Olga had taken no notice of him, and now (What could be fairer?) he took no notice of Olga. He just mentioned that she had a "pretty little cottage" at Riseholme, where she came occasionally for weekends, and there were three long sumptuous paragraphs about The Hurst, and Mr. and Mrs. Philip Lucas who had Lord Limpsfield and the wife of the member, Mrs. Garroby-Ashton, and Mrs. Alingsby staying with them. Lady Ambermere and her party from The Hall had come to tea, and it was all glorious and distinguished. Hermione had proved himself a true friend, and there was not a word about Olga and the Princess going to lunch with Georgie, or about Daisy and her absurd weedj. . . . Lucia read the luscious lines through twice, and then, as she often did, sent her copy across to Georgie, in order to help him to readjust values. Almost simultaneously Daisy sent de Vere across to him with her copy, and Mrs. Boucher did the same, calling attention to the obnoxious paragraphs with blue and red pencil respectively, and a great many exclamation marks in both cases.

Riseholme settled back into its strenuous life again when Lucia departed next morning to resume her vapid existence in London. It was not annoyed with her any more, because it had "larned" her, and was quite prepared to welcome her back if (and when) she returned in a proper spirit and behaved herself suitably. Moreover, even with its own perennial interests to attend to, it privately missed the old Lucia, who gave them a lead in everything, even though she domineered, and was absurd, and pretended to know all about everything, and put her finger into every pie within reach. But it did not miss the new shingled Lucia, the one who had come down with a party of fresh friends, and had laughed at the Museum, and had neglected her old friends altogether, till she found out that Olga and a princess were in the place: the less seen of her, the better. It was considered, also, that she had remained down here this extra day in order to propitiate those whom she had treated as pariahs, and condescend to take notice of them again, and if there was one thing that Riseholme could not stand, and did not mean to stand from anybody, it was condescension. It was therefore perfectly correct for Daisy and Mrs. Boucher to say they were engaged for lunch, and for Georgie to decline to ask her to dinner. . . . These three formed the committee of the Museum, and they met that morning to audit the accounts for the week and discuss any other business connected or uncon-

nected with their office. There was not, of course, with
so small and intimate a body, any need to have a chairman, and they all rapped the table when they wanted
to be listened to.

Mrs. Boucher was greedily counting the shillings
which had been taken from the till, while Georgie
counted the counterfoils of the tickets.

"A hundred and twenty-three," he said. "That's
nearly the best week we've had yet."

"And fifteen and four is nineteen," said Mrs.
Boucher, "and four is twenty-three which makes exactly six pounds three shillings. Well, I do call that
good. And I hear we've had a wonderful bequest made.
Most generous of our dear Olga. I think she ought not
only to be thanked, but asked to join the committee. I
always said—"

Daisy rapped the table.

"Abfou said just the same," she interrupted. "I had
a sitting this morning, and he kept writing 'committee.'
I brought the paper along with me, because I was going to propose that myself. But there's another thing
first, and that's about insurance. Robert told me he was
insuring the building and its contents separately for a
thousand pounds each. We shall have to pay a pre-
mium, of course. Oh, here's Abfou's message. 'Committee'; you see 'committee' written three times. I feel
quite sure he meant Olga."

"He spells it with only one 'm'," said Georgie, "but I
expect he meant that. There's one bit of business that
comes before that, for I have been offered another object for the Museum, and I said I would refer the offer
to the committee before I accepted it. Lucia came to
see me yesterday morning and asked—"

"The Elizabethan spit," said Mrs. Boucher. "I don't

see what we want with it, for my part, and if I had to
say what I thought, I should thank her most politely,
and beg that she would keep it herself. Most kind of
her, I'm sure. Sorry to refuse, which was just what I
said when she asked me to lunch yesterday. There'd
have been legs of cold chickens of which her friends
from London had eaten wings."

"She asked me, too," said Daisy, "and I said no. Did
she leave this morning?"

"Yes, about half past ten," said Georgie. "She
wanted me to ask her to dinner last night."

Daisy had been writing "committee" again and again
on her blotting paper. It looked very odd with two
"m's" and she would certainly have spelt it with one
herself.

"I think Abfou is right about the way to spell 'committee,' " she said, "and even if he weren't, the meaning is clear enough. But about the insurance. Robert
only advises insurance against fire, for he says no burglar in his senses—"

Mrs. Boucher rapped the table.

"But there wasn't the manuscript of *Lucrezia* then,"
she said. "And I should think that any burglar whether
in his senses or out of them would think *that* worth
taking. If it was a question of insuring an Elizabethan
spit—"

"Well, I want to know what the committee wishes
me to say about that," said Georgie. "Oh, by the way,
when we have a new edition of the catalogue, we must
bring it up to date. There'll be the manuscript of *Lucrezia*."

"And if you ask me," said Mrs. Boucher, "she only
wanted to get rid of the spit because it makes her

chimney smoke. Tell her to get her chimney swept and keep the spit."

"There's a portrait of her in the music room," said Georgie, "by Sigismund. It looks like nothing at all—"

"Of course everybody has a right to have their hair shingled," said Mrs. Boucher, "whatever their age, and there's no law to prevent you."

Daisy rapped the table.

"We were considering as to whether we should ask Mrs. Shuttleworth to join the committee," she said.

"She sang too beautifully Sunday night," said Georgie, "and what fun we had dancing. Oh, and Lucia asked for the Princess's book to sign her name in, and the only book she had brought was a book of crossword puzzles."

"No!" said both ladies together.

"She did, because Olga's parlormaid told Foljambe, and—"

"Well, I never!" said Daisy. "That served her out. Did she write Lucia across, and Peppino down?"

"I'm sure I've nothing to say against her," said Mrs. Boucher, "but people usually get what they deserve. Certainly let us have the Museum insured if that's the right thing to do, and as for asking Olga to be on the committee, why we settled that hours ago, and I have nothing more to say about the spit. Have the spit if you like, but I would no more think of insuring it than insuring a cold in the head. I've as much use for one as the other. All that stuff, too, about the gracious chatelaine at The Hurst in the *Evening Gazette*! My husband read it, and what he said was 'Faugh!' 'Tush' and 'Faugh' was what he said."

Public opinion was beginning to boil up again about Lucia, and Georgie intervened.

"I think that's all the business before the meeting," he said, "and so we accept the manuscript of *Lucrezia* and decline the spit. I'm sure it was very kind of both the donors. And Olga's to be asked to join the committee. Well, we have got through a good morning's work."

Lucia, meanwhile, was driving back to London, where she intended to make herself a busy week. There would be two nights at the opera, on the second of which Olga was singing in *The Valkyrie*, and so far from intending to depreciate her singing, or to refrain from going, by way of revenge for the slight she had suffered, she meant, even if Olga sang like a screech owl and acted like a stick, to say there had never been so perfect a presentation of Brunnhilde. She could not conceive doing anything so stupid as snubbing Olga because she had not come to her house or permitted her to enter Old Place: that would have been the height of folly.

At present, she was (or hoped to be) on the upward road, and the upward road could only be climbed by industry and appreciation. When she got to the top, it would be a different matter, but just now it was an asset, a score to allude to dear Olga and the hoppings in and out that took place all day at Riseholme: she knew, too, a good deal that Olga had done on Sunday, and that would all be useful. "Always appreciate, always admire," thought Lucia to herself as she woke Peppino up from a profound nap on their arrival at Brompton Square. "Be busy; work, work, work."

She knew already that there would be hard work in front of her before she got where she wanted to get, and she whisked off like a disturbing fly which impeded concentration the slight disappointment which her weekend had brought. If you meant to progress, you must never look back (the awful example of Lot's wife!) and never, unless you are certain it is absolutely useless, kick down a ladder which has brought you anywhere, or might in the future bring you anywhere. Already she had learned a lesson about that, for if she had only told Georgie that she had been coming down for a weekend, and had bidden him to lunch and dinner and anything else he liked, he would certainly have got Olga to pop in at The Hurst, or have said that he couldn't dine with Olga on that fateful Sunday night because he was dining with her, and then no doubt Olga would have asked them all to come in afterward. It had been a mistake to kick Riseholme down, a woeful mistake, and she would never do such a thing again. It was a mistake also to be sarcastic about anybody till you were sure they could not help you, and who could be sure of that? Even poor dear Daisy with her ridiculous Abfou had proved such an attraction at Old Place, that Georgie had barely time to get back and dress for dinner, and a benignant Daisy instead of a militant and malignant Daisy would have helped. Everything helps, thought Lucia, as she snatched up the tablets which stood by the telephone and recorded the ringings up that had taken place in her absence.

She fairly gasped at the amazing appropriateness of a message that had been received only ten minutes ago. Marcia Whitby hoped that she could dine that evening: the message was to be delivered as soon as she arrived. Obviously it was a last-moment invitation: somebody had thrown her over, and perhaps that made them thirteen. There was no great compliment in it, for Marcia, so Lucia conjectured, had already tried high and low to get another woman, and now in despair she tried Lucia. . . . Of course there were the tickets for *Henry VIII*, and it was a first night, but perhaps she could get somebody to go with Peppino. . . . Ah, she remembered Aggie Sandeman lamenting that she had been unable to secure a seat! Without a pause she rang up the Duchess of Whitby, and expressed her eager delight at coming to dine tonight. So lucky, so charmed. Then having committed herself, she rang up Aggie and hoped for the best, and Aggie jumped at the idea of a ticket for *Henry VIII*, and then she told Peppino all about it.

"*Caro*, I had to be kind," she said, tripping off into the music room where he was at tea. "Poor Marcia Whitby in despair."

"Dear me, what has happened?" asked Peppino.

"One short, one woman short, evidently, for her dinner tonight; besought me to go. But you shall have your play all the same, and a dear sweet woman to take to it. Guess! No. I'll tell you—Aggie. She was longing to go, and so it's a kindness all round. You will have somebody more exciting to talk to than your poor old *sposa*, and dearest Aggie will get her play, and Marcia will be ever so grateful to me. I shall miss the play, but I will go another night unless you tell me it is no good. . . ."

Of course the *Evening Gazette* would contain no further news of the chatelaine at The Hurst, but Lucia turned to Hermione's column with a certain eagerness, for there might be something about the Duchess's dinner this evening. Hermione did not seem to have heard of it, but if Hermione came to lunch tomorrow, he would hear of it then. She rang him up. . . .

• • •

Lucia's kindness to Marcia Whitby met with all sorts of rewards. She got there, as was her custom in London, rather early, so that she could hear the names of all the guests as they arrived, and Marcia, feeling thoroughly warmhearted to her, for she had tried dozens of women to turn her party from thirteen into fourteen, called her Lucia instead of Mrs. Lucas. It was no difficulty to Lucia to reciprocate this intimacy in a natural manner, for she had alluded to the Duchess as Marcia behind her back for weeks, and now the syllables tripped to her tongue with the familiarity of custom.

"Sweet of you to ask me, dear Marcia," she said. "Peppino and I only arrived from Riseholme an hour or two ago, and he took Aggie Sandeman to the theatre instead of me. Such a lovely Sunday at Riseholme: you must spare a weekend and come down and vegetate. Olga Shuttleworth was there with Princess Isabel, and she sang too divinely on Sunday evening, and then, would you believe it, we turned on the gramophone and danced."

"What a coincidence!" said Marcia, "because I've got a small dance tonight, and Princess Isabel is coming. But not nearly so chic as your dance at Riseholme."

She moved toward the door to receive the guests who were beginning to arrive, and Lucia, with ears open for distinguished names, had just a moment's qualm for having given the impression which she meant to give, that she had been dancing to Olga's gramophone. It was no more than momentary, and presently the Princess arrived, and was led round by her hostess, to receive curtseys.

"And of course you know Mrs. Lucas," said Marcia.

"She's been telling me about your dancing to the gramophone at her house on Sunday."

Lucia recovered from her curtsey.

"No, dear Marcia," she said. "It was at Olga's, in fact—"

The Princess fixed her with a royal eye before she passed on, as if she seemed to understand.

But that was the only catastrophe, and how small a one! The Princess liked freaks, and so Marcia had asked a star of the movies and a distinguished novelist, and a woman with a skin like a kipper from having crossed the Sahara twice on foot, or having swum the Atlantic twice, or something of the sort, and a society caricaturist, and a slim young gentleman with a soft voice, who turned out to be the bloodiest pugilist of the century, and the Prime Minister, two ambassadresses, and the great Mrs. Beaucourt who had just astounded the world by her scandalous volume of purely imaginary reminiscences. Each of these would furnish a brilliant center for a dinner party, and the idea of spreading the butter as thick as that seemed to Lucia almost criminal: she herself, indeed, was the only bit of bread to be seen anywhere. Before dinner was over, she had engaged both her neighbors, the pugilist and the cinema star, to dine with her on consecutive nights next week, and was mentally running through her list of friends to settle whom to group round them. Alf Watson, the pugilist, it appeared, when not engaged in knocking people out, spent his time in playing the flute to soothe his savage breast, while Marcelle Periscope when not impersonating impassioned lovers, played with his moderately tame lion cub. Lucia begged Alf to bring his flute, and they would have some music, but did not extend her invitation to the lion cub, which

sounded slightly Bolshevistic. . . . Later in the evening
she got hold of Herbert Alton, the social caricaturist,
who promised to lunch on Sunday, but failed to do
business with the lady from the Sahara, who was leaving
next day to swim another sea, or cross another desert.
Then the guests for the dance began to arrive, and
Lucia, already half-intoxicated by celebrities, sank rapt
in a chair at the top of the staircase and listened to the
catalogue of sonorous names. Up trooped stars and
garters and tiaras, and when she felt stronger, she clung
firmly to Lord Limpsfield, who seemed to know everybody and raked in introductions.

Lucia did not get home till three o'clock (for having
given up her play out of kindness to Marcia, she might
as well do it thoroughly), but she was busy writing invitations for her two dinner parties next week by nine
in the morning. Peppino was lunching at his club,
where he might meet the Astronomer Royal, and have
a chat about the constellations, but he was to ring her
up about a quarter past two and ascertain if she had
made any engagement for him during the afternoon.
The idea of this somehow occupied her brain as she
filled up the cards of invitation in her small exquisite
handwriting. There was a telephone in her dining
room, and she began to visualize to herself Peppino's
ringing her up, while she and the two or three friends
who were lunching with her would be still at table. It
would be at the end of lunch: they would be drinking
their coffee, which she always made herself in a glass
machine with a spirit lamp which, when it appeared to
be on the point of exploding, indicated that coffee was
ready. The servants would have left the room, and she
would go to the telephone herself. . . . She would hear
Peppino's voice, but nobody else would. They would

not know who was at the other end, and she might easily pretend that it was not Peppino, but . . . She would
give a gabbling answer, audible to her guests, but she
could divert her mouth a little away so that Peppino
could not make anything out of it, and then hang up
the receiver again. . . . Peppino, no doubt, would
think he had got hold of the wrong number and
presently call her again, and she would then tell him
anything there was to communicate. As she scribbled
away, the idea took shape and substance: there was an
attraction about it; it smiled on her.

She came to the end of her dinner invitations grouped round the cinema star and the fluting prizefighter,
and she considered whom to ask to meet Herbert Alton
on Sunday. He was working hard, he had told her, to
finish his little gallery of caricatures with which he an-
nually regaled London, and which was to open in a
fortnight. He was a licensed satirist, and all London always flocked to his show to observe with glee what he
made of them all, and what witty and pungent little remarks he affixed to their monstrous effigies. It was a
distinct *cachet*, too, to be caricatured by him, a sign
that you attracted attention and were a notable figure.
He might (in fact, he always did) make you a perfect
guy, and his captions invariably made fun of something
characteristic, but it gave you publicity. She wondered
whether he would take a commission: she wondered
whether he might be induced to do a caricature of Peppino or herself or of them both, at a handsome price,
with the proviso that it was to be on view at his exhibition. That could probably be ascertained, and then she
might approach the subject on Sunday. Anyhow, she
would ask one or two pleasant people to meet him, and
hope for the best.

Lucia's little lunch party that day consisted only of four people. Lunch, Lucia considered, was for *intimes*: you sat with your elbows on the table, and all talked together, and learned the news, just as you did on the green at Riseholme. There was something unwieldy about a large lunch party; it was a distracted affair, and in the effort to assimilate more news than you could really digest, you forgot half of it. Today, therefore, there was only Aggie Sandeman, who had been to the play last night with Peppino and was bringing her cousin Adele Brixton (whom Lucia had not yet met, but very much wanted to know), and Stephen Merriall. Lady Brixton was a lean, intelligent American of large fortune who found she got on better without a husband. But as Lord Brixton preferred living in America and she in England, satisfactory arrangements were easily made. Occasionally she had to go to see relatives in America, and he selected such periods for seeing relatives in England.

She explained the situation very good-naturedly to Lucia who rather rashly asked after her husband.

"In fact," she said, "we blow kisses to each other from the decks of Atlantic liners going in opposite directions, if it's calm, and if it's rough, we're sick into the same ocean."

Now that would never have been said at Riseholme, or if it was, it would have been very ill thought of, and a forced smile followed by a complete change of conversation would have given it a chilly welcome. Now, out of habit, Lucia smiled a forced smile, and then remembered that you could not judge London by the chaste standards of Riseholme. She turned the forced smile into a genial one.

"Too delicious!" she said. "I must tell Peppino that."

"Pep what?" asked Lady Brixton.

This was explained; it was also explained that Aggie had been with Peppino to the play last night; in fact there was rather too much explanation going on for social ease, and Lucia thought it was time to tell them all about what she had done last night. She did this in a characteristic manner.

"Dear Lady Brixton," she said, "ever since you came in, I've been wondering where I have seen you. Of course it was last night, at our darling Marcia's dance."

This seemed to introduce the desirable topic, and though it was not in the least true, it was a wonderfully good shot.

"Yes, I was there," said Adele. "What a crush. Sheer Mormonism: one man to fifty women."

"How unkind of you! I dined there first; quite a small party. Princess Isabel, who had been down at our dear little Riseholme on Sunday, staying with Olga—such a coincidence—" Lucia stopped just in time; she was about to describe the impromptu dance at Olga's on Sunday night, but remembered that Stephen knew she had not been to it. So she left the coincidence alone, and went rapidly on.

"Dear Marcia insisted on my coming," she said, "and so, really, like a true friend I gave up the play and went. Such an amusing little dinner. Marcelle—Marcelle Periscope, the Prime Minister and the Italian ambassadress, and Princess Isabel, of course, and Alf, and a few more. There's nobody like Marcia for getting up a wonderful unexpected little party like that. Alf was too delicious."

"Not Alf Watson?" asked Lady Brixton.

"Yes, I sat next him at dinner, and he's coming to dine with me next week, and is bringing his flute. He adores playing the flute. Can't I persuade you to come, Lady Brixton? Thursday, let me see, is it Thursday? Yes, Thursday. No party at all, just a few old friends, and some music. I must find some duets for the piano and flute; Alf made me promise that I would play his accompaniments for him. And Dora; Dora Beaucourt. What a lurid life! And Sigismund; no, I don't think Sigismund was there; it was at Sophy's. Such a marvellous portrait he has done of me. Is it not marvellous, Stephen? You remember it down at Riseholme. How amusing Sophy was, insisting that I should move every other picture out of my music room. I must get her to come in after dinner on Thursday; there is something primitive about the flute." So Theocritan!

Lucia suddenly remembered that she mustn't kick ladders down, and turned to Aggie. Aggie had been very useful when first she came up to London, and she might quite easily be useful again, for she knew quantities of solid people, and if her parties lacked brilliance, they were highly respectable. The people whom Sophy called "the old crusted" went there.

"Aggie dear, as soon as you get home, put down Wednesday for dining with me," she said, "and if there's an engagement there already, as there's sure to be, cross it out and have pseudo-influenza. Marcelle— Marcelle Periscope—is coming, but I didn't ask the lion cub. A lion cub, so quaint of him—And who else was there last night? Dear me, I get so mixed up with all the people one runs across."

Lucia, of course, never got mixed up at all: there was no one so clear-headed, but she had to spin things

out a little, for Peppino was rather late ringing up. The
coffee equipage had been set before her, and she kept
drawing away the spirit lamp in an absent manner just
before it boiled, for they must still be sitting in the dining room when he rang up. But even as she lamented
her muddled memory, the tinkle of the telephone bell
sounded. She rapidly rehearsed in her mind what she
was going to say.

"Ah, that telephone," she said, rising hastily so as to
get to it before one of the servants came back. "I often
tell Peppino I shall cut it out of the house, for one
never gets a moment's peace. Yes, yes, who is it?"

Lucia listened for a second, and then gave a curtsey.

"Oh, is it you, ma'am?" she said, holding the mouthpiece a little obliquely. "Yes, I'm Mrs. Lucas."

A rather gruff noise, clearly Peppino's voice, came
from the instrument, but she trusted it was inaudible to
the others, and she soon broke in again talking very
rapidly.

"Oh, that is kind of you, your Highness," she said.
"It would be too delightful. Tomorrow. Charmed, delighted."

She replaced the mouthpiece, and instantly began to
talk again from the point at which she had left off.

"Yes, and of course Herbert Alton was there," she
said. "His show opens in a fortnight, and how we shall
all meet there at the private view and laugh at each
other's caricatures! What is it that Rousseau—is it
Rousseau?—says, about our not being wholly grieved
at the misfortunes of our friends? So true! Bertie is
rather wicked sometimes though, but still one forgives
him everything. Ah, the coffee is boiling at last."

Peppino, as Lucia had foreseen, rang up again almost
immediately, and she told him he had missed the most

charming little lunch party, because he would go to his club. Her guests, of course, were burning to know to whom she had curtsied, but Lucia gave no information on the point. Adele Brixton and Aggie presently went off to a matinée, but Stephen remained behind. That looked rather well, Lucia thought, for she had noticed that often a handsome and tolerably young man lingered with the hostess when other guests had gone. There was something rather chic about it; if it happened very constantly, or if at another house they came together or went away together, people would begin to talk, quite pleasantly of course, about his devotion to her. Georgie had been just such a *cavaliere servente*. Stephen, for his part, was quite unconscious of any such scintillations in Lucia's mind: he merely knew that it was certainly convenient for an unattached man to have a very pleasant house always to go to, where he would be sure of hearing things that interested Hermione.

"Delicious little lunch party," he said. "What a charming woman Lady Brixton is."

"Dear Adele," said Lucia dreamily. "Charming, isn't she? How pleased she was at the thought of meeting Alf! Do look in after dinner that night, Stephen, I wish I could ask you to dine, but I expect to be crammed as it is. Dine on Wednesday, though. Let me see; Marcelle comes that night. What a rush next week will be!"

Stephen waited for her to allude to the voice to which she had curtsied, but he waited in vain.

7

THIS DELICIOUS little luncheon party had violently excited Adele Brixton: she was thrilled to the marrow at Lucia's curtsey to the telephone.

"My dear, she's marvellous," she said to Aggie. "She's a study. She's cosmic. The telephone, the curtsey! I've never seen the like. But why in the name of wonder didn't she tell us who the Highness was? She wasn't shy of talking about the other folk she'd met. Alf and Marcelle and Marcia and Bertie. But she made a mistake over Bertie. She shouldn't have said 'Bertie.' I've known Herbert Alton for years, and never has anybody called him anything but Herbert. 'Bertie' was a mistake, but don't tell her. I adore your Lucia. She'll go far, mark my words, and I bet you she's talking of me as Adele this moment. Don't you see how wonderful she is? I've been a climber myself, and I know. But I was a snail compared to her."

Aggie Sandeman was rather vexed at not being asked to the Alf party.

"You needn't tell me how wonderful she is," she observed with some asperity. "It's not two months since she came to London first, and she didn't know a soul. She dined with me the first night she came up, and since then she has annexed every single person she met at my house."

"She would," said Adele appreciatively. "And who was the man who looked as if he had been labelled 'Man' by mistake when he was born, and ought to have been labelled 'Lady'? I never saw such a perfect lady, though I only know him as Stephen at present. She just said, 'Stephen, do you know Lady Brixton?'"

"Stephen Merriall," said Aggie. "Just one of the men who go out to tea every day—one of the unattached."

"Well then, she's going to attach him," said Adele. "Dear me, aren't I poisonous, when I'm going to her house to meet Alf next week! But I don't feel poisonous; I feel wildly interested: I adore her. Here we are at the theatre. What a bore! And there's Tony Limpsfield. Tony, come and help me out. We've been lunching with the most marvellous—"

"I expect you mean Lucia," said Tony. "I spent Sunday with her at Riseholme."

"She curtsied to the telephone," said Adele.

"Who was at the other end?" asked Tony eagerly.

"That's what she didn't say," said Adele.

"Why not?" asked Tony.

Adele stepped briskly out of her car, followed by Aggie.

"I can't make out," she said. "Oh, do you know Mrs. Sandeman?"

"Yes, of course," said Tony. "And it couldn't have been Princess Isabel."

"Why not? She met her at Marcia's last night."

"Yes, but the Princess fled from her. She fled from her at Riseholme, too, and said she would never go to her house. It can't have been she. But she got hold of that boxer—"

"Alf Watson," said Adele. "She called him Alf, and I'm going to meet him at her house on Thursday."

"Then it's very unkind of you to crab her, Adele," said Tony.

"I'm not; I'm simply wildly interested. Anyhow, what about you? You spent a Sunday with her at Riseholme."

"And she calls you Tony," said Aggie vituperatively, still thinking about the Alf party.

"No, does she really?" said Tony. "But after all, I call her Lucia when she's not there. The bell's gone, by the way; the curtain will be up."

Adele hurried in.

"Come to my box, Tony," she said, "after the first act. I haven't been so interested in anything for years."

Adele paid no attention whatever to the gloomy play of Tchekov's. Her whole mind was concentrated on Lucia, and soon she leaned across to Aggie, and whispered:

"I believe it was Peppino who rang her up."

Aggie knitted her brows for a moment.

"Couldn't have been," she said. "He rang her up directly afterward."

Adele's face fell. Not being able to think as far ahead as Lucia, she didn't see the answer to that, and relapsed into Lucian meditation, till the moment the curtain fell, when Tony Limpsfield slid into her box.

"I don't know what the play has been about," he said, "but I must tell you why she was at Marcia's last night. Some women chucked Marcia during the afternoon and made her thirteen—"

"Marcia would like that," said Aggie.

Tony took no notice of this silly joke.

"So she rang up everybody in town—" he continued.

"Except me," said Aggie bitterly.

"Oh, never mind that," said Tony. "She rang up everybody, and couldn't get hold of anyone. Then she rang up Lucia."

"Who instantly said she was disengaged, and rang me up to go to the theatre with Peppino," said Aggie. "I suspected something of the sort, but I wanted to see the play, and I wasn't going to cut off my nose to spite Lucia's face."

"Besides, she would have got someone else, or sent Peppino to the play alone," said Tony. "And you've got hold of the wrong end of the stick, Aggie. Nobody wants to spite Lucia. We all want her to have the most glorious time."

"Aggie's vexed because she thinks she invented Lucia," observed Adele. "That's the wrong attitude altogether. Tell me about Pep."

"Simply nothing to say about him," said Tony. "He has trousers and a hat, and a telescope on the roof at Riseholme, and when you talk to him, you see he remembers what the leading articles in the *Times* said that morning. Don't introduce irrelevant matters, Adele."

"But husbands are relevant—all but mine," said Adele. "Part of the picture. And what about Stephen?"

"Oh, you always see him handing buns at tea parties. He's irrelevant, too."

"He might not be if her husband is," said Adele.

Tony exploded with laughter.

"You are off the track," he said. "You'll get nowhere if you attempt to smirch Lucia's character. How could she have time for a lover to begin with? And you misunderstand her altogether, if you think that."

"It would be frightfully picturesque," said Adele.

"No, it would spoil it altogether. . . . Oh, there's this stupid play beginning again. . . . Gracious heavens, look there!"

They followed his finger, and saw Lucia followed by Stephen coming up the central aisle of the stalls to two places in the front row. Just as she reached her place she turned round to survey the house, and caught sight of them. Then the lights were lowered, and her face slid into darkness.

This little colloquy in Adele's box was really the foundation of the secret society of the Luciaphils, and the membership of the Luciaphils began swiftly to increase. Aggie Sandeman was scarcely eligible, for complete goodwill toward Lucia was a *sine qua non* of membership, and there was in her mind a certain asperity when she thought that it was she who had given Lucia her gambit, and that already she was beginning to be relegated to second circles in Lucia's scale of social precedence. It was true that she had been asked to dine to meet Marcelle Periscope, but the party to meet Alf and his flute was clearly the smarter of the two. Adele, however, and Tony Limpsfield were real members, so too, when she came up a few days later, was Olga. Marcia Whitby was another who greedily followed her career, and such as these, whenever they met, gave eager news to each other about it. There was, of course, another camp, consisting of those whom Lucia bombarded with pleasant invitations, but who (at present) firmly refused them. They professed not to know her and not to take the slightest interest in her, which showed, as Adele said, a deplorable narrowness of mind. Types and striking characters like Lucia, who pursued undaunted and indefatigable their aim in life, were rare, and when they occurred should be studied with reverent affection. . . . Sometimes one of the old and original members of the Luciaphils discovered others, and if when Lucia's name was mentioned, an eager and a kindly light shone in their eyes and they said in a hushed whisper, "Did you hear who was there on Thursday?" they thus disclosed themselves as Luciaphils. . . . All this was gradual, but the movement went steadily on, keeping pace with her astonishing career, for the days were few on which some gratifying achievement was not recorded in the veracious columns of Hermione.

Lucia was driving home one afternoon after a day passed in the Divorce Court. She had made the acquaintance of the presiding judge not long ago, and had asked him to dinner on the evening before this trial, which was the talk of the town, was to begin, and at the third attempt had got him to give her a seat in the court. The trial had already lasted three days, and really no one seemed to think about anything else, and the papers had been full of soulful and surprising evidence. Certainly, Babs Shyton, the lady whose husband wanted to get rid of her, had written very odd letters to Woof-dog, otherwise known as Lord Middlesex, and he to her: Lucia could not imagine writing to anybody like that, and she would have been very much surprised if anyone had written to her as Woof-dog wrote to Babs. But as the trial went on, Lucia found herself growing warm with sympathy for Babs. Her husband, Colonel Shyton, must have been an impossible person to live with, for sometimes he would lie in bed all day, get up in the evening, have breakfast at 8 P.M., lunch a little after midnight, and dine heavily at 8:30 in the morning. Surely with a husband like that, any woman would want some sort of a Woof-dog to take care of her. Both Babs and he, in the extracts from the remarkable correspondence between them which were read out in court, alluded to Colonel Shyton as the S.P., which Babs (amid loud laughter) frankly confessed meant Stinkpot; and Babs had certainly written to Woof-dog to say that she was in bed and very sleepy and cross, but wished that Woof-dog was thumping his tail on the hearthrug. That was indiscreet, but there was nothing incriminating about it, and as for the row of crosses which followed Babs's signature, she explained frankly that they indicated that she was cross. There were roars of laughter again at this, and even the judge wore a broad grin as he said that if there was any more disturbance, he should clear the court. Babs had produced an excellent impression, in fact: she had looked so pretty and had answered so gaily, and the Woof-dog had been just as admirable, for he was a strong silent Englishman, and when he was asked whether he had ever kissed Babs, he said "That's a lie" in such a loud fierce voice that you felt that the jury had better believe him unless they all wanted to be knocked down. The verdict was expected next day, and Lucia meant to lose no time in asking Babs to dinner if it was in her favor.

The court had been very hot and airless, and Lucia directed her chauffeur to drive round the park before going home. She had asked one or two people to tea at five, and one or two more at half past, but there was time for a turn first, and diverting her mind from the special features of the case to the general features of such cases, she thought what an amazing and incomparable publicity they gave any woman. Of course, if the verdict went against her, such publicity would be extremely disagreeable, but given that the jury decided that there was nothing against her, Lucia could imagine being almost envious of her. She did not actually want to be placed in such a situation herself, but certainly it would convey a notoriety that could scarcely be accomplished by years of patient effort. Babs would feel that there was not a single person in any gathering who did not know who she was and all about her, and if she was innocent, that would be a wholly delightful result. Naturally Lucia only envied the outcome of such an experience, not the experience itself, for it would entail a miserable life with Peppino, and she felt sure that dinner at 8:30 in the morning would be highly indigestible, but it would be wonderful to be as well-known as Babs.

Another point that had struck her, both in the trial itself and in the torrents of talk that for the last few days had been poured out over the case, was the warm sympathy of the world in general with Babs, whether guilty or innocent. "The world always loves a lover," thought Lucia, and Woof-dog thumping his tail on the rug by her bedroom fire was a beautiful image.

Her thoughts took a more personal turn. The idea of having a real lover was, of course, absolutely abhorrent to her whole nature, and besides, she did not know whom she could get. But the reputation of having a lover was a wholly different matter, presenting no such objections or difficulties, and most decidedly it gave a woman a certain *cachet*, if a man was always seen about with her and was supposed to be deeply devoted to her. The idea had occurred to her vaguely before, but now it took more definite shape, and as to her choice of this sort of lover, there was no difficulty about that. Hitherto, she had done nothing to encourage the notion, beyond having Stephen at the house a good deal, but now she saw herself assuming an air of devoted proprietorship of him; she could see herself talking to him in a corner, and even laying her hand on his sleeve, arriving with him at an evening party, and going away with him, for Peppino hated going out after dinner. . . .

But caution was necessary in the first steps, for it would be hard to explain to Stephen what the proposed relationship was, and she could not imagine herself saying "We are going to pretend to be lovers, but we aren't." It would be quite dreadful if he misunderstood and unexpectedly imprinted on her lips or even her hand a hot lascivious kiss, but up till now he certainly had not shown the smallest desire to do anything of the sort. She would never be able to see him again if he did that, and the world would probably say that he had dropped her. But she knew she couldn't explain the proposed position to him, and he would have to guess; she could only give him a lead and must trust to his intelligence, and to the absence in him of any unsuspected amorous proclivities. She would begin gently, anyhow, and have him to dinner every day that she was at home. And really it would be very pleasant for him, for she was entertaining a great deal during this next week or two, and if he only did not yield to one of those rash and turbulent impulses of the male, all would be well. Georgie, until (so Lucia put it to herself) Olga had come between them, had done it beautifully, and Stephen was rather like Georgie. As for herself, she knew she could trust her firm slow pulses never to beat wild measures for anybody.

She reached home to find that Adele had already arrived, and pausing only to tell her servant to ring up Stephen and ask him to come round at once, she went upstairs.

"Dearest Adele," she said, "a million pardons. I have been in the Divorce Court all day. Too thrilled. Babs, dear Babs Shyton, was wonderful. They got nothing out of her at all—"

"No. Lord Middlesex has got everything out of her already," observed Adele.

"Ah, how can you say that?" said Lucia. "Lord Middlesex—Woof-dog, you know—was just as wonderful. I feel sure the jury will believe them. Dear Babs! I must get her to come here some night soon and have a friendly little party for her. Think of that horrid old man who had lunch in the middle of the night! How terrible for her to have to go back to him. Dear me, what is her address?"

"She may not have to go back to him," said Adele. "If so, 'care of Woof-dog' would probably find her."

Adele had been feeling rather cross. Her husband had announced his intention of visiting his friends and relatives in England, and she did not feel inclined to make a corresponding journey to America. But as Lucia went on, she forgot these minor troubles, and became enthralled. Though she was still talking about

Babs and Woof-dog, Adele felt sure these were only symbols, like the dreams of psychoanalysts.

"My sympathy is entirely with dear Babs," she said. "Think of her position with that dreadful old wretch. A woman surely may be pardoned, even if the jury don't believe her for—"

"Of course she may," said Adele with a final spurt of ill temper. "What she's not pardoned for is being found out."

"Now you're talking as everybody talked in that dreadful play I went to last night," said Lucia. "Dear Olga was there; she is singing tomorrow, is she not? And you are assuming that Babs is guilty. How glad I am, Adele, that you are not on the jury! I take quite the other view; a woman with a wretched home like that must have a man with whom she is friends. I think it was a pure and beautiful affection between Babs and Woof-dog, such as any woman, even if she was happily married, might be proud to enjoy. There can be no doubt of Lord Middlesex's devotion to her, and really—I hope this does not shock you—what their relations were concerns nobody but them. George Sand and Chopin, you know. Nelson and Lady Hamilton. Sir Andrew Moss—he was the Judge, you know—dined here the other night; I'm sure he is broadminded. He gave me an admission card to the court. . . . Ah, Stephen, there you are. Come in, my dear. You know Lady Brixton, don't you? We were talking of Babs Shyton. Bring up your chair. Let me see, no sugar, isn't it? How you scolded me when I put sugar into your tea by mistake the other day!"

She held Stephen's hand for as long as anybody might, or, as Browning says, "so very little longer," and Adele saw a look of faint surprise on his face. It was not alarm; it was not rapture; it was just surprise.

"Were you there?" he said. "No verdict yet, I suppose."

"Not till tomorrow, but then you will see. Adele has been quite horrid about her, quite horrid, and I have been preaching to her. I shall certainly ask Babs to dine some night soon, and you shall come, if you can spare an evening, but we won't ask Adele. Tell me the news, Stephen. I've been in court all day."

"Lucia's quite misunderstood me," said Adele. "My sympathy is entirely with Babs; all I blame her for is being found out. If you and I had an affair, Mr. Merriall, we should receive the envious sympathy of everybody, until we were officially brought to book. But then we should acquiesce in even our darling Lucia's cutting us. And if you had an affair with anybody else—I'm sure you've got hundreds—I and everybody else would be ever so pleased and interested, until—Mark that word 'until.' Now I must go, and leave you two to talk me well over."

Lucia rose, making affectionate but rather half-hearted murmurs to induce her to stop.

"Must you really be going, Adele?" she said. "Let me see, what am I doing tomorrow—Stephen, what is tomorrow, and what am I doing? Ah, yes, Bertie Alton's private view in the morning. We shall be sure to meet there, Adele. The wretch has done two caricatures of Peppino and me. I feel as if I was to be flayed in the sight of all London. Au revoir, then, dear Adele, if you're so tired of us. And then the opera in the evening: I shall hardly dare to show my face. Your motor's here, is it? Ring, Stephen, will you? Such a short visit, and I expect Olga will pop in presently. All sorts of messages to her, I suppose. Look in again, Adele; propose yourself."

On the doorstep Adele met Tony Limpsfield. She hurried him into her motor, and told the chauffeur not to drive on.

"News!" she said. "Lucia's going to have a lover."

"No!" said Tony in the Riseholme manner.

"But I tell you she is. He's with her now."

"They won't want me then," said Tony. "And yet she asked me to come at half past five."

"Nonsense, my dear. They will want you, both of them. . . . Oh, Tony, don't you see? It's a stunt."

Tony assumed the rapt expression of Luciaphils receiving intelligence.

"Tell me all about it," he said.

"I'm sure I'm right," said she. "Her poppet came in just now, and she held his hand as women do, and made him draw his chair up to her, and said he scolded her. I'm not sure that he knows yet. But I saw that he guessed something was up. I wonder if he's clever enough to do it properly. . . . I wish she had chosen you, Tony; you'd have done it perfectly. They have got—don't you understand?—to have the appearance of being lovers; everyone must think they are lovers, while all the time there's nothing at all of any sort in it. It's a stunt; it's a play; it's a glory."

"But perhaps there is something in it," said Tony. "I really think I had better not go in."

"Tony, trust me. Lucia has no more idea of keeping a real lover than of keeping a chimpanzee. She's as chaste as snow; a kiss would scorch her. Besides she hasn't time. She asked Stephen there in order to show him to me, and to show him to you. It's the most wonderful plan; and it's wonderful of me to have understood it so quickly. You must go in; there's nothing private of any kind; indeed, she thirsts for publicity."

Her confidence inspired confidence, and Tony was naturally consumed with curiosity. He got out, told Adele's chauffeur to drive on, and went upstairs. Stephen was no longer sitting in the chair next to Lucia, but on the sofa at the other side of the tea table. This rather looked as if Adele was right: it was consistent anyhow with their being lovers in public, but certainly not lovers in private.

"Dear Lord Tony," said Lucia—this appellation was a halfway house between Lord Limpsfield and Tony, and she left out the "Lord" except to him—"how nice of you to drop in. You have just missed Adele. Stephen, you know Lord Limpsfield?"

Lucia gave him his tea, and presently getting up reseated herself negligently on the sofa beside Stephen. She was a shade too close at first, and edged slightly away.

"Wonderful play of Tchekov's the other day," she said. "Such a strange, unhappy atmosphere. We came out, didn't we, Stephen, feeling as if we had been in some remote dream. I saw you there, Lord Tony, with Adele who had been lunching with me."

Tony knew that. Was not that the birthday of the Luciaphils?

"It was a dream I wasn't sorry to wake from," he said. "I found it a boring dream."

"Ah, how can you say so? Such an experience! I felt as if the woe of a thousand years had come upon me, some old anguish which I had forgotten. With the effect, too, that I wanted to live more fully and vividly than ever, till the dusk closed round."

Stephen waved his hands, as he edged a little further away from Lucia. There was something strange about Lucia today. In those few minutes when they had been alone she had been quite normal, but both before, when Adele was here, and now after Lord Limpsfield's entry, she seemed to be implying a certain intimacy, to which he felt he ought to respond.

"Morbid fancies, Lucia," he said. "I shan't let you go to a Tchekov play again."

"Horrid boy," said Lucia daringly. "But that's the way with all you men. You want women to be gay and bright and thoughtless, and have no other ideas except to amuse you. I shan't ever talk to either of you again about my real feelings. We will talk about the trial to-day. My entire sympathies are with Babs, Lord Tony. I'm sure yours are, too."

Lord Limpsfield left Stephen there when he took his leave, after a quarter of an hour's lighter conversation, and as nobody else dropped in, Lucia only asked her lover to dine on two or three nights the next week, to meet her at the private view of Herbert Alton's Exhibition next morning, and let him go in a slightly bewildered frame of mind.

Stephen walked slowly up the Brompton Road, looking into the shop windows, and puzzling this out. She had held his hand oddly, she had sat close to him on the sofa, she had waved a dozen of those little signals of intimacy which gave color to a supposition, which though it did not actually make his blood run cold, certainly did not make it run hot. . . . He and Lucia were excellent friends; they had many tastes in common; but Stephen knew that he would sooner never see her again than have an intrigue with her. He was no hand, to be-

gin with, at amorous adventures, and even if he had
been, he could not conceive a woman more ill-adapted
to dally with than Lucia. "Galahad and Artemis would
make a better job of it than Lucia and me," he muttered to himself, turning hastily away from a window
full of dainty underclothing for ladies. In vain he
searched the blameless records of his intercourse with
Lucia; he could not accuse himself of thought, word, or
deed which could possibly have given rise to any disor-
dered fancy of hers that he observed her with a lascivious eye.

"God knows I am innocent," he said to himself, and
froze with horror at the sudden sight of a large
newsboard on which was printed in large capitals
"Babs wants Woof-dog on the hearthrug."

He knew he had no taste for gallantry, and he felt
morally certain that Lucia hadn't either. . . . What
then could she mean by those little tweaks and
pressures? Conning them over for the second time, it
struck him more forcibly than before that she had only
indulged in these little licentiousnesses when there was
someone else present. Little as he knew of the ways of
lovers, he always imagined that they exchanged such
tokens chiefly in private, and in public only when
their passions had to find a small safety valve. Again, if
she had had designs on his virtue, she would surely,
having got him alone, have given a message to her servants that she was out and not have had Lord
Limpsfield admitted. . . . He felt sure she was up to
something, but to his dull male sense, it was at present
wrapped in mystery. He did not want to give up all
those charming hospitalities of hers, but he must needs
be very circumspect.

It was, however, without much misgiving that he

awaited her next morning at the doors of the little Rutland Gallery, for he felt safe in so public a place as a private view. Only a few visitors had come in when Lucia arrived, and as she passed the turnstile, showing the two cards of invitation for herself and Peppino, impersonated by Stephen, she asked for hers back, saying that she was only going to make a short visit now and would return later. She had not yet seen the caricature of herself and Peppino, for which Bertie Alton (she still stuck to this little mistake) had accepted a commission, and she made her way at once to Numbers 39 and 40, which her catalogue told her were of Mr. and Mrs. Philip Lucas. Subjoined to their names were the captions, and she read with excitement that Peppino was supposed to be saying "At whatever personal inconvenience, I must live up to Lucia" while below Number 40 was the enticing little legend "Oh, these duchesses! They give one no peace!" . . . . And there was Peppino, in the knee breeches of levee dress, tripping over his sword which had got entangled with his legs, and a cocked hat on the back of his head, with his eyes very much apart, and no nose, and a small agonized hole in his face for a mouth. . . . And there was she with a pile of opened letters on the floor, and a pile of unopened letters on the table. There was not much of her face to be seen, for she was talking into a telephone, but her skirt was very short, and so was her hair, and there was a wealth of weary resignation in the limpness of her carriage.

Lucia examined them both carefully, and then gave a long sigh of perfect happiness. That was her irrepressible comment: she could not have imagined anything more ideal. Then she gave a little peal of laughter.

"Look, Stephen," she said. "Bobbie—I mean Bertie—really is too wicked for anything—Really, outrageous! I am furious with him, and yet I can't help laughing. Poor Peppino, and poor me! Marcia will adore it. She always says she can never get hold of me nowadays."

Lucia gave a swift scrutiny to the rest of the collection, so as to be able to recognize them all without reference to her catalogue, when she came back, as she intended to do later in the morning. There was hardly anyone here at present, but the place would certainly be crowded an hour before lunch time, and she proposed to make a *soi-disant* first visit then, and know at once whom all the caricatures represented (for Bertie in his enthusiasm for caricature sometimes omitted likenesses), and go into peals of laughter at those of herself and Peppino, and say she must buy them, which of course she had already done. Stephen remained behind, for Hermione was going to say a good deal about the exhibition, but promised to wait till Lucia came back. She had not shown the smallest sign of amorousness this morning. His apprehensions were considerably relieved, and it looked as if no storm of emotion was likely to be required of him.

"Hundreds of things to do!" she said. "Let me see, half past eleven, twelve—yes, I shall be back soon after twelve, and we'll have a real look at them. And you'll lunch? Just a few people coming."

Before Lucia got back, the gallery had got thick with visitors, and Hermione was busy noting those whom he saw chatting with friends or looking lovely, or being very pleased with the new house in Park Lane, or receiving congratulations on the engagement of a daughter. There was no doubt which of the pictures excited most interest, and soon there was a regular queue waiting to look at Numbers 39 and 40. People stood in front of them regarding them gravely and consulting their catalogues and then bursting into loud cracks of laughter and looking again till the growing weight of the queue dislodged them. One of those who lingered longest and stood her ground best was Adele, who when she was eventually shoved on, ran round to the tail of the queue and herself shoved till she got opposite again. She saw Stephen.

"Ah, then Lucia won't be far off," she observed archly. "Doesn't she adore it? Where is Lucia?"

"She's been, but she's coming back," he said. "I expect her every minute. Ah! there she is."

This was rather stupid of Stephen. He ought to have guessed that Lucia's second appearance was officially intended to be her first. He grasped that when she squeezed her way through the crowd and greeted him as if they had not met before that morning.

"And dearest Adele," she said. "What a crush! Tell me quickly, where are the caricatures of Peppino and me? I'm dying to see them; and when I see them no doubt I shall wish I was dead."

The light of Luciaphilism came into Adele's intelligent eyes.

"Well look for them together," she said. "Ah thirty-nine and forty. They must be somewhere just ahead."

Lucia exerted a steady indefatigable pressure on those in front, and presently came into range.

"Well, I never!" she said. "Oh, but so like Peppino! How could Bertie have told he got his sword entangled just like that? And look what he says. . . . Oh, and then Me! Just because I met him at Marcia's party, and people were wanting to know when I had an evening free! Of all the impertinences! How I shall scold him!"

Lucia did it quite admirably in blissful unconsciousness that Adele knew she had been here before. She laughed; she looked again and laughed again (Mrs. Lucas and Lady Brixton in fits of merriment over the cartoon of Mr. Lucas and herself, thought Hermione).

"Ah, and there's Lord Hurtacombe," she said. "I'm sure that's Lord Hurtacombe, though you can't see much of him, and look, Olga surely, is it not? How does he do it?"

That was a very clever identification for one who had not previously studied the catalogue, for Olga's face consisted entirely of a large open mouth and the tip of a chin, it might have been the face of anybody yawning. Her arms were stretched wide, and she towered above a small man in shorts.

"The last scene in *Siegfried,* I'm sure," said Lucia. "What does the catalogue say, Stephen? Yes, I am right. 'Siegfried! Brunnhilde!' How wicked, is it not? But killing! Who could be cross with him?"

This was all splendid stuff for Luciaphils; it was amazing how at a first glance she recognized everybody. The gallery, too, was full of dears and darlings of a few weeks' standing, and she completed a little dinner party for next Tuesday long before she had made the circuit. All the time she kept Stephen by her side, looked over his catalogue, put a hand on his arm to direct his attention to some picture, took a speck of alien material off his sleeve, and all the time the entranced Adele felt increasingly certain that she had plumbed the depth of the adorable situation. Her sole anxiety was as to whether Stephen would plumb it, too.

He might—though he didn't look like it—welcome these little tokens of intimacy as indicating something more, and when they were alone, attempt to kiss her, and that would ruin the whole exquisite design. Luckily his demeanor was not that of a favored swain; it was, on the other hand, more the demeanor of a swain who feared to be favored, and if that shy thing took fright, the situation would be equally ruined. . . . To think that the most perfect piece of Luciaphilism was dependent on the just perceptions of Stephen! As the three made their slow progress, listening to Lucia's brilliant identifications, Adele willed Stephen to understand; she projected a perfect torrent of suggestion toward his mind. He must, he should understand. . . .

Fervent desire, so every psychist affirms, is never barren. It conveys something of its yearning to the consciousness to which it is directed, and there began to break on the dull male mind what had been so obvious to the finer feminine sense of Adele. Once again, and in the blaze of publicity, Lucia was full of touches and tweaks, and the significance of them dawned, like some pale, austere sunrise, on his darkened senses. The situation was revealed, and he saw it was one with which he could easily deal. His gloomy apprehensions brightened, and he perceived that there would be no need, when he went to stay at Riseholme next, to lock his bedroom door, a practice which was abhorrent to him for fear of fire suddenly breaking out in the house. Last night he had had a miserable dream about what had happened when he failed to lock his door at The Hurst, but now he dismissed its haunting. These little intimacies of Lucia's were purely a public performance.

"Lucia, we must be off," he said loudly and confidently. "Peppino will wonder where we are."

Lucia sighed.

"He always bullies me like that, Adele," she said. "I must go; *au revoir*, dear. Tuesday next—just a few *intimes*."

Lucia's relief was hardly less than Stephen's. He would surely not have said anything so indiscreet if he had been contemplating an indiscretion, and she had no fear that his hurry to be off was due to any passionate desire to embrace her in the privacy of her car. She believed he understood, and her belief felt justified when he proposed that the car should be opened.

Riseholme, in the last three weeks of social progress, had not occupied the front row of Lucia's thoughts, but the second row, so to speak, had been entirely filled with it, for as far as the future dimly outlined itself behind the present, the plan was to go down there early in August, and remain there, with a few brilliant excursions till autumn peopled London again. She had hoped for a dash to Aix, where there would be many pleasant people, but Peppino had told her summarily that the treasury would not stand it. Lucia had accepted that with the frankest good nature: she had made quite a gay little lament about it, when she was asked what she was going to do in August. "Ah, all you lucky rich people with money to throw about; we've got to go and live quietly at home," she used to say. "But I shall love it, though I shall miss you all dreadfully. Riseholme, dear Riseholme, you know, adorable; and all the delicious funny friends down there who spoil me so dreadfully. I shall have lovely tranquil days, with a trot across the green to order fish, and a chat on the way, and my books and my piano, and a chair in the garden, and an early bedtime, instead of all these late hours. An anchorite life, but if you have a weekend to spare between your Aix and your yacht and your Scotland, ah, how nice it would be if you just sent a postcard!"

Before they became anchorites, however, there was a long weekend for her and Peppino over the August bank holiday, and Lucia looked forward to that with unusual excitement. Adele was the hostess, and the scene that immense country house of hers in Essex. The whole world, apparently, was to be there, for Adele had said the house would be full; and it was to be a final reunion of the choicest spirits before the annual dispersion. Mrs. Garroby-Ashton had longed to be bidden, but was not, and though Lucia was sorry for dear Millicent's disappointment, she could not but look down on it, as a sort of perch far below her that showed how dizzily she herself had gone upward. But she had no intention of dropping good kind Millie who was hopping about below; she must certainly come to The Hurst for a Sunday—that would be nice for her, and she would learn all about Adele's party.

There were yet ten days before that, and the morning after the triumphant affair at the Rutland Gallery, Lucia heard a faint rumor, coming from nowhere in particular, that Marcia Whitby was going to give a very small and very wonderful dance to wind up the season. She had not seen much of Marcia lately; in other words, she had seen nothing at all, and Lucia's last three invitations to her had been declined, one through a secretary, and two through a telephone. Lucia continued, however, to talk about her with unabated familiarity and affection. The next day the rumor became slightly more solid; Adele let slip some allusion to Marcia's ball, and hurriedly covered it up with talk of her own weekend. Lucia fixed her with a penetrating eye for a moment, but the eye failed apparently to penetrate: Adele went on gabbling about her own party, and took not the slightest notice of it.

But in truth Adele's gabble was a frenzied and feverish maneuver to get away from the subject of Marcia's ball. Marcia was no true Luciaphil; instead of feeling entranced pleasure in Lucia's successes and failures, her schemes and attainments and ambitions, she had lately been taking a high severe line about her.

"She's beyond a joke, Adele," she said. "I hear she's got a scrapbook, and puts in picture postcards and photographs of country houses, with dates below them to indicate she has been there—"

"No!" said Adele. "How heavenly of her. I must see it, or did you make it up?"

"Indeed I didn't," said the injured Marcia. "And she's got in it a picture postcard of the moat garden at Whitby with the date of the Sunday before last, when I had a party there and didn't ask her. Besides, she was in London at the time. And there's one of Buckingham Palace Garden, with the date of the last garden party. Was she asked?"

"I haven't heard she was," said Adele.

"Then you may be sure she wasn't. She's beyond a joke, I tell you, and I'm not going to ask her to my dance. I won't, I won't—I will not. And she asked me to dine three times last week. It isn't fair; it's bullying. A weak-minded person would have submitted, but I'm not weak-minded, and I won't be bullied. I won't be forcibly fed, and I won't ask her to my dance. There!"

"Don't be so unkind," said Adele. "Besides, you'll meet her down at my house only a few days afterward, and it will be awkward. Everybody else will have been."

"Well, then she can pretend she has been exclusive," said Marcia snappily, "and she'll like that. . . ."

The rumors solidified into fact, and soon Lucia was forced to the dreadful conclusion that Marcia's ball was to take place without her. That was an intolerable thought, and she gave Marcia one more chance by ringing her up and inviting her to dinner on that night (so as to remind her she knew nothing about the ball), but Marcia's stony voice replied that most unfortunately she had a few people to dinner herself. Wherever she went (and where now did Lucia not go?), she heard talk of the ball, and the plethora of princes and princesses that were to attend it.

For a moment the thought of princesses lightened the depression of this topic. Princess Isabel was rather seriously ill with influenza, so Lucia, driving down Park Lane, thought it would not be amiss to call and enquire how she was, for she had noticed that sometimes the papers recorded the names of enquirers. She did not any longer care in the least how Princess Isabel was; whether she died or recovered was a matter of complete indifference to her in her present embittered frame of mind, for the Princess had not taken the smallest notice of her all these weeks. However, there was the front door open, for there were other enquirers on the threshold, and Lucia joined them. She presented her card, and asked in a trembling voice what news there was, and was told that the Princess was no better. Lucia bowed her head in resignation, and then, after faltering a moment in her walk, pulled herself together, and with a firmer step went back to her motor.

After this interlude her mind returned to the terrible topic. She was due at a drawing-room meeting at Sophy Alingsby's house to hear a lecture on psychoanaly-

sis, and she really hardly felt up to it. But there would
certainly be a quantity of interesting people there, and
the lecture itself might possibly be of interest, and so before long she found herself in the black dining room,
which had been cleared for the purpose. With the self-
effacing instincts of the English, the audience had left the
front-row chairs completely unoccupied, and she got a
very good place. The lecture had just begun, and so
her entry was not unmarked. Stephen was there, and as
she seated herself, she nodded to him, and patted the
empty chair by her side with a beckoning gesture. Her
lover, therefore, sidled up to her and took it.

Lucia whistled her thoughts away from such ephe-
meral and frivolous subjects as dances, and tried to
give Professor Bonstetter her attention. She felt that
she had been living a very hectic life lately; the world
and its empty vanities had been too much with her,
and she needed some intellectual tonic. She had seen
no pictures lately, except Bobbie (or was it Bertie?)
Alton's; she had heard no music; she had not touched
the piano herself for weeks; she had read no books,
and at the most had skimmed the reviews of such as
had lately appeared in order to be up to date and be
able to reproduce a short but striking criticism or two
if the talk became literary. She must not let the mere
froth of living entirely conceal by its winking headiness
of foam the true beverage below it. There was Sophy,
with her hair over her eyes and her chin in her hand,
dressed in a faded rainbow, weird beyond description,
but rapt in concentration, while she herself was letting
the notion of a dance to which she had not been asked
and was clearly not to be asked, drive like a mist between her and these cosmic facts about dreams and the
unconscious self. How curious that if you dreamed

about boiled rabbit, it meant that sometime in early childhood you had been kissed by a poacher in a railway carriage, and had forgotten all about it! What a magnificent subject for excited research psychoanalysis would have been in those keen intellectual days at Riseholme. . . . She thought of them now with a vague yearning for their simplicity and absorbing earnestness; of the hours she had spent with Georgie over piano duets, of Daisy Quantock's Ouija board and planchette, of the Museum with its mittens. Riseholme presented itself now as an abode of sweet peace, where there were no disappointments or heartburnings, for sooner or later she had always managed to assert her will and constitute herself priestess of the current interests. . . . Suddenly the solution of her present difficulty flashed upon her: Riseholme. She would go to Riseholme; that would explain her absence from Marcia's stupid ball.

The lecture came to an end, and with others she buzzed for a little while round Professor Bonstetter, and had a few words with her hostess.

"Too interesting. Marvellous, was it not, dear Sophy? Boiled rabbit! How curious! And the outcropping of the unconscious in dreams. Explains so much about phobias; people who can't go in the tube. So pleased to have heard it. Ah, there's Aggie. Aggie darling! What a treat, wasn't it? Such a refreshment from our bustlings and runnings about to get back into origins. I've got to fly, but I couldn't miss this. Dreadful overlapping all this afternoon, and poor Princess Isabel is no better. I just called on my way here, but I wasn't allowed to see her. Stephen, where is Stephen? See if my motor is there, dear. Au revoir, dear Sophy. We must meet again very soon. Are you going to Adele's next week? No? How tiresome! Wonderful lecture! Calming!"

Lucia edged herself out of the room with these very hurried greetings, for she was really eager to get home. She found Peppino there, having tea peacefully all by himself, and sank exhausted in a chair.

"Give me a cup of tea, strong tea, Peppino," she said. "I've been racketing about all day, and I feel done for. How I shall get through these next two or three days, I really don't know. And London is stifling. You look worn out too, my dear."

Peppino acknowledged the truth of this. He had hardly had time even to go to his club this last day or two, and had been reflecting on the enormous strength of the weaker sex. But for Lucia to confess herself done for was a portentous thing: he could not remember such a thing happening before.

"Well, there are not many more days of it," he said. "Three more this week, and then Lady Brixton's party."

He gave several loud sneezes.

"Not a cold?" asked Lucia.

"Something extraordinarily like one," said he.

Lucia became suddenly alert again. She was sorry for Peppino's cold, but it gave her an admirable gambit for what she had made up her mind to do.

"My dear, that's enough," she said. "I won't have you flying about London with a bad cold coming on. I shall take you down to Riseholme tomorrow."

"Oh, but you can't, my dear," said he. "You've got your engagement book full for the next three days."

"Oh, a lot of stupid things," said she. "And really, I tell you, quite honestly, I'm fairly worn out. It'll do us both good to have a rest for a day or two. Now don't make objections. Let us see what I've got to do."

The days were pretty full (though, alas, Thursday

evening was deplorably empty), and Lucia had a brisk half hour at the telephone. To those who had been bidden here, and to those to whom she had been bidden, she gave the same excuse, namely, that she had been advised (by herself) two or three days' complete rest.

She rang up The Hurst, to say that they were coming down tomorrow, and would bring the necessary attendants; she rang up Georgie (for she was not going to fall into *that* error again) and in a mixture of baby language and Italian, which he found very hard to understand, asked him to dine tomorrow night, and finally she scribbled a short paragraph to the leading morning papers to say that Mrs. Philip Lucas had been ordered to leave London for two or three days' complete rest. She had hesitated a moment over the wording of that, for it was Peppino who was much more in need of rest than she, but it would have been rather ludicrous to say that Mr. and Mrs. Philip Lucas were in need of a complete rest. . . . These announcements she sent by hand so that there might be no miscarriage in their appearance tomorrow morning. And then, as an afterthought, she rang up Daisy Quantock and asked her and Robert to lunch tomorrow.

She felt much happier. She would not be at the fell Marcia's ball, because she was resting in the country.

8

A FEW MINUTES before Lucia and Peppino drove off next morning from Brompton Square, Marcia observed Lucia's announcement in the *Morning Post*. She was a good-natured woman, but she had been goaded, and now that Lucia could goad her no more for the present, she saw no objection to asking her to her ball. She thought of telephoning, but there was the chance that Lucia had not yet started, so she sent her a card instead, directing it to 25 Brompton Square, saying that she was At Home, dancing, to have the honor to meet a string of exalted personages. If she had telephoned, no one knows what would have happened, whether Daisy would have had any lunch that day or Georgie any dinner that night, and what excuse Lucia would have made to them. . . . Adele and Tony Limpsfield, the most adept of all the Luciaphils, subsequently argued the matter out with much heat, but never arrived at a solution that they felt was satisfactory. But then Marcia did not telephone. . . .

The news that the two were coming down was, of course, all over Riseholme a few minutes after Lucia had rung Georgie up. He was in his study when the telephone bell rang, in the fawn-colored Oxford trousers, which had been cut down from their monstrous proportions and fitted quite nicely, though there had been a sad waste of stuff. Robert Quantock, the wag who had danced a hornpipe when Georgie had appeared in the original voluminousness, was waggish again, when he saw the abbreviated garments, and *à propos* of nothing in particular had said, "Home is the sailor, home from sea," and that was the epitaph on the Oxford trousers.

Georgie had been busy indoors this afternoon, for he had been attending to his hair, and it was not quite dry yet, and the smell of the auburn mixture still clung to it. But the telephone was a trunk call, and whether his hair was dry or not, it must be attended to. Since Lucia had disappeared after that weekend party, he had had a line from her once or twice, saying that they must really settle when he would come and spend a few days in London, but she had never descended to the sordid mention of dates.

A trunk call, as far as he knew, could only be Lucia or Olga, and one would be interesting and the other delightful. It proved to be the interesting one, and though rather difficult to understand because of the aforesaid mixture of baby talk and Italian, it certainly conveyed the gist of the originator's intention.

"Me so tired," Lucia said, "and it will be divine to get to Riseholme again. So come to 'ickle quiet din-din

with me and Peppino tomorrow, Georgino. Shall want
to hear all *novelle*—"

"What?" said Georgie.

"All the news," said Lucia.

Georgie sat in the draught—it was very hot today—
until the auburn mixture dried. He knew that Daisy
Quantock and Robert were playing clock golf on the
other side of his garden paling, for their voices had
been very audible. Daisy had not been weeding much
lately but had taken to golf, and since all the authori-
ties said that matches were entirely won or lost on the
putting green, she with her usual wisdom devoted herself to the winning factor in the game. Presently she
would learn to drive and approach and niblick and that
sort of thing, and then they would see. . . . She wondered how good Miss Wethered really was.

Georgie, now dry, tripped out into the garden and
shouted, "May I come in?" That meant, of course,
might he look over the garden paling and talk.

Daisy missed a very short putt, owing to the interruption.

"Yes, do," she said icily. "I supposed you would
give me that, Robert."

"You supposed wrong," said Robert, who was now
two up.

Georgie stepped on a beautiful pansy.

"Lucia's coming down tomorrow," he said.

Daisy dropped her putter.

"No!" she exclaimed.

"And Peppino," went on Georgie. "She says she's
very tired."

"All those duchesses," said Daisy. Herbert Alton's
cartoon had been reproduced in an illustrated weekly,

but Riseholme up to this moment had been absolutely silent about it. It was beneath notice.

"And she's asked me to dinner tomorrow," said Georgie.

"So she's not bringing down a party?" said Daisy.

"I don't know," remarked Robert, "if you are going on putting, or if you give me the match."

"Pouf!" said Daisy, just like that. "But tired, Georgie? What does that mean?"

"I don't know," said Georgie, "but that's what she said."

"It means something else," said Daisy. "I can't tell you what, but it doesn't mean that. I suppose you've said you're engaged."

"No I haven't," said Georgie.

De Vere came out from the house. In this dry weather her heels made no indentations on the lawn.

"Trunk call, ma'am," she said to Daisy.

"These tiresome interruptions," said Daisy, hurrying indoors with great alacrity.

Georgie lingered. He longed to know what the trunk call was, and was determined to remain with his head on the top of the paling till Daisy came back. So he made conversation.

"Your lawn is better than mine," he said pleasantly to Robert.

Robert was cross at this delay.

"That's not saying much," he observed.

"I can't say any more," said Georgie, rather nettled. "And there's the leather-jacket grub, I see, has begun on yours. I daresay there won't be a blade of grass left presently."

Robert changed the conversation: there were bare patches. "The Museum insurance," he said. "I got the fire policy this morning. The contents are the property of the four trustees: me and you and Daisy and Mrs. Boucher. The building is Colonel Boucher's, and that's insured separately. If you had a spark of enterprise about you, you would take a match, set light to the mittens, and hope for the best."

"You're very tarsome and cross," said Georgie. "I should like to take a match and set light to you."

Georgie hated rude conversations like this, but when Robert was in such a mood, it was best to be playful. He did not mean, in any case, to cease leaning over the garden paling till Daisy came back from her trunk call.

"Beyond the mittens," began Robert, "and, of course, those three sketches of yours, which I daresay are masterpieces—"

Daisy bowled out of the dining room and came with such speed down the steps that she nearly fell into the circular bed where the broccoli had been. (The mignonette there was poorish.)

"At half past one or two," said she, bursting with the news and at the same time unable to suppress her gift for withering sarcasm. "Lunch tomorrow. Just a picnic, you know, as soon as she happens to arrive. So kind of her. More notice than she took of me last time."

"Lucia?" asked Georgie.

"Yes. Let me see, I was putting, wasn't I?"

"If you call it putting," said Robert. He was not often two up, and he made the most of it.

"So I suppose you said you were engaged," said Georgie.

Daisy did not trouble to reply at all. She merely went on putting. That was the way to deal with inquisitive questions.

This news, therefore, was very soon all over Riseholme, and next morning it was supplemented by the amazing announcement in the *Times, Morning Post, Daily Telegraph,* and *Daily Mail* that Mrs. Philip Lucas had left London for two or three days' complete rest. It sounded incredible to Riseholme, but of course it might be true and, as Daisy had said, that the duchesses had been too much for her. (This was nearer the mark than the sarcastic Daisy had known, for it was absolutely and literally true that one duchess had been too much for her. . . .) In any case, Lucia was coming back to them again, and though Riseholme was still a little dignified and reticent, Georgie's acceptance of his dinner invitation, and Daisy's of her lunch invitation, were symptomatic of Riseholme's feelings. Lucia had foully deserted them; she had been down here only once since that fatal accession to fortune, and on that occasion had evidently intended to see nothing of her old friends while that Yahoo party ("Yahoo" was the only word for Mrs. Alingsby) was with her; she had laughed at their Museum; she had courted the vulgar publicity of the press to record her movements in London; but Riseholme was really perfectly willing to forget and forgive if she behaved properly now. For though no one would have confessed it, they missed her more and more. In spite of all her bullying monarchical ways, she had initiative; and though the excitement of the Museum and the sagas from Abfou had kept them going for a while, it was really in relation to Lucia that these enterprises had been interesting. Since then, too, Abfou had been full of vain repetitions, and no one could go on being excited by his denunciation of Lucia as a snob, indefinitely. Lucia had personality, and if she had been here and had taken to golf, Riseholme would have been thrilled at her skill, and have exulted over her want of it, whereas Daisy's wonderful scores at clock golf (she was off her game today) produced no real interest. Degrading, too, as were the records of Lucia's movements in the columns of Hermione, Riseholme had been thrilled (though disgusted) by them, because they were about Lucia, and though she was coming down now for complete rest (whatever that might mean), the mere fact of her being here would make things hum. This time, too, she had behaved properly (perhaps she had learned wisdom) and had announced her coming, and asked old friends in.

Forgiveness, therefore, and excitement were the prevalent emotions in the morning parliament on the green next day. Mrs. Boucher alone expressed grave doubts on the situation.

"I don't believe she's ill," she said. "If she's ill, I shall be very sorry, but I don't believe it. If she is, Mr. Georgie, I'm all for accepting her gift of the spit to the Museum, for it would be unkind not to. You can write and say that the Committee have reconsidered it and would be very glad to have it. But let's wait to see if she's ill first. In fact, wait to see if she's coming at all first."

Piggy came whizzing up with news, while Goosie shouted into her mother's ear-trumpet. Before Piggy could come out with it, Goosie's announcement was audible everywhere.

"A cab from the station has arrived at The Hurst, Mamma," she yelled, "with the cook and the housemaid, and a quantity of luggage."

"Oh, Mrs. Boucher, have you heard the news?" panted Piggy.

"Yes, my dear, I've just heard it," said Mrs. Boucher, "and it looks as if they were coming. That's all I can say. And if the cook's come by half past eleven, I don't see why you shouldn't get a proper lunch, Daisy. No need for a cup of strong soup or a sandwich, which I should have recommended if there had been no further news since you were asked to a picnic lunch. But if the cook's here now. . . ."

Daisy was too excited to go home and have any serious putting and went off to the Museum. Mr. Rushbold, the Vicar, had just presented his unique collection of walking sticks to it, and though the Committee felt it would be unkind not to accept them, it was difficult to know how to deal with them. They could not all be stacked together in one immense stick stand, for then they could not be appreciated. The handles of many were curiously carved, some with gargoyle heads of monsters putting out their tongues and leering, some with images of birds and fish, and there was one rather indelicate one, of a young man and a girl passionately embracing. . . . On the other hand, if they were spaced and leaned against the wall, some slight disturbance upset the equilibrium of one, and it fell against the next, and the whole lot went down like ninepins. In fact, the boy at the turnstile said his entire time was occupied with picking them up. Daisy had a scheme of stretching an old lawn-tennis net against the wall, and tastefully entangling them in its meshes. . . .

Riseholme lingered on the green that morning long after one o'clock, which was its usual lunchtime, and at precisely twenty-five minutes past, they were rewarded. Out of the motor stepped Peppino in a very thick coat and a large muffler. He sneezed twice as he held out his arm to assist Lucia to alight. She clung to it, and

leaning heavily on it, went with faltering steps past
Perdita's garden into the house. So she was ill.

Ten minutes later, Daisy and Robert Quantock were
seated at lunch with them. Lucia certainly looked very
well, and she ate her lunch very properly, but she
spoke in a slightly faded voice, as befitted one who had
come here for complete rest. "But Riseholme, dear
Riseholme will soon put me all right again," she said.
"Such a joy to be here! Any news, Daisy?"

Really there was very little. Daisy ran through such
topics as had interested Riseholme during those last
weeks, and felt that the only thing which had attracted
true, feverish, Riseholme attention was the record of
Lucia's own movements. Apart from this there was
only her own putting, and the embarrassing gift of
walking sticks to the Museum. . . . But then she
remembered that the Committee had authorized the acceptance of the Elizabethan spit, if Lucia seemed ill,
and she rather precipitately decided that she was ill
enough.

"Well, we've been busy over the Museum," she began.

"Ah, the dear Museum," said Lucia wistfully.

That quite settled it.

"We should so like to accept the Elizabethan spit, if
we may," said Daisy. "It would be a great acquisition."

"Of course; delighted," said Lucia. "I will have it
sent over. Any other gifts?"

Daisy went on to the walking sticks, omitting all
mention of the indelicate one in the presence of gentlemen, and described the difficulty of placing them satis-
factorily. There were eighty-one (including the
indelicacy), and a lawn-tennis net would barely hold
them. The invalid took but a wan interest in this, and

Daisy's putting did not rouse much keener enthusiasm. But soon she recovered a greater animation and was more herself. Indeed, before the end of lunch it had struck Daisy that Peppino was really the invalid of the two. He certainly had a prodigious cold, and spoke in a throaty wheeze that was scarcely audible. She wondered if she had been a little hasty about accepting the spit, for that gave Lucia a sort of footing in the Museum.

Lucia recovered still further when her guests had gone, and her habitual energy began to assert itself. She had made her impressive invalid entry into Riseholme, which justified the announcement in the papers, and now, quietly, she must be on the move again. She might begin by getting rid, without delay, of that tiresome spit.

"I think I shall go out for a little drive, Peppino," she said, "though if I were you I would nurse my cold and get it all right before Saturday when we go to Adele's. The gardener, I think, could take the spit out of the chimney for me, and put it in the motor, and I would drop it at the Museum. I thought they would want it before long. . . . And that clock golf of Daisy's; it sounds amusing; the sort of thing for Sunday afternoon if we have guests with us. I think she said that you could get the apparatus at the Stores. Little tournaments might be rather fun."

The spit was easily removed, and Lucia, having written to the Stores for a set of clock golf, had it loaded up on the motor, and conveyed to the Museum. So that was done. She waved and fluttered a hand of greeting to Piggy and Goosie who were gambolling on the green, and set forth into the country, satisfied that she had behaved wisely in leaving London rather than being left out in London. Apart from that, too, it had been politic to come down to Riseholme again like this, to give them a taste of her quality before she resumed, in August, as she entirely meant to do, her ancient sway. She guessed from the paucity of news which that arch-gossip, dear Daisy, had to give, that things had been remarkably dull in her absence, and though she had made a sad mistake over her weekend party, a little propitiation would soon put that right. And Daisy had had nothing to say about Abfou; they seemed to have got a little tired of Abfou. But Abfou might be revived: clock golf and a revival of Ouija would start August very pleasantly. She would have liked Aix better, but Peppino was quite clear about that. . . .

Georgie was agreeably surprised to find her so much herself when he came over for dinner. Peppino, whose cold was still extremely heavy, went to bed very soon after, and he and Lucia settled themselves in the music room.

"First a little chat, Georgie," she said, "and then I insist on our having some music. I've played nothing lately; you will find me terribly out of practice, but you mustn't scold me. Yes, the spit has gone; dear Daisy said the Museum was most anxious to get it, and I took it across myself this afternoon. I must see what else I can find worthy of it."

This was all rather splendid. Lucia had a glorious way of completely disregarding the past, and pushing on ahead into the future.

"And have you been playing much lately?" she asked.

"Hardly a note," said Georgie; "there is nobody to

play with. Piggy wanted to do some duets, but I said, 'No, thanks.' "

"Georgie, you've been lazy," she said. "There's been nobody to keep you up to the mark. And Olga? Has Olga been down?"

"Not since—not since that Sunday when you were both down together," said he.

"Very wrong of her to have deserted Riseholme. But just as wrong of me, you will say. But now we must put our heads together and make great plans for August. I shall be here to bully you all August. Just one visit, which Peppino and I are paying to dear Adele Brixton on Saturday, and then you will have me here solidly. London? Yes, it has been great fun, though you and I never managed to arrange a date for your stay with us. That must come in the autumn when we go up in November. But, oh, how tired I was when we settled to leave town yesterday. Not a kick left in me. Lots of engagements, too, and I just scrapped them. But people must be kind to me and forgive me. And sometimes I feel that I've been wasting time terribly. I've done nothing but see people, people, people. All sorts, from Alf Watson the pugilist—"

"No!" said Georgie, beginning to feel the thrill of Lucia again.

"Yes, he came to dine with me, such a little duck, and brought his flute. There was a great deal of talk about my party for Alf, and how the women buzzed round him!"

"Who else?" said Georgie greedily.

"My dear, who *not* else? Marcelle—Marcelle Periscope came another night, Adele, Sophy Alingsby, Bertie Alton, Aggie—I must ask dear Aggie down here; Tony—Tony Limpsfield; a thousand others. And then, of course, dear Marcia Whitby often. She is giving a ball tomorrow night. I should like to have been there, but I was just *finito*. Ah, and your friend Princess Isabel. Very bad influenza. You should ring up her house, Georgie, and ask how she is. I called there yesterday. So sad! But let us talk of more cheerful things. Daisy's clock golf: I must pop in and see her at it tomorrow. She is wonderful, I suppose. I have ordered a set from the Stores, and we will have great games."

"She's been doing nothing else for weeks," said Georgie. "I daresay she's very good, but nobody takes any interest in it. She's rather a bore about it—"

"Georgie, don't be unkind about poor Daisy," said Lucia. "We must start little competitions, with prizes. Do you have partners? You and I will be partners at mixed putting. And what about Abfou?"

It seemed to Georgie that this was just the old Lucia, and so no doubt it was. She was intending to bag any employments that happened to be going about and claim them as her own. It was larceny, intellectual and physical larceny, no doubt, but Lucia breathed life into those dead bones and made them interesting. It was weary work to watch Daisy dabbing away with her putter and then trying to beat her score without caring the least whether you beat it or not. And Daisy even telephoned her more marvellous feats, and nobody cared how marvellous they were. But it would be altogether different if Lucia was the goddess of putting. . . .

"I haven't Abfou'd for ages," said Georgie. "I fancy she has dropped it."

"Well, we must pick everything up again," said Lucia briskly, "and you shan't be lazy any more, Georgie. Come and play duets. My dear piano! What shall we do?"

They did quantities of things, and then Lucia played the slow movement of the "Moonlight Sonata," and Georgie sighed as usual, and eventually Lucia let him out and walked with him to the garden gate. There were quantities of stars, and as usual she quoted "See how the floor of heaven is thick inlaid . . ." and said she must ring him up in the morning, after a good night's rest.

There was a light in Daisy's drawing room, and just as he came opposite it, she heard his step, for which she had long been listening and looked out.

"Is it Georgie?" she said, knowing perfectly well that it must be.

"Yes," said Georgie. "How late you are."

"And how is Lucia?" asked Daisy.

Georgie quite forgot for the moment that Lucia was having complete rest.

"Excellent form," he said. "Such a talk, and such a music."

"There you are, then!" said Daisy. "There's nothing the matter with her. She doesn't want rest any more— than the moon. What does it mean, Georgie? Mark my words; it means something."

Lucia, indeed, seemed in no need whatever of complete rest the next day. She popped into Daisy's very soon after breakfast, and asked to be taught how to putt. Daisy gave her a demonstration, and told her how to hold the putter and where to place her feet, and said it was absolutely essential to stand like a rock and to concentrate. Nobody could putt if anyone spoke. Eventually Lucia was allowed to try, and she stood all wrong and grasped her putter like an umbrella, and holed out of the longest of putts in the middle of an uninterrupted sentence. Then they had a match; Daisy proposing to give her four strokes in the round, which Lucia refused, and Daisy, dithering with excitement and superiority, couldn't putt at all. Lucia won easily, with Robert looking on, and she praised Daisy's putter, and said it was beautifully balanced, though where she picked that up, Daisy couldn't imagine.

"And now I must fly," said Lucia, "and we must have a return match sometime. So amusing! I have sent for a set, and you will have to give me lessons. Goodby, dear Daisy. I'm away for the Sunday at dear Adele Brixton's, but after that how lovely to settle down at Riseholme again! You must show me your Ouija board, too. I feel quite rested this morning. Shall I help you with the walking sticks later on?"

Daisy went uneasily back to her putting: it was too awful that Lucia in that amateurish manner should have beaten a serious exponent of the art, and already, in dark anticipation, she saw Lucia as the impresario of clock golf, popularizing it in Riseholme. She herself would have to learn to drive and approach without delay, and make Riseholme take up real golf, instead of merely putting.

Lucia visited the Museum next, and arranged the spit in an empty and prominent place between Daisy's fossils and Colonel Boucher's fragments of Samian ware. She attended the morning parliament on the green, and walked beside Mrs. Boucher's Bath chair. She shouted into Mrs. Antrobus's ear-trumpet; she dallied with Piggy and Goosie, and never so much as mentioned a duchess. All her thoughts seemed wrapped up in Riseholme; just one tiresome visit lay in front of her, and then, oh, the joy of settling down here again! Even Mrs. Boucher felt disarmed; little as she

would have thought it, there was something in Lucia
beyond mere snobbery.

Georgie popped in that afternoon about teatime. The
afternoon was rather chilly, and Lucia had a fire lit in
the grate of the music room, which now that the spit
had been removed, burned beautifully. Peppino,
drowsy with his cold, sat by it, while the other two
played duets. Already Lucia had taken down
Sigismund's portrait and installed Georgie's water
colors again by the piano. They had had a fine tussle
over the Mozart duet, and Georgie had promised to
practise it, and Lucia had promised to practise it, and
she had called him an idle boy, and he had called her a
lazy girl, quite in the old style, while Peppino dozed.
Just then the evening post came in, with the evening
paper, and Lucia picked up the latter to see what Hermione had said about her departure from London.
Even as she turned back the page her eye fell on two
or three letters, which had been forwarded from
Brompton Square. The top one was a large square envelope, the sort of fine thick envelope that contained a
rich card of invitation, and she opened it. Next moment she sprang from her seat.

"Peppino, dear," she cried. "Marcia! Her ball. Marcia's ball tonight!"

Peppino roused himself a little.

"Ball? What ball?" he said. "No ball. Riseholme."

Lucia pushed by Georgie on the treble music stool,
without seeming to notice that he was there.

"No, dear, of course you won't go," she said. "But
do you know, I think I shall go up and pop in for an
hour. Georgie will come to dine with you, won't you,
Georgie, and you'll go to bed early. Half past six! Yes,
I can be in town by ten. That will be heaps of time. I

shall dress at Brompton Square. Just a sandwich to take with me and eat it in the car."

She wheeled round to Georgie, pressing the bell in her circumvolution.

"Marcia Whitby," she said. "Winding up the season. So easy to pop up there, and dear Marcia would be hurt if I didn't come. Let me see, shall I come back tomorrow, Peppino? Perhaps it would be simpler if I stayed up there and sent the car back. Then you could come up in comfort next day, and we would go on to Adele's together. I have a host of things to do in London tomorrow. That party at Aggie's. I will telephone to Aggie to say that I can come after all. My maid, my chauffeur," she said to the butler, rather in the style of Shylock. "I want my maid and my chauffeur and my car. Let him have his dinner quickly—no, he can get his dinner at Brompton Square. Tell him to come round at once."

Georgie sat positively aghast, for Lucia ran on like a thing demented. Mozart, Ouija, putting, the Elizabethan spit—all the simple joys of Riseholme fizzled out like damp fireworks. Gone, too, utterly gone was her need of complete rest; she had never been so full of raw, blatant, savage vitality.

"Dear Marcia," she said. "I felt it must be an oversight from the first, but naturally, Georgie, though she and I are such friends, I could not dream of reminding her. What a blessing that my delicious day at Riseholme has so rested me: I feel I could go to fifty balls without fatigue. Such a wonderful house, Georgie; when you come up to stay with us in the autumn, I must take you there. Peppino, is it not lucky that I only brought down here just enough for a couple of nights, and left everything in London to pick up as we came through to go to Adele's? What a sight it will be, all the royal family almost I believe, and the whole of the diplomatic corps; my Gioconda, I know, is going. Not a large ball though at all; not one of those great promiscuous affairs, which I hate so. How dear Marcia was besieged for invitations! How vulgar people are and how pushing! Good-by; mind you practise your Mozart, Georgie. Oh, and tell Daisy that I shan't be able to have another of those delicious puttings with her tomorrow. Back on Tuesday after the weekend at Adele's, and then weeks and weeks of dear Riseholme. How long they are! I will just go and hurry my maid up."

Georgie tripped off, as soon as she had gone, to see Daisy, and narrated to her open-mouthed disgust this amazing scene.

"And the question is," he said, "about the complete rest that was ordered her. I don't believe she was ordered any rest at all. I believe—"

Daisy gave a triumphant crow: inductive reasoning had led her to precisely the same point at precisely the same moment.

"Why, of course!" she said. "I always felt there was something behind that complete rest. I told you it meant something different. She wasn't asked, and so—"

"And so she came down here for rest," said Georgie in a loud voice. He was determined to bring that out first. "Because she wasn't asked—"

"And the moment she was asked she flew," said Daisy. "Nothing could be plainer. No more rest, thank you."

"She's wonderful," said Georgie. "Too interesting!"

• • •

Lucia sped through the summer evening on this errand of her own reprieve too excited to eat and too happy to wonder how it had happened like this. How wise, too, she had been to hold her tongue and give way to no passionate laments at her exclusion from the paradise toward which she was now hastening. Not one word of abuse had she uttered against Marcia; she had asked nobody to intercede; she had joined in all the talk about the ball as if she were going, and finally had made it impossible for herself to go by announcing that she had been ordered a few days of complete rest. She could (and would) explain her appearance perfectly: she had felt much better—doctors were such fussers— and at the last moment had made just a little effort, and here she was.

A loud explosion interrupted these agreeable reflections and the car drew up. A tire had burst, but they carried an extra wheel, and though the delay seemed terribly long, they were soon on their way again. They traversed another ten miles, and now in the northeast the smoldering glow of London reddened the toneless hue of the summer night. The stars burned bright, and she pictured Peppino at his telescope—no, Peppino had a really bad cold, and would not be at his telescope. Then there came another explosion—was it those disgusting stars in their courses that were fighting against her?—and again the car drew up by the side of the empty road.

"What has happened?" asked Lucia in a strangled voice.

"Another tire gone, ma'am," said the chauffeur. "Never knew such a thing."

Lucia looked at her clock. It was ten already, and she ought now to be in Brompton Square. There was no further wheel that could be put on, and the tire had to be taken off and mended. The minutes passed like hours. . . . Lucia, outwardly composed, sat on a rug at the edge of the road, and tried unsuccessfully not to curse Almighty Providence. The moon rose, like a gelatine lozenge.

She began to count the hours that intervened between the tragic present and, say, four o'clock in the morning, and she determined that whatever further disasters might befall, she would go to Whitby House, even if it was in a dustman's cart, so long as there was a chance of a single guest being left there. She would go. . . .

And all the time, if she had only known it, the stars were fighting not against her but for her. The tire was mended, and she got to Brompton Square at exactly a quarter past eleven. Cupboards were torn open, drawers ransacked, her goaded maid burst into tears. Aunt Amy's pearls were clasped round her neck, Peppino's hair in the shrine of gold sausage that had once been Beethoven's was pinned on, and at five minutes past twelve she hurried up the great stairs at Whitby House. Precisely as she came to the door of the ballroom, there emerged the head of the procession going down to supper. Marcia for a moment stared at her as if she were a ghost, but Lucia was so busy curtseying that she gave no thought to that. Seven times in rapid succession did she curtsey. It almost became a habit, and she nearly curtseyed to Adele who (so like Adele) followed immediately after.

"Just up from Riseholme, dearest Adele," she said. "I felt quite rested—How are you, Lord Tony?—and

so I made a little effort. Peppino urged me to come.
How nice to see your Excellency! Millie! Dearest Olga!
What a lot of friends! How is poor Princess Isabel?
Marcia looked so handsome. Brilliant! Such a delicious
drive; I felt I had to pop in. . . ."

9

POOR PEPPINO'S cold next day, instead of being better, was a good deal worse. He had aches and pains, and felt feverish, and sent for the doctor, who peremptorily ordered him to go to bed. There was nothing in the least to cause alarm, but it would be the height of folly to go to any weekend party at all. Bed.

Peppino telegraphed to Lady Brixton with many regrets for the unavoidable, and rang up Lucia. The state of his voice made it difficult to catch what he said, but she quite understood that there was nothing to be anxious about, and that he hoped she would go to Adele's without him. Her voice on the other hand was marvellously distinct, and he heard a great deal about the misfortunes which had come to so brilliant a conclusion last night. There followed a string of seven Christian names, and Lucia said a flashlight photograph had

245

been permitted during supper. She thought she was in
it, though rather in the background.

Lucia was very sorry for Peppino's indisposition,
but, as ordered, had no anxiety about him. She felt too,
that he wouldn't personally miss very much by being
prevented from coming to Adele's party, for it was to
be a very large party, and Peppino—bless him—occasionally got a little dazed at these brilliant gatherings.
He did not grasp who people were with the speed and
certainty which were needful, and he had been known
to grasp the hand of an eminent author and tell him
how much he had admired his fine picture at the
Academy. (Lucia constantly did that sort of thing herself, but then she got herself out of the holes she had
herself digged with so brilliant a maneuver that it
didn't matter, whereas Peppino was only dazed the
more by his misfortunes.) Moreover she knew that
Peppino's presence somehow hampered her style: she
could not be the brilliant mondaine, when his patient
but proud eye was on her, with quite the dash that
was hers when he was not there. There was always the
sense that he knew her best in her Riseholme incarna-
tion, in her duets with Georgie, and her rendering of
the slow movement of the "Moonlight Sonata," and her
grabbing of all Daisy's little stunts. She electrified him
as the superb butterfly, but the electrification was ac-
companied by slight shocks and surprises. When she
referred by her Christian name to some woman with
whom her only bond was that she had refused to dine
at Brompton Square, that puzzled Peppino. . . . In the
autumn she must be a little more serious, have some
quiet dinner parties of ordinary people, for really up
till now there had scarcely been an "ordinary" person

at Brompton Square at all, such noble lions of every species had been entrapped there. And Adele's party was to be of a very leonine kind; the smart world was to be there, and some highbrows and some politicians, and she was aware that she herself would have to do her very best, and be elusive, and pretend to know what she didn't know, and seem to swim in very distinguished currents. Dear Peppino wasn't up to that sort of thing, he couldn't grapple with it, and she grappled with it best without him. . . . At the moment of that vainglorious thought it is probable that Nemesis fixed her inexorable eye on Lucia.

Lucia unconscious of this deadly scrutiny turned to her immediate affairs. Her engagement book pleasantly informed her that she had many things to do on the day when the need for complete rest overtook her, and now she heralded through the telephone the glad tidings that she could lunch here and drop in there, and dine with Aggie. All went well with these restorations, and the day would be full, and tomorrow also, down to the hour of her departure for Adele's. Having despatched this agreeable business, she was on the point of ringing up Stephen, to fit him in for the spare three-quarters of an hour that was left, when she was rung up and it was Stephen's voice that greeted her.

"*Stephano mio,*" she said. "How did you guess I was back?"

"Because I rang up Riseholme first," said he, "and heard you had gone to town. Were you there last night?"

There was no cause to ask where "there" was. There had only been one place in London last night.

"Yes; delicious dance," said Lucia. "I was just going

to ring you up and see if you could come round for a chat at four forty-five, I am free till five thirty. Such fun it was. A flashlight photograph."

"No!" said Stephen in the Riseholme manner. "I long to hear about it. And were there really seven of them?"

"Quite," said Lucia magnificently.

"Wonderful! But four forty-five is no use for me. Can't you give me another time?"

"My dear, impossible," said Lucia. "You know what London is in these last days. Such a scrimmage."

"Well, we shall meet tomorrow then," said he.

"But, alas, I go to Adele's tomorrow," she said.

"Yes, but so do I," said Stephen. "She asked me this morning. I was wondering if you would drive me down, if you're going in your car. Would there be room for you and Peppino and me?"

Lucia rapidly reviewed the situation. It was perfectly clear to her that Adele had asked Stephen, at the last moment, to fill Peppino's place. But naturally she had not told him that, and Lucia determined not to do so either. It would spoil his pleasure (at least it would have spoiled hers) to know that. . . . And what a wonderful entry it would make for her—rather daring—to drive down alone with her lover. She could tell him about Peppino's indisposition tomorrow, as if it had just occurred.

"Yes, Stephano, heaps of room," she said. "Delighted. I'll call for you, shall I, on my way down, soon after three?"

"Angelic," he said. "What fun we shall have."

And it is probable that Nemesis at that precise moment licked her dry lips. "Fun!" thought Nemesis.

• • •

Marcia Whitby was of the party. She went down in the morning, and lunched alone with Adele. Their main topic of conversation was obvious.

"I saw her announcement in the *Morning Post*," said the infuriated Marcia, "that she had gone for a few days' complete rest into the country, and naturally I thought I was safe. I was determined she shouldn't come to my ball, and when I saw that, I thought she couldn't. So out of sheer good nature I sent her a card, so that she could tell everybody she had been asked. Never did I dream that there was a possibility of her coming. Instead of which, she made the most conspicuous entry that she could have made. I believe she timed it: I believe she waited on the stairs till she saw we were going down to supper."

"I wonder!" said Adele. "Genius, if it was that. She curtseyed seven times, too. I can't do that without loud cracks from my aged knees."

"And she stopped till the very end," said Marcia. "She was positively the last to go. I shall never do a kind thing again."

"You're horrid about her," said Adele. "Besides, what has she done? You asked her and she came. You don't rave at your guests for coming when they're asked. You wouldn't like it if none of them came."

"That's different," said Marcia. "I shouldn't wonder if she announced she was ordered complete rest in order that I should fall into her trap."

Adele sighed, but shook her head.

"Oh, my dear, that *would* have been magnificent," she said. "But I'm afraid I can't hope to believe that. I daresay she went into the country because you hadn't asked her, and that was pretty good. But the other, No. However, we'll ask Tony what he thinks."

"What's Tony got to do with it?" said Marcia.

"Why, he's even more wrapped up in her than I am," said Adele. "He thinks of nothing else."

Marcia was silent a moment. Then a sort of softer gleam came into her angry eye.

"Tell me some more about her," she said.

Adele clapped her hands.

"Ah, that's splendid," she said. "You're beginning to feel kinder. What we would do without our Lucia, I can't imagine. I don't know what there would be to talk about."

"She's ridiculous!" said Marcia, relapsing a little.

"No, you mustn't feel that," said Adele. "You mustn't laugh at her ever. You must just richly enjoy her."

"She's a snob!" said Marcia, as if this was a tremendous discovery.

"So am I; so are you; so are we all," said Adele. "We all run after distinguished people like—like Alf and Marcelle. The difference between you and Lucia is entirely in her favor, for you pretend you're not a snob, and she is perfectly frank and open about it. Besides, what is a duchess like you for except to give pleasure to snobs? That's your work in the world, darling; that's why you were sent here. Don't shirk it, or when you're old, you will suffer agonies of remorse. And you're a snob, too. You like having seven—or was it seventy?—royals at your dance."

"Well, tell me some more about Lucia," said Marcia, rather struck by this ingenious presentation of the case.

"Indeed, I will; I long for your conversion to Lucia-philism. Now today there are going to be marvellous happenings. You see Lucia has got a lover—"

"Quite absolutely impossible!" said Marcia firmly.

"Oh, don't interrupt. Of course he is only an official lover, a public lover, and his name is Stephen Merriall. A perfect lady. Now Peppino, Lucia's husband, was coming down with her today, but he's got a very bad cold and has put me off. I'm rather glad; Lucia has got more—more dash when he's not there. So I've asked her lover instead—"

"No!" said Marcia. "Go on."

"My dear, they are much better than any play I have ever seen. They do it beautifully; they give each other little glances and smiles, and then begin to talk hurriedly to someone else. Of course, they're both as chaste as snow, chaster if possible. I think poor Babs's case put it into Lucia's head that in this naughty world it gave a *cachet* to a woman to have the reputation of having a lover. So safe, too: there's nothing to expose. They only behave like lovers strictly in public. I was terrified when it began that Mr. Merriall would think she meant something, and try to kiss her when they were alone, and so rub the delicate bloom completely off, but I'm sure he's tumbled to it."

"How perfect!" said Marcia.

"Isn't it? Aren't you feeling more Luciaphil? I'm sure you are. You must enjoy her; it shows such a want of humor to be annoyed with her. And really I've taken a great deal of trouble to get people she will revel in. There's the Prime Minister; there's you; there's Greatorex the pianist who's the only person who can play Stravinski; there's Professor Bonstetter the psychoanalyst; there's the Italian Ambassador, there's her lover; there's Tony. . . . I can't go on. Oh, and I must remember to tell her that Archie Singleton is Babs's brother, or she may say something dreadful.

And then there are lots who will revel in Lucia, and I the foremost. I'm devoted to her; I am really, Marcia. She's got character; she's got an iron will; and I like strong talkative women so much better than strong silent men."

"Yes, she's got will," said Marcia. "She determined to come to my ball, and she came. I allow I gave her the chance."

"Those are the chances that come to gifted people," said Adele. "They don't come to ordinary people."

"Suppose I flirted violently with her lover?" said Marcia.

Adele's eyes grew bright with thought.

"I can't imagine what she would do," she said. "But I'm sure she would do something that scored. Otherwise she wouldn't be Lucia. But you mustn't do it."

"Just one evening," said Marcia. "Just for an hour or two. It's not poaching, you see, because her lover isn't her lover. He's just a stunt."

Adele wavered.

"It would be wonderful to know what she would do," she said. "And it's true that he's only a stunt. . . . Perhaps for an hour or two tomorrow, and then give him back."

Adele did not expect any of her guests till teatime, and Marcia and she both retired for after-lunch siestas. Adele had been down here for the last four or five days, driving up to Marcia's ball and back in the very early morning, and had three days before settled everything in connection with her party, assigning rooms, discussing questions of high importance with her chef, and arranging to meet as many trains as possible. It so happened, therefore, that Stephen Merriall, since the house was full, was to occupy the spacious dressing room, furnished as a bedroom, next to Lucia's room, which had been originally allotted to Peppino. Adele had told her butler that Mr. Lucas was not coming, but that his room would be occupied by Mr. Merriall, thought no more about it, and omitted to substitute a new card on his door. These two rooms were halfway down a long corridor of bedrooms and bathrooms that ran the whole length of the house, a spacious oak-boarded corridor, rather dark, with the broad staircase coming up at the end of it. Below was the suite of public rooms, a library at the end, a big music room, a long gallery of a drawing room, and the dining room. These all opened on to a paved terrace overlooking the gardens and tennis courts, and it was here, with the shadow of the house lying coolly across it, that her guests began to assemble. In ones and twos they gathered, some motoring down from London, others arriving by train, and it was not till there were some dozen of them, among whom were the most fervent Luciaphils, that the object of their devotion, attended by her lover, made her appearance, evidently at the top of her form.

"Dearest Adele," she said. "How delicious to get into the cool country again. Marcia dear! Such adventures I had on my way up to your ball: two burst tires; I thought I should never get there. How are you, your Excellency? I saw you at the Duchess's, but couldn't get a word with you. Aggie darling! Ah, Lord Tony! Yes, a cup of tea would be delicious; no sugar, Stephen, thanks."

Lucia had not noticed quite everybody. There were one or two people rather retired from the tea table, but they did not seem to be of much importance, and certainly the Prime Minister was not among them. Stephen hovered, loverlike, just behind her chair, and she turned to the Italian Ambassador.

"I was afraid of a motor accident all the way down," she said, "because last night I dreamed I broke a looking glass. Quaint things dreams are, though really the psychoanalysts who interpret them are quainter. I went to a meeting at Sophy's, dear Sophy Alingsby, the other day—your Excellency I am sure knows Sophy Alingsby—and heard a lecture on it. Let me see: boiled rabbit, if you dream of boiled rabbit—"

Lucia suddenly became aware of a sort of tension. Just a tension. She looked quickly round, and recognized one of the men she had not paid much attention to. She sprang from her chair.

"Professor Bonstetter," she said. "How are you? I know you won't remember me, but I did have the honor of shaking hands with you after your enthralling lecture the other day. Do come and tell his Excellency and me a little more about it. There were so many questions I longed to ask you."

Adele wanted to applaud, but she had to be content with catching Marcia's eye. Was Lucia great, or was she not? Stephen, too; how exactly right she was to hand him her empty cup when she had finished with it, without a word, and how perfectly he took it! "More?" he said, and Lucia just shook her head without withdrawing her attention from Professor Bonstetter. Then the Prime Minister arrived, and she said how lovely Chequers must be looking. She did not annex him; she just hovered and hinted, and made no direct suggestion; and sure enough, within five minutes he had asked her if she knew Chequers. Of course she did, but only as a tourist—and so one thing led to another. It

would be a nice break in her long drive down to Riseholme on Tuesday to lunch at Chequers, and not more
than forty miles out of her way.

People dispersed and strolled on the terrace, and
gathered again, and some went off to their rooms. Lucia had one little turn up and down with the Ambassador, and spoke with great tact of Mussolini, and
another with Lord Tony, and not for a long time did
she let Stephen join her. But then they wandered off
into the garden, and were seen standing very close together and arguing publicly about a flower, and Lucia,
seeing they were observed, called to Adele to know if it
wasn't Dropmore Borage. They came back very soon,
and Stephen went up to his room while Lucia remained
downstairs. Adele showed her the library and the
music room, and the long drawing room, and then vanished. Lucia gravitated to the music room, opened the
piano, and began the slow movement of the "Moonlight Sonata."

About halfway through it, she became aware that
somebody had come into the room. But her eyes were
fixed dreamily on the usual point at the edge of the
ceiling, and her fingers faultlessly doled out the slow
triplets. She gave a little sigh when she had finished,
pressed her fingers to her eyes, and slowly awoke, as
from some melodious anesthetic.

It was a man who had come in and who had seated
himself not far from the keyboard.

"Charming!" he said. "Thank you."

Lucia didn't remember seeing him on the terrace;
perhaps he had only just arrived. She had a vague idea,
however, that whether on the terrace or elsewhere, she
had seen him before. She gave a pretty little start. "Ah,
I had no idea I had an audience," she said. "I should

never have ventured to go on playing. So dreadfully
out of practice."

"Please have a little more practice then," said the
polite stranger.

She ran her hands, butterfly fashion, over the keys.

"A little morsel of Stravinski?" she said.

It was in the middle of the morsel that Adele came
in and found Lucia playing Stravinski to Mr.
Greatorex. The position seemed to be away, away beyond her orbit altogether, and she merely waited with
undiminished faith in Lucia, to see what would happen
when Lucia became aware of to whom she was playing. . . . It was a longish morsel, too: more like a
meal than a morsel, and it was also remarkably like a
muddle. Finally, Lucia made an optimistic attempt at
the double chromatic scale in divergent directions
which brought it to an end, and laughed gaily.

"My poor fingers," she said. "Delicious piano, dear
Adele. I love a Bechstein; that was a little morsel of
Stravinski. Hectic perhaps, do you think? But so true
to the modern idea: little feverish excursions, little bits
of tunes, and nothing worked out. But I always say
that there is something in Stravinski, if you study him.
How I worked on that little piece, and I'm afraid it's
far from perfect yet."

Lucia played one more little run with her right hand,
while she cudgelled her brain to remember where she
had seen this man before, and turned round on the
music stool. She felt sure he was an artist of some
kind, and she did not want to ask Adele to introduce
him, for that would look as if she did not know everybody. She tried pictures next.

"In Art I always think that the Stravinski school is
represented by the post-cubists," she said. "They give

us pattern in lines, just as Stravinski gives us patterns in notes, and the modern poet patterns in words. At Sophy Alingsby's the other night we had a feast of patterns. Dear Sophy—what a curious mixture of tastes! She cares only for the ultra-primitive in music, and the ultra-modern in art. Just before you came in, Adele, I was trying to remember the first movement of Beethoven's "Moonlight," those triplets though they look easy have to be kept so level. And yet Sophy considers Beethoven a positive decadent. I ought to have taken her to Diva's little concert—Diva Dalrymple—for I assure you really that Stravinski sounded classical compared to the rest of the program. It was very creditably placed, too. Mr."—what was his name?—"Mr. Greatorex."

She had actually said the word before her brain made the connection. She gave her little peal of laughter.

"Ah, you wicked people," she cried. "A plot—clearly a plot. Mr. Greatorex, how could you? Adele told you to come in here when she heard me begin my little strummings, and told you to sit down and encourage me. Don't deny it, Adele! I know it was like that. I shall tell everybody how unkind you've been, unless Mr. Greatorex sits down instantly and magically restores to life what I have just murdered."

Adele denied nothing. In fact there was no time to deny anything, for Lucia positively thrust Mr. Greatorex on to the music stool, and instantly put on her rapt musical face, chin in hand, and eyes looking dreamily upward. There was Nemesis, you would have thought, dealing thrusts at her, but Nemesis was no match for her amazing quickness. She parried and thrust again, and here—what richness of future reminiscence—was Mr. Greatorex playing Stravinski to her, before no audience but herself and Adele, who really didn't count for the only tune she liked was "Land of Hope and Glory." . . . Great was Lucia!

Adele left the two, warning them that it was getting on for dressing time, but there was some more Stravinski first, for Lucia's sole ear. Adele had told her the direction of her room, and said her name was on the door, and Lucia found it at once. A beautiful room it was, with a bathroom on one side, and a magnificent Charles II bed draped at the back with woolwork tapestry. It was a little late for Lucia's Elizabethan taste, and she noticed that the big wardrobe was Chippendale, which was later still. There was a Chinese paper on the wall, and fine Persian rugs on the floor, and though she could have criticized, it was easy to admire. And there for herself was a very smart dress, and for decoration Aunt Amy's pearls, and the Beethoven brooch. But she decided to avoid all possible chance of competition, and put the pearls back into her jewel case. The Beethoven brooch, she was sure, need fear no rival.

Lucia felt that dinner, as far as she went, was a huge success. Stephen was seated just opposite her, and now and then she exchanged little distant smiles with him. Next her on one side was Lord Tony, who adored her story about Stravinski and Greatorex. She told him also what the Italian Ambassador had said about Mussolini, and the Prime Minister about Chequers: she was going to pop in to lunch on her way down to Riseholme after this delicious party. Then conversation shifted, and she turned left, and talked to the only man whose identity she had not grasped. But, as matter of public knowledge, she began about poor Babs and her own admiration of her demeanor at that wicked trial, which had ended so disastrously. And once again there was slight tension.

Bridge and Mah-Jong followed, and rich allusive conversation and the sense, so dear to Lucia, of being in the very center of everything that was distinguished. When the women went upstairs, she hurried to her room, made a swift change into greater simplicity, and by invitation, sought out Marcia's room, at the far end of the passage, for a chat. Adele was there, and dear (rather common) Aggie was there, and Aggie was being just a shade sycophantic over the six rows of Whitby pearls. Lucia was glad she had limited her splendors to the Beethoven brooch.

"But why didn't you wear your pearls, Lucia?" asked Adele. "I was hoping to see them." (She had heard talk of Aunt Amy's pearls, but had not noticed them on the night of Marcia's ball.)

"My little seedlings!" said Lucia. "Just seedlings, compared to Marcia's marbles. Little trumperies!"

Aggie had seen them, and she knew Lucia did not overstate their minuteness. Like a true Luciaphil, she changed a subject that might prove embarrassing.

"Take away your baubles, Marcia," said Aggie. "They are only diseases of a common shellfish which you eat when it's healthy and wear when it's got a tumor. . . . How wretched it is to think that all of us aren't going to meet day after day as we have been doing! There's Adele going to America, and there's Marcia going to Scotland—what a foul spot, Marcia, come to Marienbad instead with me. And what are you going to do, Lucia?"

"Oh, my dear, how I wanted to go to Aix or Marienbad," she said. "But my Peppino says it's impossible.

We've got to stop quiet at Riseholme. Shekels, tiresome shekels."

"There she goes, talking about Riseholme as if it was some dreadful penance to go there," said Adele. "You adore Riseholme, Lucia; at least if you don't, you ought to. Olga raves about it. She says she's never really happy away from it. When are you going to ask me there?"

"Adele, as if you didn't know that you weren't always welcome," said Lucia.

"Me, too," said Marcia.

"A standing invitation to both of you always," said Lucia. "Dear Marcia, how sweet of you to want to come! I go there on Tuesday, and there I remain. But it's true; I do adore it. No balls, no parties, and such dear Arcadians. You couldn't believe in them without seeing them. Life at its very simplest, dears."

"It can't be simpler than Scotland," said Marcia. "In Scotland you kill birds and fish all day, and eat them at night. That's all."

Lucia through these months of strenuous effort had never perhaps felt herself so amply rewarded as she was at this moment. All evening she had talked in an effortless dishabille of mind to the great ones of the country, the noble, the distinguished, the accomplished, and now here she was in a duchess's bedroom having a good-night talk. This was nearer Nirvana than even Marcia's ball. And the three women there seemed to be grouped round her; they waited—there was no mistaking it—listening for something from her, just as Riseholme used to wait for her lead. She felt that she was truly attaining, and put her chin in her hand and looked a little upward.

"I shall get tremendously put in my place when I go

back to Riseholme again," she said. "I'm sure Riseholme thinks I have been wasting my time in idle frivolities. It sees perhaps in an evening paper that I have been to Aggie's party, or Adele's house, or Marcia's ball, and I assure you it will be very suspicious of me. Just as if I didn't know that all these delightful things were symbols."

Adele had got the cataleptic look of a figure in a stained-glass window, so rapt she was. But she wanted to grasp this with full appreciation.

"Lucia, don't be so dreadfully clever," she said. "You're talking high over my head; you're like the whirr of an airplane. Explain what you mean by symbols."

"My dear, you know," she said. "All our runnings about, all our gaieties, are symbols of affection; we love to see each other because we partake of each other. Interesting people, distinguished people, obscure people, ordinary people, we long to bring them all into our lives in order to widen our horizons. We learn, or we try to learn, of other interests besides our own. I shall have to make Riseholme understand that dear little Alf, playing the flute at my house, or half a dozen princes eating quails at Marcia's mansion, it's all the same, isn't it? We get to know the point of view of prizefighters and princes. And it seems to me, it seems to me—"

Lucia's gaze grew a shade more lost and aloof.

"It seems to me that we extend our very souls," she said, "by letting them flow into other lives. How badly I put it! But when Eric Greatorex—so charming of him—played those delicious pieces of Stravinski to me before dinner, I felt I was stepping over some sort of frontier *into* Stravinski. Eric made out my passport. A multiplication of experience. I think that is what I mean."

None of those present could have said with any precision what Lucia had meant, but the general drift seemed to be that an hour with a burglar or a cannibal was valuable for the amplification of the soul.

"Odd types, too," she said. "How good for one to be put into touch with something quite remote. Marcelle—Marcelle Periscope—you met him at my house, didn't you, Aggie—"

"Why wasn't I asked?" said Marcia.

Lucia gave a little quick smile, as at some sweet child's interruption.

"Darling Marcia, why didn't you propose yourself? Surely you know me well enough to do that. Yes, Marcelle, a cinema artist. A fresh horizon, a fresh attitude toward life. So good for me: it helps me not to be narrow. *Dio mio!* how I pray I shall never be narrow. To be shocked, too! How shocking to be shocked. If you all had fifty lovers apiece, I should merely think it a privilege to know about them all."

Marcia longed, with almost the imperativeness of a longing to sneeze, to allude directly to Stephen. She raised her eyes for a half second to Adele, the priestess of this cult in which she knew she was rapidly becoming a worshipper, but if ever an emphatic negative was wordlessly bawled at a tentative enquirer, it was bawled now. If Lucia chose to say anything about Stephen it would indeed be manna, but to ask—never! Aggie, seated sideways to them, had not seen this telegraphy, and spoke unwisely with her lips.

"If an ordinary good-looking woman," she said, "tells me that she hasn't got a lover or a man who wants to be her lover, I always say, 'You lie!' So she does. You shall begin, Lucia, about your lovers."

Nothing could have been more unfortunate. Adele could have hurled the entire six rows of the Whitby pearls at Aggie's face. Lucia had no lover, but only the wraith of a lover, on whom direct light must never be flashed. Such a little reflection should have shown Aggie that. The effect of her carelessness was that Lucia became visibly embarrassed, looked at the clock, and got up in a violent hurry.

"Good gracious me!" she said. "What a time of night! Who could have thought that our little chat had lasted so long? Yes, dear Adele, I know my room, on the left with my name on the door. Don't dream of coming to show it me."

Lucia distributed little pressures and kisses and clingings, and holding her very smart pale-blue wrapper close about her, slid noiselessly out in her slippers into the corridor. It was late; the house was quite quiet; for a quarter of an hour they had heard the creaking of men's footsteps going to their rooms. The main lights had been put out; only here and there down the long silent aisle there burned a single small illumination. Past half a dozen doors Lucia tiptoed, until she came to one on which she could just see the name Philip Lucas preceded by a dim hieroglyph which of course was "Mrs." She turned the handle and went in.

Two yards in front of her, by the side of the bed, was standing Stephen, voluptuous in honey-colored pyjamas. For one awful second—for she felt sure this was her room *(and so did he)*—they stared at each other in dead silence.

"How dare you?" said Stephen, so agitated that he could scarcely form the syllables.

"And how dare *you?*" hissed Lucia. "Go out of. my room instantly."

"Get out of mine!" said Stephen.

Lucia's indignant eye left his horror-stricken face and swept round the room. There was no Chinese paper on the wall, but a pretty Morris paper; there was no Charles II bed with tapestry, but a brass-testered couch; there was no Chippendale wardrobe, but something useful from Tottenham Court Road. She gave one little squeal, of a pitch between the music of the slate pencil and of the bat, and closed his door again. She staggered on to the next room where again the legend "Philip Lucas" was legible, popped in, and locked the door. She hurried to the door of communication between this and the fatal chamber next it, and as she locked that also, she heard from the other side of it the bolt violently pulled forward.

She sat down on her bed in a state of painful agitation. Her excursion into the fatal chamber had been an awful, a hideous mistake; none knew that better than herself, but how was she to explain that to her lover? For weeks they had been advertising the guilt of their blameless relationship, and now it seemed to her impossible ever to resume it. Every time she gave Stephen one of those little smiles or glances, at which she had become so perfect an adept, there would start into her mind that moment of speechless horror, and her smile would turn to a tragic grimace, and her sick glance recoil from him. Worse than that, how was she ever to speak of it to him, or passionately protest her innocence? He had thought that she had come to his room (indeed she had) when the house was quiet, on the sinister errand of love, and though, when he had repudiated her, she had followed suit, she saw the recoiling indignation of her lover. If only, just now, she had kept her head, if only she had said at once, "I beg your pardon, I mistook my room," all might have been well, but how nerve herself to say it afterward? And in spite of the entire integrity of her moral nature, which was puritanical to the verge of prudishness, she had not liked (no woman could) his unfeigned horror at her irruption.

Stephen next door was in little better plight. He had had a severe shock. For weeks Lucia had encouraged him to play the lover, and had (so he awfully asked himself) this pleasant public stunt become a reality to her, a need of her nature? She had made it appear, when he so rightly repulsed her, that she had come to his room by mistake, but was that pretence? Had she really come with a terrible motive? It was her business, anyhow, to explain, and insist on her innocence, if she was innocent, and he would only be too thankful to believe her. But at present and without that, the idea of resuming the public loverlike demeanor was frankly beyond him. She might be encouraged again. . . . Though now he was safe with locked and bolted doors, he knew he would not be able to sleep, and he took a large dose of aspirin.

Lucia was far more thorough; she never shelved difficulties, but faced them. She still sat on the edge of her bed, long after Stephen's nerves were quieted, and as she herself calmed down, thought it all out. For the present, loverlike relations in public were impossible, and it was lucky that in a couple of days more she would be interned at Riseholme. Then, with a flash of genius, there occurred to her the interesting attitude to

adopt in the interval. She would give the impression
that there had been a lovers' quarrel. The more she
thought of that, the more it commended itself to her.
People would notice it, and wonder what it was all
about, and their curiosity would never be gratified, for
Lucia felt sure, from the horror depicted on Stephen's
face, that he as well as she would be for ever dumb on
the subject of that midnight encounter. She must not
look unhappy; she must on the other hand be more
vivid and eager than ever, and just completely ignore
Stephen. But there would be no lift for him in her car
back to London; he would have to go by train.

The ex-lovers both came down very late next day,
for fear of meeting each other alone, and thus they sat
in adjoining rooms half the morning. Stephen had some
Hermione-work on hand, for this party would run to
several paragraphs, but, however many it ran to, Hermione was utterly determined not to mention Lucia in
any of them. Hermione knew, however, that Mr. Stephen Merriall was there, and said so. . . . By one of
those malignant strokes, which are rained on those
whom Nemesis desires to chastise, they came out of
their rooms at precisely the same moment, and had to
walk downstairs together, coldly congratulating each
other on the beauty of the morning. Luckily there were
people on the terrace, among whom was Marcia. She
thought this was an excellent opportunity for beginning
her flirtation with Stephen, and instantly carried him
off to the kitchen garden, for unless she ate gooseberries on Sunday morning she died. Lucia seemed sub-
limely unaware of their departure, and joined a select
little group round the Prime Minister. Between a dis-
cussion of the housing problem with him, a stroll with

Lord Tony, who begged her to drop the "lord," and a little more Stravinski alone with Greatorex, the short morning passed very agreeably. But she saw when she went into lunch rather late that Marcia and Stephen had not returned from their gooseberrying. There was a gap of just three places at the table, and it thus became a certainty that Stephen would sit next her.

Lunch was fully half over before they appeared, Marcia profusely apologetic.

"Wretchedly rude of me, dear Adele," she said, "but we had no idea it was so late, did we, Mr. Merriall? We went to the gooseberries, and—and I suppose we must have stopped there. Your fault, Mr. Merriall; you men have no idea of time."

"Who could, Duchess, when he was with you?" said Stephen most adroitly.

"Sweet of you," said she. "Now do go on. You were in the middle of telling me something quite thrilling. And please, Adele, let nobody wait for us. I see you are all at the end of lunch, and I haven't begun, and gooseberries, as usual, have given me an enormous appetite. Yes, Mr. Merriall?"

Adele looked in vain, when throughout the afternoon Marcia continued in possession of Lucia's lover, for the smallest sign of resentment or uneasiness on her part. There was simply none; it was impossible to detect a thing that had no existence. Lucia seemed completely unconscious of any annexation, or indeed of Stephen's existence. There she sat, just now with Tony and herself, talking of Marcia's ball, and the last volume of risqué memoirs, of which she had read a review in the Sunday paper, and Sophy's black room and Alf; never had she been more equipped at all points, more prosperously central. Marcia, thought Adele, was being

wonderfully worsted, if she imagined she could produce
any sign of emotion on Lucia's part. The lovers understood each other too well. . . . Or, she suddenly conjectured, had they quarrelled? It really looked rather
like it. Though she and Tony were having a good Luciaphil meeting, she almost wanted Lucia to go away, in
order to go into committee over this entrancing possibility. And how naturally she Tony'd him; she must
have been practising on her maid.

Somewhere in the house a telephone bell rang, and a
footman came out on to the terrace.

"Lucia, I know that's for you," said Adele. "Wherever you are, somebody wants you on the telephone. If
you were in the middle of the Sahara, a telephone
would ring for you from the sands of the desert. Yes?
Who is it for?" she said to the footman.

"Mrs. Lucas, my lady," he said.

Lucia got up, quite delighted.

"You're always chaffing me, Adele," she said.
"What a nuisance the telephone is. One never gets a
rest from it. But I won't be a moment."

She tripped off.

"Tony, there's a great deal to talk about," said
Adele quickly. "Now what's the situation between the
lovers? Perfect understanding or a quarrel? And who
has been ringing her up? What would you bet that it
was—"

"Alf," said Tony.

"I wonder. Tony, about the lovers. There's something. I never saw such superb indifference. How I
shall laugh at Marcia. She's producing no effect at all.
Lucia doesn't take the slightest notice. I knew she
would be great. Last night we had a wonderful talk in

Marcia's room, till Aggie was an ass. There she is again. Now we shall know."

Lucia came quickly along the terrace.

"Adele dear," she said. "Would it be dreadful of me if I left this afternoon? They've rung me up from Rise-holme. Georgie rang me up. My Peppino is very far from well. Nothing really anxious; but he's in bed and he's alone. I think I had better go."

"Oh, my dear," said Adele, "of course you shall do precisely as you wish. I'm dreadfully sorry; so shall we all be if you go. But if you feel you would be easier in your mind—"

Lucia looked around on all the brilliant little groups. She was leaving the most wonderful party: it was the highest perch she had reached yet. On the other hand, she was leaving her lover, which was a compensation. But she truly didn't think of any of these things.

"My poor old Peppino," she said. "I must go, Adele."

10

Today, the last of August, Peppino had been allowed for the first time to go out and have a half-hour's quiet strolling in the garden and sit in the sun. His illness which had caused Lucia to recall herself had been serious, and for a few days he had been dangerously ill with pneumonia. After turning a bad corner, he had made satisfactory progress.

Lucia, who for these weeks had been wholly admirable, would have gone out with him now, but the doctor, after his visit, had said he wanted to have a talk with her, and for twenty minutes or so they had held colloquy in the music room. Then, on his departure, she sat there a few minutes more, arranged her ideas, and went to join Peppino.

"Such a good cheering talk, *caro*," she said. "There never was such a perfect convalescer—my dear, what a word—as you. You're a prize patient. All you've got to do is to go on exactly as you're going, doing a little more, and a little more every day, and in a month's time you'll be ever so strong again. Such a good constitution."

"And no sea voyage?" asked Peppino. The dread prospect had been dangled before him at one time.

"Not unless they think a month or two on the Riviera in the winter might be advisable. Then the sea voyage from Dover to Calais, but no more than that. Now I know what you're thinking about. You told me that we couldn't manage Aix this August because of expense, so how are we to manage two months of Cannes?"

Lucia paused a moment.

"That delicious story of dear Marcia's," she said, "about those cousins of hers who had to retrench. After talking everything over, they decided that all the retrenchment they could possibly make was to have no coffee after lunch. But we can manage better than that. . . ."

Lucia paused again. Peppino had had enough of movement under his own steam, and they had seated themselves in the sunny little arbor by the sundial, which had so many appropriate mottoes carved on it.

"The doctor told me, too, that it would be most unwise of you to attempt to live in London for any solid period," she said. "Fogs, sunlessness, damp darkness—all bad. And I know again what's in your kind head. You think I adore London, and can spend a month or two there in the autumn, and in the spring, coming down here for weekends. But I haven't the slightest intention of doing anything of the kind. I'm not going to be up there alone. Besides, where are the dibs, as that sweet little Alf said, where are the dibs to come from for our Riviera?"

"Let the house for the winter then?" said Peppino.

"Excellent idea, if we could be certain of letting it. But we can't be certain of letting it, and all the time a stream of rates and taxes, and caretakers. It would be wretched to be always anxious about it, and always counting the dibs. I've been going into what we spent there this summer, *caro,* and it staggered me. What I vote for is to sell it. I'm not going to use it without you, and you're not going to use it at all. You know how I looked forward to being there for your sake, your club, the Reading Room at the British Museum, the Astronomer Royal, but now that's all kaput, as Tony says. We'll bring down here anything that's particularly connected with dear Auntie: her portrait by Sargent, of course, though Sargents are fetching immense prices; or the walnut bureau, or the Chippendale chairs, or that little worsted rug in her bedroom; but I vote for selling it all, freehold, furniture, everything. As if I couldn't go up to Claridge's now and then, when I want to have a luncheon party or two of all our friends! And then we shall have no more anxieties, and if they say you must get away from the cold and the damp, we shall know we're doing nothing on the margin of our means. That would be hateful; we mustn't do that."

"But you'll never be able to be content with Riseholme again," said Peppino. "After your balls and your parties and all that, what will you find to do here?"

Lucia turned her gimlet eye on him.

"I shall be a great fool if I don't find something to do," she said. "Was I so idle and unoccupied before we went to London? Good gracious, I was always worked to death here. Don't you bother your head about that, Peppino, for if you do, it will show you don't understand me at all. And our dear Riseholme, let me tell you, has got very slack and inert in our absence, and I feel very guilty about that. There's nothing going on: there's none of the old fizz and bubble and Excelsior there used to be. They're vegetating; they're dry-rotting; and Georgie's getting fat. There's never any news. All that happens is that Daisy slashes a golf ball about the green for practice in the morning, and then goes down to the links in the afternoon, and positively the only news next day is whether she has been round under a thousand strokes, whatever that means."

Lucia gave a little indulgent sigh.

"Dear Daisy has ideas sometimes," she said, "and I don't deny that. She had the idea of Ouija; she had the idea of the Museum; and though she said that came from Abfou, she had the idea of Abfou. Also she had the idea of golf. But she doesn't carry her ideas out in a vivid manner that excites interest and keeps people on the boil. On the boil! That's what we all ought to be, with a thousand things to do that seem immensely important and which are important because they seem so. You want a certain touch to give importance to things, which dear Daisy hasn't got. Whatever poor Daisy does seems trivial. But they shall see that I've come home. What does it matter to me whether it's Marcia's ball, or playing Alf's accompaniments, or playing golf with Daisy, or playing duets with poor dear Georgie, whose fingers have all become thumbs, so long as I find it thrilling? If I find it dull, *caro*, I shall be, as Adele once said, a bloody fool. Dear Adele, she has always that little vein of coarseness."

Lucia encountered more opposition from Peppino

than she anticipated, for he had taken a huge pride in her triumphant summer campaign in London, and though at times he had felt bewildered and buffeted in this high gale of social activity, and had, so to speak, to close his streaming eyes and hold his hat on, he gloried in the incessant and tireless blowing of it, which stripped the choicest fruits from the trees. He thought they could manage, without encroaching on financial margins, to keep the house open for another year yet, anyhow: he acknowledged that he had been unduly pessimistic about going to Aix; he even alluded to the memories of Aunt Amy which were twined about 25 Brompton Square, and which he would be so sorry to sever. But Lucia, in that talk with his doctor, had made up her mind: she rejected at once the idea of pursuing her victorious career in London if all the time she would have to be careful and thrifty, and if, far more importantly, she would be leaving Peppino down at Riseholme. That was not to be thought of—affection no less than decency made it impossible—and so having made up her mind, she set about the attainment of her object with all her usual energy. She knew, too, the value of incessant attack: smash little Alf, for instance, when he had landed a useful blow on his opponent's face, did not wait for him to recover, but instantly followed it up with another and yet another till his victim collapsed and was counted out. Lucia behaved in precisely the same way with Peppino; she produced rows of figures to show they were living beyond their means: she quoted (or invented) something the Prime Minister had said about the probability of an increase in income tax: she assumed that they would go to the Riviera for certain, and was appalled at the price of tickets in the Blue Train, and of the tariff at hotels.

"And with all our friends in London, Peppino," she said in the decisive round of these combats, "who are longing to come down to Riseholme and spend a week with us, our expenses here will go up. You mustn't forget that. We shall be having a succession of visitors in October, and indeed till we go south. Then there's the meadow at the bottom of the garden; you've not bought that yet, and on that I really have set my heart. A spring garden there. A profusion of daffodils, and a paved walk. You promised me that. I described what it would be like to Tony, and he is wildly jealous. I'm sure I don't wonder. Your new telescope, too. I insist on that telescope, and I'm sure I don't know where the money's to come from. My dear old piano also: it's on its very last legs, and won't last much longer, and I know you don't expect me to live, literally keep alive, without a good piano in the house."

Peppino was weakening. Even when he was perfectly well and strong, he was no match for her, and this rain of blows was visibly staggering him.

"I don't want to urge you, *caro*," she continued. "You know I never urge you to do what you don't feel is best."

"But you are urging me," said Peppino.

"Only to do what you feel is best. As for the memories of Aunt Amy in Brompton Square, you must not allow false sentiment to come in. You never saw her there since you were a boy, and if you brought down here her portrait, and the woolwork rug which you remember her putting over her knees, I should say, without urging you, mind, that that was ample. . . . What a sweet morning! Come to the end of the garden and imagine what the meadow will look like with a paved walk and a blaze of daffodils. . . . The Chippendale chairs, I think I should sell."

Lucia did not really want Aunt Amy's portrait either, for she was aware she had said a good deal from time to time about Aunt Amy's pearls, which were there, a little collar of very little seeds, faultlessly portrayed. But then Georgie had seen them on the night of the opera, and Lucia felt that she knew Riseholme very poorly if it was not perfectly acquainted by now with the nature and minuteness of Aunt Amy's pearls. The pearls had better be sold, too, and also, she thought, her own portrait by Sigismund, for the post-cubists were not making much of a mark.

The determining factor in her mind, over this abandonment of her London career, to which in a few days, by incessant battering, she had got Peppino to consent, was Peppino himself. He could not be with her in London, and she could not leave him week after week (for nothing less than that, if you were to make any solid progress in London, was any good) alone in Riseholme. But a large factor, also, was the discovery of how little at present she counted for in Riseholme, and that could not be tolerated. Riseholme had deposed her; Riseholme was not intending to be managed by her from Brompton Square. The throne was vacant, for poor Daisy, and for the matter of that poor Georgie, were not the sort of people who could occupy thrones at all. She longed to queen it there again, and though she was aware that her utmost energies would be required, what were energies for except to get you what you wanted?

Just now she was nothing in Riseholme: they had been sorry for her because Peppino had been so ill, but as his steady convalescence proceeded, and she began to ring people up, and pop in, and make plans for them, she became aware that she mattered no more than Piggy and Goosie. . . . There on the green, as she saw from the window of her hall, was Daisy, whirling her arms madly, and hitting a ball with a stick which had a steel blade at the end, and Georgie, she was rather horrified to observe, was there, too, trying to do the same. Was Daisy reaping the reward of her persistence, and getting somebody interested in golf? And, good heavens, there were Piggy and Goosie also smacking away. Riseholme was clearly devoting itself to golf.

"I shall have to take to golf," thought Lucia. "What a bore! Such a foolish game."

At this moment a small white ball bounded over her yew hedge, and tapped smartly against the front door.

"What an immense distance to have hit a ball," she thought. "I wonder which of them did that?"

It was soon clear, for Daisy came tripping through the garden after it, and Lucia, all smiles, went out to meet her.

"Good morning, dear Daisy," she said. "Did you hit that ball that immense distance? How wonderful! No harm done at all. But what a splendid player you must be!"

"So sorry," panted Daisy, "but I thought I would have a hit with a driver. Very wrong of me; I had no idea it would go so far or so crooked."

"A marvellous shot," said Lucia. "I remember how beautifully you putted. And this is all part of golf, too? Do let me see you do it again."

Daisy could not reproduce that particular masterpiece, but she sent the ball high in the air, or skimming along the ground, and explained that one was a lofted shot, and the other a wind-cheater.

"I like the wind-cheater best," said Lucia. "Do let me see if I can do that."

She missed the ball once or twice, and then made a lovely wind-cheater, only this time Daisy called it a top. Daisy had three clubs, two of which she put down when she used the third, and then forgot about them, so that they had to go back for them. . . . And up came Georgie, who was making wind-cheaters, too.

"Good morning, Lucia," he said. "It's so tarsome not to be able to hit the ball, but it's great fun if you do. Have you put down your clock golf yet? There, didn't that go?"

Lucia had forgotten all about the clock golf. It was somewhere in what was called the "game cupboard," which contained bowls (as being Elizabethan) and some old tennis rackets, and a cricket bat Peppino had used at school.

"I'll put it down this afternoon," she said. "Come in after lunch, Georgie, and play a game with me. You, too, Daisy."

"Thanks, but Georgie and I were going to have a real round on the links," said Daisy in a rather superior manner.

"What fun!" said Lucia sycophantically. "I shall walk down and look at you. I think I must learn. I never saw anything so interesting as golf."

This was gratifying: Daisy was by no means reluctant to show Lucia the way to do anything, but behind that, she was not quite sure whether she liked this sudden interest in golf. Now that practically the whole of Riseholme was taking to it, and she herself could beat them all, having had a good start, she was hoping that

Lucia would despise it, and find herself left quite alone on these lovely afternoons. Everybody went down to the little nine-hole course now after lunch, the Vicar (Mr. Rumbold) and his wife, the curate, Colonel Boucher, Georgie, Mrs. Antrobus (who discarded her ear-trumpet for these athletics and never could hear you call "Fore"), and Piggy and Goosie, and often Mrs. Boucher was wheeled down in her Bath chair, and applauded the beautiful putts made on the last green. Indeed, Daisy had started instruction classes in her garden, and Riseholme stood in rows and practised swinging and keeping its eye on a particular blade of grass; golf in fact promised to make Riseholme busy and happy again just as the establishment of the Museum had done. Of course, if Lucia was wanting to learn (and not learn too much) Daisy would be very happy to instruct her, but at the back of Daisy's mind was a strange uneasiness. She consoled herself, however, by supposing that Lucia would go back to London again in the autumn, and by giving Georgie an awful drubbing.

Lucia did not accompany them far on their round, but turned back to the little shed of a clubhouse, where she gathered information about the club. It was quite new, having been started only last spring by the tradesmen and townspeople of Riseholme and the neighboring little town of Blitton. She then entered into pleasant conversation with the landlord of the Ambermere Arms, who had just finished his round and said how pleased they all were that the gentry had taken to golf.

"There's Mrs. Quantock, ma'am," said he. "She comes down every afternoon and practises on the green every morning. Walking over the green now of a morning is to take your life in your hand. Such keenness I never saw, and she'll never be able to hit the ball at all."

"Oh, but you mustn't discourage us, Mr. Stratton," said Lucia. "I'm going to devote myself to golf this autumn."

"You'll make a better hand at it, I'll be bound," said Mr. Stratton obsequiously. "They say Mrs. Quantock putts very nicely when she gets near the hole, but it takes her so many strokes to get there. She's lost the hole, in a manner of speaking, before she has a chance of winning it."

Lucia thought hard for a minute.

"I must see about joining at once," she said. "Who—who are the committee?"

"Well, we are going to reconstitute it next October," he said, "seeing that the ladies and gentlemen of Rise-holme are joining. We should like to have one of you ladies as president, and one of the gentlemen on the committee."

Lucia made no hesitation about this.

"I should be delighted," she said, "if the present committee did me the honor to ask me. And how about Mr. Pillson? I would sound him if you like. But we must say nothing about it, till your committee meets."

That was beautifully settled then; Mr. Stratton knew how gratified the committee would be, and Lucia, long before Georgie and Daisy returned, had bought four clubs, and was having a lesson from a small wiry caddie.

Every morning while Daisy was swanking away on the green, teaching Georgie and Piggy and Goosie how to play, Lucia went surreptitiously down the hill and learned, while after tea she humbly took her place in

Daisy's class and observed Daisy doing everything all wrong. She putted away at her clock golf; she bought a beautiful book with pictures and studied them; and all the time she said nothing whatever about it. In her heart she utterly despised golf, but golf just now was the stunt, and she had to get hold of Riseholme again. . . .

Georgie popped in one morning after she had come back from her lesson, and found her in the act of holing out from the very longest of the stations.

"My dear, what a beautiful putt!" he said. "I believe you're getting quite keen on it."

"Indeed I am," said she. "It's great fun. I go down sometimes to the links and knock the ball about. Be very kind to me this afternoon and come round with me."

Georgie readily promised to do so.

"Of course I will," he said, "and I should be delighted to give you a hint or two, if I can. I won two holes from Daisy yesterday."

"How clever of you, Georgie! Any news?"

Georgie said the sound that is spelt *t-u-t*.

"I quite forgot," he said. "I came round to tell you. Neither Mrs. Boucher nor Daisy nor I know *what* to do."

("That's the Museum Committee," thought Lucia.)

"What is it, Georgie?" she said. "See if poor Lucia can help."

"Well," said Georgie, "You know Pug?"

"That mangy little thing of Lady Ambermere's?" asked Lucia.

"Yes. Pug died, I don't know what of—"

"Cream, I should think," said Lucia. "And cake."

"Well, it may have been. Anyhow, Lady Ambermere

had him stuffed, and while I was out this morning, she left him in a glass case at my house, as a present for the Museum. There he is lying on a blue cushion, with one ear cocked, and a great watery eye, and the end of his horrid tongue between his lips."

"No!" said Lucia.

"I assure you. And we don't know what to do. We can't put him in the Museum, can we? And we're afraid she'll take the mittens away if we don't. But, how can we refuse? She wrote me a note about 'her precious Pug.'"

Lucia remembered how they had refused an Elizabethan spit, though they had subsequently accepted it. But she was not going to remind Georgie of that. She wanted to get a better footing in the Museum than an Elizabethan spit had given her.

"What a dreadful thing!" she said. "And so you came to see if your poor old Lucia could help you."

"Well, we all wondered if you might be able to think of something," said he.

Lucia enjoyed this: the Museum was wanting her. . . . She fixed Georgie with her eye.

"Perhaps I can get you out of your hole," she said. "What I imagine is, Georgie, that you want *me* to take that awful Pug back to her. I see what's happened. She had him stuffed, and then found he was too dreadful an object to keep, and so thought she'd be generous to the Museum. We—I should say 'you,' for I've got nothing to do with it—you don't care about the Museum being made a dump for all the rubbish that people don't want in their houses. Do you?"

"No, certainly not," said Georgie. (Did Lucia mean anything by that? Apparently she did.) She became brisk and voluble.

"Of course, if you asked my opinion," said Lucia, "I should say that there has been a little too much dumping done already. But that is not the point, is it? And it's not my business either. Anyhow, you don't want any more rubbish to be dumped. As for withdrawing the mittens—only lent, aren't they?—she won't do anything of the kind. She likes taking people over and showing them. Yes, Georgie, I'll help you; tell Mrs. Boucher and Daisy that I'll help you. I'll drive over this afternoon—no, I won't, for I'm going to have a lovely game of golf with you—I'll drive over tomorrow and take Pug back, with the Committee's regrets that they are not taxidermists. Or, if you like, I'll do it on my own authority. How odd to be afraid of poor old Lady Ambermere! Never mind; I'm not. How all you people bully me into doing just what you want! I always was Riseholme's slave. Put Pug's case in a nice piece of brown paper, Georgie, for I don't want to see the horrid little abortion, and don't think anything more about it. Now let's have a good little putting match till lunchtime."

Georgie was nowhere in the good little putting match, and he was even less anywhere when it came to their game in the afternoon. Lucia made magnificent swipes from the tee, the least of which, if she happened to hit it, must have gone well over a hundred yards, whereas Daisy considered eighty yards from the tee a most respectable shot, and was positively pleased if she went into a bunker at a greater distance than that, and said the bunker ought to be put further off for the sake of the longer hitters. And when Lucia came near the green, she gave a smart little dig with her mashie, and when this remarkable stroke came off, though she certainly hit the ground, the ball went beautifully, whereas when Daisy hit the ground the ball didn't go at all. All the time she was lighthearted and talkative, and even up to the moment of striking, would be saying "Now oo naughty ickle ball: Lucia's going to give you such a spank!" whereas when Daisy was playing, her opponent and the caddies had all to be dumb and turned to stone, while she drew a long breath and waved her club with a pendulum-like movement over the ball.

"But you're marvellous," said Georgie as, three down, he stood on the fourth tee, and watched Lucia's ball sail away over a sheep that looked quite small in the distance. "It's only three weeks or so since you began to play at all. You are clever! I believe you'd nearly beat Daisy."

"Georgie, I'm afraid you're a flatterer," said Lucia. "Now give your ball a good bang, and then there's something I want to talk to you about."

"Let's see; it's slow back, isn't it?" said Georgie. "Or is it quick back? I believe Daisy says sometimes one and sometimes the other."

Daisy and Piggy, starting before them, were playing in a parallel and opposite direction. Daisy had no luck with her first shot, and very little with her second. Lucia just got out of the way of her third, and Daisy hurried by them.

"Such a slice!" she said. "How are you getting on, Lucia? How many have you played to get there?"

"One at present, dear," said Lucia. "But isn't it difficult?"

Daisy's face fell.

"One?" she said.

Lucia kissed her hand.

"That's all," she said. "And has Georgie told you that I'll manage about Pug for you?"

Daisy looked round severely. She had begun to address her ball, and nobody must talk.

Lucia watched Daisy do it again, and rejoined Georgie who was in a "tarsome" place, and tufts of grass flew in the air.

"Georgie, I had a little talk with Mr. Stratton the other day," she said. "There's a new golf committee being elected in October, and they would so like to have you on it. Now be good-natured and say you will."

Georgie had no intention of saying anything else.

"And they want poor little me to be president," said Lucia. "So shall I send Mr. Stratton a line and say we will? It would be kind, Georgie. Oh, by the way, do come and dine tonight. Peppino—so much better, thanks—Peppino told me to ask you. He would enjoy it. Just one of our dear little evenings again."

Lucia, in fact, was bringing her batteries into action, and Georgie was the immediate though not the ultimate objective. He longed to be on the golf committee; he was intensely grateful for the promised removal of Pug; and it was much more amusing to play golf with Lucia than to be dragooned round by Daisy, who told him after every stroke what he ought to have done and could never do it herself. A game should not be a lecture.

Lucia thought it was time to confide in him about the abandoning of Brompton Square. Georgie would love knowing what nobody else knew yet. She waited till he had failed to hole a short putt, and gave him the subsequent one, which Daisy never did.

"I hope we shall have many of our little evenings, Georgie," she said. "We shall be here till Christmas.

No, no more London for us, though it's a secret at present."

"What?" said Georgie.

"Wait a moment," said Lucia, teeing up for the last hole. "Now ickle ballie, fly away home. There! . . ." And ickle ballie flew at about right angles to home, but ever such a long way.

She walked with him to cover point, where he had gone, too.

"Peppino must never live in London again," she said. "All going to be sold, Georgie. The house and the furniture and the pearls. You must put up with your poor old Lucia at Riseholme again. Nobody knows yet but you, but now it is all settled. Am I sorry? Yes, Georgie, course I am. So many dear friends in London. But then there are dear friends in Riseholm. Oh, what a beautiful bang, Georgie. You nearly hit Daisy. Call, 'Five!' isn't that what they do?"

Lucia was feeling much surer of her ground. Georgie, bribed by a place on the golf committee and by her admiration of his golf, and by her nobility with regard to Pug, was trotting back quick to her, and that was something. Next morning she had a hectic interview with Lady Ambermere. . . .

Lady Ambermere was said to be not at home, though Lucia had seen her majestic face at the window of the pink saloon. So she asked for Miss Lyall, the downtrodden companion, and waited in the hall. Her chauffeur had deposited the large brown-paper parcel with Pug inside on the much-admired tessellated pavement.

"Oh, Miss Lyall," said Lucia. "So sad that dear Lady Ambermere is out, for I wanted to convey the grateful thanks of the Museum Committee to her for her beautiful gift of poor Pug. But they feel they can't. . . . Yes, that's Pug in the brown-paper parcel. So sweet. But will you, on Lady Ambermere's return, make it quite clear?"

Miss Lyall, looking like a mouse, considered what her duty was in this difficult situation. She felt that Lady Ambermere ought to know Lucia's mission and deal with it in person.

"I'll see if Lady Ambermere has come in, Mrs. Lucas," she said. "She may have come in. Just out in the garden, you know. Might like to know what you've brought. Oh, dear me!"

Poor Miss Lyall scuttled away, and presently the door of the pink saloon was thrown open. After an impressive pause Lady Ambermere appeared, looking vexed. The purport of this astounding mission had evidently been conveyed to her.

"Mrs. Lucas, I believe," she said, just as if she wasn't sure.

Now Lucia after all her duchesses was not going to stand that. Lady Ambermere might have a Roman nose, but she hadn't any manners.

"Lady Ambermere, I presume," she retorted. So there they were.

Lady Ambermere glared at her in a way that should have turned her to stone. It made no impression.

"You have come, I believe, with a message from the Committee of your little Museum at Riseholme, which I may have misunderstood."

Lucia knew she was doing what neither Mrs. Boucher nor Daisy in their most courageous moments would have dared to do. As for Georgie. . . .

"No, Lady Ambermere," she said. "I don't think you've misunderstood it. A stuffed dog on a cushion;

they felt that the Museum was not quite the place for it. I have brought it back to you with their thanks and regrets. So kind of you and—and so sorry of them. This is the parcel. That is all, I think."

It wasn't quite all. . . .

"Are you aware, Mrs. Lucas," said Lady Ambermere, "that the mittens of the late Queen Charlotte are my loan to your little Museum?"

Lucia put her finger to her forehead.

"Mittens?" she said. "Yes, I believe there are some mittens. I think I have seen them. No doubt, those are the ones. Yes?"

That was brilliant: it implied complete indifference on the part of the Committee (to which Lucia felt sure she would presently belong) as to what Lady Ambermere might think fit to do about mittens.

"The Committee shall hear from me," said Lady Ambermere, and walked majestically back to the pink saloon.

Lucia felt sorry for Miss Lyall; Miss Lyall would probably not have a very pleasant day, but she had no real apprehensions, so she explained to the Committee, who were anxiously awaiting her return on the green, about the withdrawal of these worsted relics.

"Bluff, just bluff," she said. "And even if it wasn't—Surely, dear Daisy, it's better to have no mittens and no Pug than both. Pug—I caught a peep of him through a hole in the brown paper—Pug would have made your Museum a laughing-stock."

"Was she very dreadful?" asked Georgie.

Lucia gave her little silvery laugh.

"Yes, dear Georgie, quite dreadful. You would have collapsed if she had said to you, 'Mr. Pillson, I believe.' Wouldn't you, Georgie? Don't pretend to be braver than you are."

"Well, I think we ought all to be much obliged to you, Mrs. Lucas," said Mrs. Boucher. "And I'm sure we are. I should never have stood up to her like that! And if she takes the mittens away, I should be much inclined to put another pair in the case, for the case belongs to us and not to her, with just the label 'These Mittens did not belong to Queen Charlotte, and were not presented by Lady Ambermere.' That would serve her out."

Lucia laughed gaily again.

"So glad to have been of use," she said. "And now, dear Daisy, will you be as kind to me as Georgie was yesterday and give me a little game of golf this afternoon? Not much fun for you, but so good for me."

Daisy had observed some of Lucia's powerful strokes yesterday, and she was rather dreading this invitation for fear it should not be, as Lucia said, much fun for her. Luckily, she and Georgie had already arranged to play today, and she had, in anticipation of the dread event, engaged Piggy, Goosie, Mrs. Antrobus, and Colonel Boucher to play with her on all the remaining days of the week. She meant to practise like anything in the interval. And then, like a raven croaking disaster, the infamous Georgie let her down.

"I'd sooner not play this afternoon," he said. "I'd sooner just stroll out with you."

"Sure, Georgie?" said Lucia. "That will be nice then. Oh, how nervous I shall be."

Daisy made one final effort to avert her downfall, by offering, as they went out that afternoon, to give Lucia a stroke a hole. Lucia said she knew she could do it, but might they, just for fun, play level? And as the round proceeded, Lucia's kindness was almost intolerable. She could see, she said, that Daisy was completely off her game, when Daisy wasn't in the least off her game. She said, "Oh, that was bad luck!" when Daisy missed short putts; she begged her to pick her ball out of bushes and not count it. . . . At half past four Riseholme knew that Daisy had halved four holes and lost the other five. Her short reign as Queen of Golf had come to an end.

The Museum Committee met after tea at Mrs. Boucher's (Daisy did not hold her golfing class in the garden that day), and tact, Georgie felt, seemed to indicate that Lucia's name should not be suggested as a new member of the Committee so swiftly on the heels of Daisy's disaster. Mrs. Boucher, privately consulted, concurred, though with some rather stinging remarks as to Daisy's having deceived them all about her golf, and the business of the meeting was chiefly concerned with the proposed closing down of the Museum for the winter. The tourist season was over, no char-a-bancs came any more with visitors, and for three days not a soul had passed the turnstile.

"So where's the use," asked Mrs. Boucher, "of paying a boy to let people into the Museum when nobody wants to be let in? I call it throwing money away. Far better close it till the spring, and have no more expense, except to pay him a shilling a week to open the windows and air it, say on Tuesday and Friday, or Wednesday and Saturday."

"I should suggest Monday and Thursday," said Daisy very decisively. If she couldn't have it all her own way on the links, she could make herself felt on committees.

"Very well, Monday and Thursday," said Mrs. Boucher. "And then there's another thing. It's getting so damp in there, that if you wanted a cold bath, you might undress and stand there. The water's pouring off the walls. A couple of oil stoves, I suggest, every day except when it's being aired. The boy will attend to them, and make it half a crown instead of a shilling. I'm going to Blitton tomorrow, and if that's your wish, I'll order them. No, I'll bring them back with me, and I'll have them lit tomorrow morning. But unless you want to have nothing to show next spring but mildew, don't let us delay about it. A crop of mildew won't be sufficient attraction to visitors, and there'll be nothing else."

Georgie rapped the table.

"And I vote we take the manuscript of *Lucrezia* out, and that one of us keeps it till we open again," he said.

"I should be happy to keep it," said Daisy.

Georgie wanted it himself, but it was better not to thwart Daisy today. Besides he was in a hurry, as Lucia had asked him to bring round his planchette and see if Abfou would not like a little attention. Nobody had talked to Abfou for weeks.

"Very well," he said, "and if that's all—"

"I'm not sure I shouldn't feel happier if it was at the bank," said Mrs. Boucher. "Supposing it was stolen."

Georgie magnanimously took Daisy's side; he knew how Daisy was feeling. Mrs. Boucher was outvoted, and he got up.

"If that's all then, I'll be off," he said.

Daisy had a sort of conviction that he was going to do something with Lucia, perhaps have a lesson at golf.

"Come in presently?" he said.

"I can't, I'm afraid," he said. "I'm busy till dinner."

And of course, on her way home, she saw him hurrying across to The Hurst with his planchette.

11

LUCIA MADE no allusion whatever to her athletic triumph in the afternoon when Georgie appeared. That was not her way; she just triumphed, and left other people to talk about it. But her principles did not prevent her speaking about golf in the abstract.

"We must get more businesslike when you and I are on the committee, Georgie," she said. "We must have competitions and handicaps, and I will give a small silver cup, the President's Cup, to be competed for. There's no organization at present, you see: great fun, but no organization. We shall have to put our heads together over that. And foursomes—I have been reading about foursomes, when two people on one side hit the ball in turn. Peppino, I'm sure, would give a little cup for foursomes, the Lucas Cup. . . . And you've brought the planchette? You must teach me how to use it. What a good employment for winter evenings, Georgie. And we must have some bridge tournaments. Wet afternoons, you know, and then tea, and then some more bridge. But we will talk about all that presently, only I warn you I shall expect you to get up all sorts of diversions for Peppino."

Lucia gave a little sigh.

"Peppino adored London," she said, "and we must cheer him up, Georgie, and not let him feel dull. You must think of lots of little diversions. Little pleasant bustling things for these long evenings: music, and bridge, and some planchette. Then I shall get up some Shakespeare readings, selections from plays, with a small part for Peppino and another for poor Daisy. I foresee already that I shall have a very busy autumn. But you must all be very kind and come here for our little entertainments. Madness for Peppino to go out after sunset. Now let us get to our planchette. How I do chatter, Georgie!"

Georgie explained the technique of planchette, how important it was not to push, but on the other hand not to resist its independent motions. As he spoke, Lucia glanced over the directions for planchette which he had brought with him.

"We may not get anything," he said. "Abfou was very disappointing sometimes. We can go on talking; indeed, it is better not to attend to what it does."

"I see," said Lucia. "Let us go on talking then. How late you are, Georgie. I expected you half an hour ago. Oh, you said you might be detained by a Museum Committee meeting."

"Yes, we settled to shut the Museum up for the winter," he said. "Just an oil stove or two to keep it dry. I wanted—and so did Mrs. Boucher, I know—to ask you—"

He stopped, for Planchette had already begun to throb in a very extraordinary manner.

"I believe something is going to happen," he said.

"No! How interesting!" said Lucia. "What do we do?"

"Nothing," said Georgie. "Just let it do what it likes. Let's concentrate: that means thinking of nothing at all."

Georgie of course had noticed and inwardly applauded the lofty reticence which Lucia had shown about Daisy's disaster this afternoon. But he had the strongest suspicion of her wish to weedj, and he fully expected that if Abfou "came through" and talked anything but Arabic, he would express his scorn of Daisy's golf. There would be scathing remarks, corresponding to "Snob" and those rude things about Lucia's shingling of her hair, and then he would feel that Lucia had pushed. She might say she hadn't, just as Daisy said she hadn't, but it would be very unconvincing if Abfou talked about golf. He hoped it wouldn't happen, for the very appositeness of Abfou's remarks before had strangely shaken his faith in Abfou. He had been willing to believe that it was Daisy's subconscious self that had inspired Abfou—or at any rate he tried to believe it—but it had been impossible to dissociate the complete Daisy from these violent criticisms.

Planchette began to move.

"Probably it's Arabic," said Georgie. "You never quite know. Empty your mind of everything, Lucia."

She did not answer, and he looked up at her. She had that far-away expression which he associated with renderings of the "Moonlight Sonata." Then her eyes closed.

Planchette was moving quietly and steadily along.

When it came near the edge of the paper, it ran back
and began again, and Georgie felt quite sure he wasn't
pushing; he only wanted it not to waste its energy on
the tablecloth. Once he felt almost certain that it traced
out the word "drive," but one couldn't be sure. And
was that "committee"? His heart rather sank: it would
be such a pity if Abfou was only talking about the golf
club which no doubt was filling Lucia's subconscious as
well as conscious mind. . . . Then suddenly he got
rather alarmed, for Lucia's head was sunk forward,
and she breathed with strange rapidity.

"Lucia!" he said sharply.

Lucia lifted her head, and Planchette stopped.

"Dear me, I felt quite dreamy," she said. "Let us go
on talking, Georgie. Lady Ambermere this morning; I
wish you could have seen her."

"Planchette has been writing," said Georgie.

"No!" said Lucia. "Has it? May we look?"

Georgie lifted the machine. There was no Arabic at
all, nor was it Abfou's writing, which in quaint little
ways resembled Daisy's when he wrote quickly.

"Vittoria," he read. "I am Vittoria."

"Georgie, how silly," said Lucia, "or is it the
Queen?"

"Let's see what she says," said Georgie. "I am Vittoria. I come to Riseholme. For proof, there is a dog
and a Vecchia—"

"That's Italian," said Lucia excitedly. "You see, *Vittoria* is Italian. *Vecchia* means—let me see; yes, of
course, it means 'old woman,' 'A dog, and an old
woman who is angry.' Oh, Georgie, you did that! You
were thinking about Pug and Lady Ambermere."

"I swear I wasn't," said Georgie. "It never entered
my head. Let's see what else. 'And Vittoria comes to

tell you of fire and water, of fire and water. The strong elements that burn and soak. Fire and water and moonlight.' "

"Oh, Georgie, what gibberish," said Lucia. "It's as silly as Abfou. What does it mean? Moonlight! I suppose you would say I pushed and was thinking of the 'Moonlight Sonata.' "

That base thought had occurred to Georgie's mind, but where did fire and water come in? Suddenly a stupendous interpretation struck him.

"It's most extraordinary!" he said. "We had a Museum Committee meeting just now, and Mrs. Boucher said the place was streaming wet. We settled to get some oil stoves to keep it dry. There's fire and water for you!" Georgie had mentioned this fact about the Museum Committee, but so casually that he had quite forgotten he had done so. Lucia did not remind him of it.

"Well, I do call that remarkable!" she said. "But I daresay it's only a coincidence."

"I don't think so at all," said Georgie. "I think it's most curious, for I wasn't thinking about that a bit. What else does it say? 'Vittoria bids you keep love and loyalty alive in your hearts. Vittoria has suffered, and bids you be kind to the suffering.' "

"That's curious!" said Lucia. "That might apply to Peppino, mightn't it? . . . Oh, Georgie, why, of course, that was in both of our minds, we had just been talking about it. I don't say you pushed intentionally, and you mustn't say I did, but that might easily have come from us."

"I think it's very strange," said Georgie. "And then, what came over you, Lucia? You looked only half conscious. I believe it was what the planchette directions call light hypnosis."

"No!" said Lucia. "Light hypnosis, that means half-asleep, doesn't it? I did feel drowsy."

"It's a condition of trance," said Georgie. "Let's try again."

Lucia seemed reluctant.

"I think I won't, Georgie," she said. "It is so strange. I'm not sure that I like it."

"It can't hurt you if you approach it in the right spirit," said Georgie, quoting from the directions.

"Not again this evening, Georgie," she said. "Tomorrow perhaps. It is interesting; it is curious; and somehow I don't think Vittoria would hurt us. She seemed kind. There's something noble, indeed, about her message."

"Much nobler than Abfou," said Georgie, "and much more powerful. Why, she came through at once, without pages of scribbles first! I never felt quite certain that Abfou's scribbles were Arabic."

Lucia gave a little indulgent smile.

"There didn't seem much evidence for it from what you told me," she said. "All you could be certain of was that they weren't English."

Georgie left his planchette with Lucia, in case she would consent to sit again tomorrow, and hurried back, it is unnecessary to state, not to his own house, but to Daisy's. Vittoria was worth two of Abfou, he thought . . . that communication about fire and water, that kindness to the suffering, and hardly less, the keeping of loyalty alive. That made him feel rather guilty, for certainly loyalty to Lucia had flickered somewhat in consequence of her behavior during the summer.

He gave a short account of these remarkable proceedings (omitting the loyalty) to Daisy, who took a superior and scornful attitude.

"Vittoria, indeed!" she said, "and Vecchia. Isn't that Lucia all over, lugging in easy Italian like that? And Pug and the angry old lady. Glorifying herself, I call it. Why, that wasn't even subconscious; her mind was full of it."

"But how about the fire and water?" asked Georgie. "It does apply to the damp in the Museum and the oil stoves."

Daisy knew that her position as priestess of Abfou was tottering. It was true that she had not celebrated the mysteries of late, for Riseholme (and she) had got rather tired of Abfou, but it was gall and wormwood to think that Lucia should steal (steal was the word) her invention and bring it out under the patronage of Vittoria as something quite new.

"A pure fluke," said Daisy. "If she'd written mutton and music, you would have found some interpretation for it. Such far-fetched nonsense!"

Georgie was getting rather heated. He remembered how when Abfou had written "death" it was held to apply to the mulberry tree which Daisy believed she had killed by amateur root pruning, so if it came to talking about far-fetched nonsense, he could have something to say. Besides, the mulberry tree hadn't died at all, so that if Abfou meant that he was wrong. But there was no good in indulging in recriminations with Daisy, not only for the sake of peace and quietness, but because Georgie could guess very well all she was feeling.

"But she didn't write about mutton and music," he observed, "so we needn't discuss that. Then there was moonlight. I don't know what that means."

"I should call it moonshine," said Daisy brightly.

"Well, it wrote moonlight," said Georgie. "Of course there's the 'Moonlight Sonata' which might have been in Lucia's mind, but it's all curious. And I believe Lucia was in a condition of light hypnosis—"

"Light fiddlesticks!" said Daisy. . . . (Why hadn't she thought of going into a condition of light hypnosis when she was Abfouing? So much more impressive!) "We can all shut our eyes and droop our heads."

"Well, I think it was light hypnosis," said Georgie firmly. "It was very curious to see. I hope she'll consent to sit again. She didn't much want to."

Daisy profoundly hoped that Lucia would not consent to sit again, for she felt Abfouism slipping out of her fingers. In any case, she would instantly resuscitate Abfou, for Vittoria shouldn't have it all her own way. She got up.

"Georgie, why shouldn't we see if Abfou has anything to say about it?" she asked. "After all, Abfou told us to make a Museum, and that hasn't turned out so badly. Abfou was practical; what he suggested led to something."

Though the notion that Daisy had thought of the Museum and pushed flitted through Georgie's mind, there was something in what she said, for certainly Abfou had written Museum (if it wasn't "mouse") and there was the Museum which had turned out so profitably for the Committee.

"We might try," he said.

Daisy instantly got out her planchette, which sadly wanted dusting, and it began to move almost as soon as they laid their hands on it: Abfou was in a rather inartistic hurry. And it really wasn't very wise of Daisy to close her eyes and snort; it was indeed light fiddle-

sticks to do that. It was a sheer unconvincing plagiarism
from Lucia, and his distrust of Daisy and Abfou im-
measurably deepened. Furiously the pencil scribbled,
going off the paper occasionally and writing on the
table till Georgie could insert the paper under it; it was
evident that Abfou was very indignant about something, and there was no need to enquire what that was.
For some time the writing seemed to feel to Georgie
like Arabic, but presently the pencil slowed down, and
he thought some English was coming through. Finally
Abfou gave a great scrawl, as he usually did when the
message was complete, and Daisy looked dreamily up.

"Anything?" she said.

"It's been writing hard," said Georgie.

They examined the script. It began, as he had expected, with quantities of Arabic, and then (as he had
expected) dropped into English, which was quite legible.

"Beware of charlatans," wrote Abfou, "beware of
Southern charlatans. All spirits are not true and faith-
ful like Abfou, who instituted your Museum. False
guides deceive. A warning from Abfou."

"Well, if that isn't convincing, I don't know what
is," said Daisy.

Georgie thought it convincing, too.

The din of battle began to rise. It was known that
very evening, for Colonel and Mrs. Boucher dined with
Georgie, that he and Lucia (for Georgie did not give
all the credit to Lucia) had received that remarkable
message from Vittoria about fire and water and the dog
and the angry old woman, and it was agreed that
Abfou cut a very poor figure, and had a jealous temper. Why hadn't Abfou done something better than
merely warn them against Southern charlatans?

"If it comes to that," said Mrs. Boucher, "Egypt is
in the south, and charlatans can come from Egypt as
much as from Italy. Fire and water! Very remarkable.
There's the water there now, plenty of it, and the fire
will be there tomorrow. I must get out my planchette
again, for I put it away. I got sick of writing nothing
but Arabic, even if it was Arabic. I call it very strange.
And not a word about golf from Vittoria. I consider
that's most important. If Lucia had been pushing, she'd
have written about her golf with Daisy. Abfou and Vittoria! I wonder which will win."

That summed it up pretty well, for it was felt that
Abfou and Vittoria could not both direct the affairs of
Riseholme from the other world, unless they acted
jointly; and Abfou's remarks about the Southern char-
latan and false spirits put the idea of a coalition out of
the question. All the time, firm in the consciousness of
Riseholme, but never under any circumstances spoken
of, was the feeling that Abfou and Vittoria (as well as
standing for themselves) were pseudonyms: they stood
also for Daisy and Lucia. And how much finer and bigger, how much more gifted of the two in every way
was Vittoria-Lucia. Lucia quickly got over her disin-
clination to weedj, and messages, not very definite, but
of high moral significance, came from this exalted
spirit. There was never a word about golf, and there
was never a word about Abfou, nor any ravings
concerning inferior and untrustworthy spirits. Vittoria
was clearly above all that (indeed, she was probably in
some sphere miles away above Abfou), whereas
Abfou's pages (Daisy sat with her planchette morning
after morning and obtained sheets of the most voluble
English) were blistered with denunciations of low and

earthborn intelligences and dark with awful warnings for those who trusted them.

Riseholme, in fact, had never been at a higher pitch of excited activity; even the arrival of the *Evening Gazette* during those weeks when Hermione had recorded so much about Mrs. Philip Lucas hadn't roused such emotions as the reception of a new message from Abfou or Vittoria. And it was Lucia again who was the cause of it all. No one for months had cared what Abfou said, till Lucia became the recipient of Vittoria's messages. She had invested planchette with the interest that attached to all she did. On the other hand it was felt that Abfou (though certainly he lowered himself by these pointed recriminations) had done something. Abfou-Daisy had invented the Museum, whereas Vittoria-Lucia, apart from giving utterance to high moral sentiments, had invented nothing (high moral sentiments couldn't count as an invention). To be sure, there was the remarkable piece about Pug and angry Lady Ambermere, but the facts of that were already known to Lucia, and as for the communication about fire, water, and moonlight, though there were new oil stoves in the damp Museum, that was not as remarkable as inventing the Museum, and moonlight unless it meant the Sonata was quite unexplained. Over this cavilling objection, rather timidly put forward by Georgie, who longed for some striking vindication of Vittoria, Lucia was superb.

"Yes, Georgie, I can't tell you what it means," she said. "I am only the humble scribe. It is quite mysterious to me. For myself, I am content to be Vittoria's medium. I feel it a high honor. Perhaps some day it will be explained, and we shall see."

They saw.

Meanwhile, since no one can live entirely on messages from the unseen, other interests were not neglected. There were bridge parties at The Hurst; there was much music; there was a reading of *Hamlet* at which Lucia doubled several of the principal parts and Daisy declined to be the Ghost. The new committee of the golf club was formed, and at the first meeting Lucia announced her gift of the President's Cup, and Peppino's of the Lucas Cup for foursomes. Notice of these was duly put up in the clubhouse, and Daisy's face was of such a grimness when she read them that something very savage from Abfou might be confidently expected. She went out for a round soon after with Colonel Boucher, who wore a scared and worried look when he returned. Daisy had got into a bunker, and had simply hewed her ball to pieces. . . . Peppino's convalescence proceeded well; Lucia laid down the law a good deal at auction bridge, and the oil stoves at the Museum were satisfactory. They were certainly making headway against the large patches of damp on the walls, and Daisy, one evening, recollecting that she had not made a personal inspection of them, went in just before dinner to look at them. The boy in charge of them had put them out, for they only burned during the day, and certainly they were doing their work well. Daisy felt she would not be able to bring forward any objection to them at the next Committee meeting, as she had rather hoped to do. In order to hurry on the drying process, she filled them both up and lit them so that they should burn all night. She spilt a little paraffin, but that would soon evaporate.

* * *

Georgie was tripping back across the green from a visit to Mrs. Boucher, and they walked homeward together.

Georgie had dined at home that night, and working at a crossword puzzle was amazed to see how late it was. He had pored long over a map of South America, trying to find a river of seven letters with *p-t* in the middle, but he determined to do no more at it tonight.

"The tarsome thing," he said, "if I could get that, I'm sure it would give me thirty-one across."

He strolled to the window and pushed aside the blind. It was a moonlight night with a high wind and a few scudding clouds. Just as he was about to let the blind drop again, he saw a reddish light in the sky, immediately above his tall yew hedge, and wondered what it was. His curiosity combined with the fact that a breath of air was always pleasant before going to bed, led him to open the front door and look out. He gave a wild gasp of dismay and horror.

The windows of the Museum were vividly illuminated by a red glow. Smoke poured out of one which apparently was broken, and across the smoke shot tongues of flame. He bounded to his telephone, and with great presence of mind rang up the fire station at Blitton. "Riseholme," he called. "House on fire; send engine at once." He ran into his garden again, and seeing a light still in the drawing room next door (Daisy was getting some sulphurous expressions from Abfou), tapped at the pane. "The Museum's burning," he cried, and set off across the green to the scene of the fire.

By this time others had seen it, too, and were coming out of their houses, looking like little black ants on a red tablecloth. The fire had evidently caught strong hold, and now a piece of the roof fell in, and the flames roared upward. In the building itself there was no apparatus for extinguishing fire, nor if there had been, could anyone have reached it. A hose was fetched from the Ambermere Arms, but that was not long enough, and there was nothing to be done except wait for the arrival of the fire engine from Blitton. Luckily the Museum stood well apart from other houses, and there seemed little danger of the fire spreading.

Soon the bell of the approaching engine was heard, but already it was clear that nothing could be saved. The rest of the roof crashed in; a wall tottered and fell. The longer hose was adjusted, and the stream of water directed through the windows, now here, now there, where the fire was fiercest, and clouds of steam mingled with the smoke. But all efforts to save anything were absolutely vain; all that could be done, as the fire burned itself out, was to quench the glowing embers of the conflagration. . . . As he watched, three words suddenly repeated themselves in Georgie's mind. "Fire, water, moonlight," he said aloud in an awed tone. . . . Victorious Vittoria!

The Committee, of course, met next morning, and Robert as financial adviser was specially asked to attend. Georgie arrived at Mrs. Boucher's house, where the meeting was held, before Daisy and Robert got there, and Mrs. Boucher could hardly greet him; so excited was she.

"I call it most remarkable," she said. "Dog and angry old woman never convinced me, but this is beyond anything. Fire, water, moonlight! It's prophecy, nothing less than prophecy. I shall believe anything Vittoria says, for the future. As for Abfou—well—"

She tactfully broke off at Daisy's and Robert's entrance.

"Good morning," she said. "And good morning, Mr. Robert. This is a disaster, indeed. All Mr. Georgie's sketches, and the walking sticks, and the mittens and the spit. Nothing left at all."

Robert seemed amazingly cheerful.

"I don't see it as such a disaster," he said. "Lucky I had those insurances executed. We get two thousand pounds from the company, of which five hundred goes to Colonel Boucher for his barn—I mean the Museum."

"Well, that's something," said Mrs. Boucher. "And the rest? I never could understand about insurances. They've always been a sealed book to me."

"Well, the rest belongs to those who put the money up to equip the Museum," he said. "In proportion, of course, to the sums they advanced. Altogether four hundred and fifty pounds was put up. You and Daisy and Georgie each put in fifty; the rest—well, I advanced the rest."

There were some rapid and silent calculations made. It seemed rather hard that Robert should get such a lot. Business always seemed to favor the rich. But Robert didn't seem the least ashamed of that. He treated it as a perfect matter of course.

"The—the treasures in the Museum almost all belonged to the Committee," he went on. "They were given to the Museum, which was the property of the Committee. Quite simple. If it had been a loan collection now—well, we shouldn't be finding quite such a bright lining to our cloud. I'll manage the insurance business for you, and pay you pleasant little cheques all round. The company, no doubt, will ask a few questions as to the origin of the fire."

"Ah, there's a mystery for you," said Mrs. Boucher. "The oil stoves were always put out in the evening, after burning all day, and how a fire broke out in the middle of the night beats me."

Daisy's mouth twitched. Then she pulled herself together.

"Most mysterious," she said, and looked carelessly out of the window to where the debris of the Museum was still steaming. Simultaneously Georgie gave a little start, and instantly changed the subject, rapping on the table.

"There's one thing we've forgotten," said he. "It wasn't entirely our property. Queen Charlotte's mittens were only a loan."

The faces of the Committee fell slightly.

"A shilling or two," said Mrs. Boucher hopefully. "I'm only glad we didn't have Pug as well. Lucia got us out of that!"

Instantly the words of Vittoria about the dog and the angry old woman, and fire and water and moonlight occurred to everybody. Most of all they occurred to Daisy, and there was a slight pause, which might have become awkward if it had continued. It was broken by the entry of Mrs. Boucher's parlormaid, who carried a letter in a large square envelope with a deep mourning border, and a huge coronet on the flap.

"Addressed to the Museum Committee, ma'am," she said.

Mrs. Boucher opened it, and her face flushed.

"Well, she's lost no time," she said. "Lady Ambermere. I think I had better read it."

"Please," said everybody in rather strained voices.

Mrs. Boucher read:

LADIES AND GENTLEMEN OF THE COMMITTEE OF RISEHOLME MUSEUM—

Your little Museum, I hear, has been totally destroyed with all its contents by fire. I have to remind you therefore that the mittens of her late Majesty Queen Charlotte were there on loan, as lent by me. No equivalent in money can really make up for the loss of so irreplaceable a relic, but I should be glad to know, as soon as possible, what compensation you propose to offer me.

The figure that has been suggested to me is £50, and an early cheque would oblige.

Faithfully yours,
CORNELIA AMBERMERE

A dead silence succeeded, broken by Mrs. Boucher as soon as her indignation allowed her to speak.

"I would sooner," she said, "go to law about it, and appeal if it went against us, and carry it up to the House of Lords, than pay fifty pounds for those rubbishy things. Why the whole contents of the Museum weren't worth more than—well, leave it at that."

The figure at which the contents of the Museum had been insured floated into everybody's mind, and it was more dignified to "leave it at that," and not let the imagination play over the probable end of Mrs. Boucher's sentence.

The meeting entirely concurred, but nobody, not even Robert, knew what to do next.

"I propose offering her ten pounds," said Georgie at last, "and I call that handsome."

"Five," said Daisy, like an auction reversed.

Robert rubbed the top of his head, as was his custom in perplexity.

"Difficult to know what to do," he said. "I don't

know of any standard of valuation for the old clothes of deceased queens."

"Two," said Mrs. Boucher, continuing the auction, "and that's a fancy price. What would Pug have been, I wonder, if we're asked fifty pounds for two old mittens. A pound each, I say, and that's a monstrous price. And if you want to know who suggested to Lady Ambermere to ask fifty, I can tell you, and her name was Cornelia Ambermere."

This proposal of Lady Ambermere's rather damped the secret exaltation of the Committee, though it stirred a pleasant feeling of rage. Fifty pounds was a paltry sum compared to what they would receive from the insurance company, but the sense of the attempt to impose on them caused laudable resentment. They broke up, to consider separately what was to be done, and to poke about the ashes of the Museum, all feeling very rich. The rest of Riseholme were there, of course, also poking about, Piggy and Goosie skipping over smoldering heaps of ash, and Mrs. Antrobus, and the Vicar and the Curate, and Mr. Stratton. Only Lucia was absent, and Georgie, after satisfying himself that nothing whatever remained of his sketches, popped in to The Hurst.

Lucia was in the music room reading the paper. She had heard, of course, about the total destruction of the Museum, that ridiculous invention of Daisy and Abfou, but not a shadow of exultation betrayed itself.

"My dear, too sad about the Museum," she said. "All your beautiful things. Poor Daisy, too, her idea."

Georgie explained about the silver lining to the cloud.

"But what's so marvellous," he said, "is Vittoria. Fire, water, moonlight. I never heard of anything so extraordinary, and I thought it only meant the damp on the walls, and the new oil stoves. It was prophetical, Lucia, and Mrs. Boucher thinks so, too."

Lucia still showed no elation. Oddly enough, she had thought it meant damp and oil stoves, too, for she did remember what Georgie had forgotten that he had told her just before the epiphany of Vittoria. But now this stupendous fulfillment of Vittoria's communication of which she had never dreamed, had happened. As for Abfou, it was a mere waste of time to give another thought to poor, dear, malicious Abfou. She sighed.

"Yes, Georgie, it was strange," she said. "That was our first sitting, wasn't it? When I got so drowsy and felt so queer. Very strange indeed—convincing, I think. But whether I shall go on sitting now, I hardly know."

"Oh, but you must," said Georgie. "After all the rubbish—"

Lucia held up her finger.

"Now, Georgie, don't be unkind," she said. "Let us say, 'Poor Daisy,' and leave it there. That's all. Any other news?"

Georgie retailed the monstrous demand of Lady Ambermere.

"And, as Robert says, it's so hard to know what to offer her," he concluded.

Lucia gave the gayest of laughs.

"Georgie, what would poor Riseholme do without me?" she said. "I seem to be made to pull you all out of difficulties. That mismanaged golf club, Pug, and now there's this. Well, shall I be kind and help you once more?"

She turned over the leaves of her paper.

"Ah, that's it," she said. "Listen, Georgie. Sale at

Pemberton's auction rooms in Knightsbridge yesterday. Various items. Autograph of Crippen the murderer. Dear me, what horrid minds people have! Mother-of-pearl brooch belonging to the wife of the poet Mr. Robert Montgomery; a pair of razors belonging to Carlyle; all odds and ends of trumpery, you see. . . . Ah, yes, here it is. Pair of riding gaiters, in good condition, belonging to his Majesty King George the Fourth. That seems a sort of guide, doesn't it, to the value of Queen Charlotte's mittens. And what do you think they fetched? A terrific sum, Georgie; fifty pounds is nowhere near it. They fetched ten shillings and sixpence."

"No!" said Georgie. "And Lady Ambermere asked fifty pounds!"

Lucia laughed again.

"Well, Georgie, I suppose I must be good-natured," she said. "I'll draft a little letter for your committee to Lady Ambermere. How you all bully me and work me to death! Why, only yesterday I said to Peppino that those months we spent in London seemed a holiday compared to what I have to do here. Dear old Riseholme! I'm sure I'm very glad to help it out of its little holes."

Georgie gave a gasp of admiration. It was but a month or two ago that all Riseholme rejoiced when Abfou called her a snob, and now here they all were again (with the exception of Daisy) going to her for help and guidance in all those employments and excitements in which Riseholme revelled. Golf competitions and bridge tournament, and duets, and real séances, and deliverance from Lady Ambermere, and above all, the excitement supplied by her personality.

"You're too wonderful," he said; "indeed, I don't know what we should do without you."

Lucia got up.

"Well, I'll scribble a little letter for you," she said, "bringing in the price of George the Fourth's gaiters in good condition. What shall we—I mean what shall you offer? I think you must be generous, Georgie, and not calculate the exact difference between the value of a pair of gaiters in good condition belonging to a king, and that of a pair of moth-eaten mittens belonging to a queen consort. Offer her the same; in fact, I think I should enclose a treasury note for ten shillings and six stamps. That will be more than generous; it will be munificent."

Lucia sat down at her writing table, and after a few minutes' thought, scribbled a couple of sides of note-paper in that neat handwriting that bore no resemblance to Vittoria's. She read them through, and approved.

"I think that will settle it," she said. "If there is any further bother with the Vecchia, let me know. There's one more thing, Georgie, and then let us have a little music. How do you think the fire broke out?"

Georgie felt her penetrating eye on him. She had not asked that question quite idly. He tried to answer it quite idly.

"It's most mysterious," he said. "The oil stoves are always put out quite early in the evening, and lit again next morning. The boy says he put them out as usual."

Lucia's eye was still on him.

"Georgie, how do you think the fire broke out?" she repeated.

This time Georgie felt thoroughly uncomfortable. Had Lucia the power of divination? . . .

"I don't know," he said. "Have you any idea about it?"

"Yes," said Lucia. "And so have you. I'll tell you my idea if you like. I saw our poor misguided Daisy coming out of the Museum close on seven o'clock last night."

"So did I," said Georgie in a whisper.

"Well, the oil stoves must have been put out long before that," said Lucia. "Mustn't they?"

"Yes," said Georgie.

"Then how was it that there was a light coming out of the Museum windows? Not much of a light, but a little light, I saw it. What do you make of that?"

"I don't know," said Georgie.

Lucia held up a censuring finger.

"Georgie, you must be very dull this morning," she said. "What I make of it is that our poor Daisy lit the oil stoves again. And then probably in her fumbling way, she spilt some oil. Something of the sort, anyhow. In fact, I'm afraid Daisy burned down the Museum."

There was a terrible pause.

"What are we to do?" said Georgie.

Lucia laughed.

"Do?" she said. "Nothing, except never know anything about it. We know quite well that poor Daisy didn't do it on purpose. She hasn't got the pluck or the invention to be an incendiary. It was only her muddling, meddling ways."

"But the insurance money?" said Georgie.

"What about it? The fire was an accident, whether Daisy confessed what she had done or not. Poor Daisy! We must be nice to Daisy, Georgie. Her golf, her Abfou! Such disappointments. I think I will ask her to be my partner in the foursome for the Lucas Cup. And perhaps if there was another place on the golf committee, we might propose her for it."

Lucia sighed, smiling wistfully.

"A pity she is not a little wiser," she said.

Lucia sat looking wistful for a moment. Then to Georgie's immense surprise she burst out into peals of laughter.

"My dear, what is the matter?" said Georgie.

Lucia was helpless for a little, but she gasped and recovered and wiped her eyes.

"Georgie, you *are* dull this morning!" she said. "Don't you see? Poor Daisy's meddling has made the reputation of Vittoria and crumpled up Abfou. Fire, water, moonlight: Vittoria's prophecy. Vittoria owes it all to poor dear Daisy!"

Georgie's laughter set Lucia off again, and Peppino coming in found both at it.

"Good morning, Georgie," he said. "Terrible about the Museum. A sad loss. What are you laughing at?"

"Nothing, *caro*," said Lucia. "Just a little joke of Daisy's. Not worth repeating, but it amused Georgie and me. Come, Georgie, half an hour's good practice of celestial Mozartino. We have been lazy lately."

ALL TIME BESTSELLERS
FROM POPULAR LIBRARY

☐ THE BERLIN CONNECTION—Simmel	08607-6	1.95
☐ THE BEST PEOPLE—Van Slyke	08456-1	1.75
☐ A BRIDGE TOO FAR—Ryan	08373-5	2.50
☐ THE CAESAR CODE—Simmel	08413-8	1.95
☐ DO BLACK PATENT LEATHER SHOES REALLY REFLECT UP?—Powers	08490-1	1.75
☐ ELIZABETH—Hamilton	04013-0	1.75
☐ THE FURY—Farris	08620-3	2.25
☐ THE HAB THEORY—Eckerty	08597-5	2.50
☐ HARDACRE—Skelton	04026-2	2.25
☐ THE HEART LISTENS—Van Slyke	08520-7	1.95
☐ TO KILL A MOCKINGBIRD—Lee	08376-X	1.50
☐ THE LAST BATTLE—Ryan	08381-6	2.25
☐ THE LAST CATHOLIC IN AMERICA—Powers	08528-2	1.50
☐ THE LONGEST DAY—Ryan	08380-8	1.95
☐ LOVE'S WILD DESIRE—Blake	08616-5	1.95
☐ THE MIXED BLESSING—Van Slyke	08491-X	1.95
☐ MORWENNA—Goring	08604-1	1.95
☐ THE RICH AND THE RIGHTEOUS —Van Slyke	08585-1	1.95

Dorothy Dunnett
THE LYMOND CHRONICLE

THE GREATEST HISTORICAL SAGA OF OUR AGE BY A WRITER "AS GOOD AS MARY RENAULT" (*Sunday Times,* London), "AS POPULAR AS TOLKIEN" (Cleveland Magazine), WHO "COULD TEACH SCHEHERAZADE A THING OR TWO ABOUT SUSPENSE, PACE AND INVENTION" (*New York Times*), AND WHO IS "ONE OF THE GREATEST TALE-SPINNERS SINCE DUMAS" (*Cleveland Plain Dealer*).